ORDER OF VENGEANCE

MOTORCYCLE CLUB

ALEX J FISCHER

For my Family and Friends

1

Garret pulled a seat up to the table. He was surrounded by his brothers-in-arms. He looked to the right. "We can't let this stand. If we don't answer back, we're just inviting them to do even more the next time."

"Agreed," said the bearded man wearing a bandana who was sitting beside him on his right. "We need to send a message."

The man at the end of the table spoke up. "Agreed. Tony, do you have any ideas?"

Tony ran a few fingers through his beard. He pointed at the nearby door. "I got a great idea, Pres. We could send the prospect in plain clothes to their club. What was it called? 'The Enclave'? He'd fit right in there with his bald ass."

A man with a purple mohawk from across the table burst into laughter. "He would fit into that neo-Nazi compound. Still, I vote not to get the prospect killed. He's scheduled to pick me up some weed tomorrow. I'd hate to lose that."

The entire group chuckled. The president spoke above the laughs. "We'd hate for that to happen, wouldn't we? We can't have that. Besides, he's supposed to pick up my dry-cleaning tomorrow." The president's other hand fell to the table. He knocked on the wooden table. "Come on, people. We're not letting this one slide. What are we doing about it?"

"We could always go with the old standby," Garret said. "There's nothing quite like a little murder to get the point across. We ride over to their turf, grab some scumbag that's kicking up a vig, and take out that revenue stream permanently. It doesn't start an immediate war, and we still get the point across."

Vinny nodded. "I know just the guy too."

"Who is it?" the president asked.

"I know a jackass that lives over there," Vinny said. "He used to date my sister. He deals in coke, meth, and crack. You name it, and he's probably got it. He's killed a lot of people over the years with that poison. He nearly got my sister with that sickness. I broke his thumbs the last time I saw him. It's why he moved like a bitch to Knight territory."

"I like it," the president said. "They take out one of our dealers, we do the same. Show of hands - who votes we retaliate?"

Every man around the table raised their hands.

"We're agreed." He turned his attention to Garret. "Garret, I want you, Vinny, and Skuz to go take care of this. Try to be subtle."

"We're the kings of low-key, boss," Skuz said, reaching a gloved fist over the table toward Garret.

Garret bumped knuckles and smiled. "Don't worry, Rich. We've got this."

"I want it done by tonight," Richard said. "There will be no mistakes, gentlemen. I trust you to deliver. Do it right the first time. Don't rush."

"We've got it, Boss." Vinny clapped his hands. "I'll just need to find him. We'll head right out as soon as we can."

"Good," Richard said. "Now on to other business. One of our prospects' year is nearly up. What do you all feel about Irving?"

A red-faced man to Garret's left spoke up. "I think Irving's showed a lot of balls this past year. He's never shied away from any task I've given him. I'm talking the nastiest shit I could come up with. He may be a skinhead, but he works as hard as a dog."

"Agreed, Lucien," Garret said. He looked to his right at the President. "He's never given us any lip. He'd make a good addition to the roster." He gave a sideways glance at Skuz. "It doesn't hurt that he can actually aim, unlike some people."

Skuz raised a middle finger. "I keep telling you I had redeye that day. Screw range tests. What matters is actual battles."

"Easy, boys," Richard said. "That vote's a little while off yet. We'll get to it eventually. I just wanted to see where we were at. For now, we focus on the immediate issues. We piss on the Hurons' shoes, and show them we won't take any further aggression lying down. So get to finding him, and head out when you're ready." He banged the gavel down on the wooden saucer. "Dismissed."

The men all pushed their seats out and filed out the double doors, except for the President who remained seated. He watched his men leave one by one until Garret got close to the door. "Garret, hold up a minute."

Garret stopped and shut the door. He took a seat beside Richard. "What's up, Pres?"

Richard stood up and moved to the glass windows connecting the meeting room and the bar. He twisted the

3

cylinder hanging there, causing the blinds to open. "I want you to take Irving with you."

"The prospect? Are you sure? If he talks..."

"If he talks, we'll take care of him," Richard said. "He needs to know what this life entails. You watch him. Keep him in line."

"One thing's for sure, I'm not leaving him on driving duty," Garret said.

Richard turned around, a wry smile adorning his face. "What's the matter? Afraid he'll leave you high and dry after the hit? I don't blame you. I'd put him up front to make sure I could watch him the whole time. I leave it up to you. You became a full-fledged member not too long ago as I recall. If anyone knows how to make a new guy feel welcome, it'd be you."

"You think this is a good idea?" Garret asked. "He's just a prospect. He still thinks all we do is shake people down and occasionally deliver a beat down. This is throwing him in the deep end and trusting he doesn't drown here."

"There is a reason for my decision," Richard said, his voice growing tense. "Think about it for a minute. What better way to get someone used to his first blood than this instance?" He saw Irving taking a shot at the billiards table outside the window as he talked. "You're going after a dealer who's killed dozens with his heroin, not to mention everything else. He'll see us as the righteous avengers of the community. There's no way he'll decide we're in the wrong. Humans are capable of incalculable cruelty if they think they're on the right side."

"Damn. That's some gradual frog boiling stuff right there," Garret said. "That's deep. It makes sense too. Alright, I'll go get his ass ready then. Anything else?"

Richard turned back to Garret. "Yeah. Dump the body

inside Huron territory. We may as well screw up their equilibrium while we're at it. We can't let them get too cozy. Make them sweat and juggle. That's when people make mistakes - mistakes we can take advantage of."

"Right outside of their compound or inside the city limits?" Garret asked, leaning forward toward Richard. "They'd be hard pressed to explain a body right outside of their clubhouse."

"Inside Victoria Falls county limits will do just fine." Richard moved back to his seat at the head of the table and leaned back. "No need exposing yourselves to that degree of risk. Make their local police deal with it. Their first guess will be the Hurons. It will still put pressure on them. In fact, putting it right outside would look a little suspicious, if I had to guess."

"I'll make it happen." Garret slid his chair out. "I'll go help Skuz find the dude, and we'll head out in the van."

Richard got to his feet and took a step toward Garret. They both wrapped their arms around each other and slapped the other's back. "You be careful, brother. I'm trusting you with our little brother here. Don't let us down."

"You know I won't. Now let me go make sure that jackass even knows how to find him before we're stuck here all night."

"I'll join you." Richard walked side by side with Garret through the double doors into the bar area. "Besides, I need a beer." He veered off toward the bar while Garret continued toward the lone desk in the corner of the room.

Skuz sat in front of it typing. "How the hell hard can it be to find one guy on the internet?" He pushed the keyboard away. "This makes no sense."

"You didn't just type the guy's name in a search engine, did you? That's no way to find anyone." Garret twisted around and threw his arm in the air. "Hey, Vinny, why don't you come over here and help us with something."

Vinny climbed off the stool, upended his drink, and sidled over. "What's up, boys?"

"Our local punk here can't find our target." Garret slapped Skuz's shoulder. "Do you remember his old address?"

"Yeah, move over." Vinny shoved Skuz over and typed. "There. That's where I last remember him living. Does that even help, considering he doesn't live there anymore?"

"It's a start," Garret said. "With this we can head over there and find out where he moved from his neighbors."

Skuz angled his head up. "What if they don't feel too forthcoming, Garret, old friend? We can't just cause a scene in the middle of that neighborhood. The cops would be there inside of ten minutes."

"We don't have a choice," Garret said, leaning over the chair and staring at the screen. "I'll be extra nice so that doesn't happen."

"Oh boy." Skuz shook his head. "I know what that means."

"What does that mean, exactly?" Vinny asked.

"You'll see when we get there." Garret pulled Skuz out of the chair. "Now let's go. We don't have all day to get this done. We still need to find the worm first." He saw Irving out of the corner of his eye as they moved toward the exit. He stopped. "I'll be just a minute.." He cupped a hand over his mouth. "Hey, prospect, come over here."

Irving dropped the broom in his hands and hurried over. "Yes, Mr. Garret?"

"You're with us." He nodded toward the door. "Come on, you're driving. It's the President's orders."

Irving peeked over his shoulder. "Shouldn't I finish cleaning the clubhouse? I mean Lucien was pretty specific."

"Now, prospect." Garret grabbed Irving's ear and dragged him away. "Lucien will get over it. If nothing else, you have something to look forward to when we get back."

"Okay then." Irving hunched his shoulders and followed behind Garret out the door...

Twenty Minutes Later

"Take a right up here." Vinnie pointed out the windshield. "Yeah, this is it. We're here. See that white picket fence and yellow place? That's our boy's house. Pull over here on the side of the road, prospect."

Skuz ran a hand over the shaved sides of his head. "It seems like a pretty normal suburb to me." He stopped fiddling with his hair and leaned forward between the seats. "You're sure he's here?"

Garret pushed Skuz back into his seat and took his place. "Vinny said he moved before. Do you not pay attention? We're here to find out where he moved from his neighbors."

"Should we take off our kuttes?" Irving asked. "These people will probably freak out to see a bunch of bikers walking up to random houses asking questions."

Garret slapped the back of Irving's head. "Obviously, kid. You don't wear your colors when you're breaking the law. You don't sully the kutte. There's a little change to that plan though. I'm going in by myself. You all stay here and cover me. I think we'll have better luck if we don't go door to door in a group."

Skuz pushed Garret back into his seat. "Screw that, brother. I'm going with you. Who knows what could happen?"

"In the middle of white suburbia?" Garret chuckled. "Fine, be my guest. I guess a pair isn't much worse." He turned his head toward Vinny. "Now as soon as we leave, you're taking the prospect's place as driver. Once we get back, you'll take us wherever they tell us. We'll get this done in time for dinner so Irving here," he flicked Irving's ear, "can get me my fucking drugs on time for once."

"I'm getting antsy." Skuz bounced in his seat. "Let's go already. I want to get back to the clubhouse early."

"Anxious to get your dick wet?" Garret asked. "That bitch from last night was a ten, I'll give her that. What happened? Couldn't close the deal with that sweet piece of ass?"

"As if," Skuz said. "I was just too hammered."

"Sure," Vinny said. "That's why your dick wouldn't work, right? It had nothing to do with you being impotent?"

Skuz kicked the back of Vinny's seat. "Fuck you."

The entire group, minus Irving, got a chuckle out of the exchange.

"Alright. Enough screwing around," Garret said removing his kutte and placing it on the seat beside him. "Let's go." Garret slid open the back door, the sun boring down on his white t-shirt. Skuz climbed out in his black shirt behind him.

"I always feel naked without my colors." Skuz pulled on his shirt. "Is that normal?"

"Kind of." Garret took the lead. "You'll get used to it eventually. Now follow my lead."

"I have a bad feeling about this."

Garret marched up to the house beside their target's old

home. He pushed an index finger on the doorbell. "Watch and learn."

A haggard woman in her mid-forties opened the door. "Yeah? What do you want?"

Garret smiled. "Yes, I was wondering if you knew where your old neighbors next door moved?"

"Why should I tell you?" She asked. "What's in it for me?"

"How much do you want?"

"Excuse me?"

Garret pulled out his wallet. "A couple hundred alright?"

"Try a few more bills." She said with a lick of her lips.

"Don't push your luck, lady," Garret said. "You'll get three hundred if you tell us where they moved. I want a full address for three hundred. None of this vague location bologna."

"Deal," she said. "They moved to the east side of town. The address is 1893 Blackwood Drive." Her hand reached out and took the cash. "Have a good one." She slammed the door shut on the two.

"Well, that sucked," Skuz said from over Garret's shoulder. "You're out three hundred, and we don't even know if it's reliable intel."

"It's reliable," Garret said, turning back to the van.

"How do you know that?" Skuz asked, jogging to catch up. "She could have been lying for the money. Did you think of that?"

"If she's lying, we'll just have to come back and ask for further clarification." He pushed Skuz away by the shoulder. "Won't we?"

"Fine." Skuz dashed past Garret and slid open the door. "We got our place, gentlemen. We're heading to Blackwood Drive on the east side. It's time to go to work."

"Work?" Irving asked. He peeked around the passenger's seat. "What are we doing? No one ever told me."

"For good reason, prospect." Garret slammed the sliding door shut. "You need to see how the life is. It's not all metal, bikes, and women. You're about to see how we provide for our own, as ugly as it may be. We need the respect, fear, and space that we use to operate. Lately, the Hurons haven't given us any of that. We're fixing that today. You're helping."

"Aww." Skuz leaned forward and rubbed the top of Irving's bald head. "Look at the cute little prospect scared of the real work. You better suck it up. This is a test. You don't want to fail."

"You do have your piece, right?" Vinny asked.

"My piece?" Irving asked.

"Your weapon, prospect. You did bring your gun, right?" Garret asked. "What kind of a man is unarmed?"

"Oh," Irving said. "I didn't know I'd need it for this. You never really told me I'd need it."

Skuz brought a hand to his face with a groan. "What kind of a man doesn't carry a weapon on him?" He leaned forward, grabbed Irving's ear, and yanked. "You always carry a weapon to protect your brothers and yourself. Never leave the clubhouse without one." He released him and leaned back in the seat. "Hell, you should probably even be armed in there to be safe." He pulled a handgun out of his shoulder holster and handed it over. "I expect it back after this."

"Yes, sir."

"Be careful with that. It's loaded and the safety's off." Garret looked to his left past the cityscape zooming by. "I assume you know how to use that?"

"Or do we have to hold your dick for you too?" Vinny asked.

"I'm good," Irving said.

"We'll see about that." Skuz reclined his seat. "Words are cheap. Actions prove mettle."

———

On the East Side

"Prospect, you, me, and Skuz are going up there," Garret said. "We get them to open the door and force ourselves inside. Now, Irving, you're going to be our lookout once we're inside. Make damned sure no one interrupts us."

"How are we dealing with the cleanup, brother?" Skuz asked. "We can't just leave a body lying around stinking up the house."

"We're going to be parking right in front of their garage like we own the joint. Once we're inside, we open the garage and place the corpse in the back. It'll be wrapped, so if anyone's watching it'll just look like we're helping them move something like a sleeping bag. It's perfect. Once we're loaded up, we take it out of town and bury it six feet deep."

"This sounds like it'll take all day," Irving said.

"Don't bitch, prospect," Vinny said. "It makes you look like a pussy. We all put in the work. You're no exception." He reached across the aisle and pushed Irving into the window. "Now get ready. We're almost there."

A crack pierced the air.

"Did you fellas hear that?" Skuz rolled down the window.

"Sounded like..." Garret leaned forward.

"A gunshot," Vinny finished.

"Everybody strap up." Garret readied his weapon and pulled back the hammer. "Sounds like someone's hosting a party."

"Park in the driveway like the original plan?" Vinny asked. "We just pulled onto the street."

"Place us across the street. If we open the garage, bring it in. Keep your piece handy. You never know."

Vinny brought the van to a stop. "You don't need to tell me twice." Vinny placed his hand gun in his lap. "I've got your backs from here if it goes down."

"Let's find out what's going on." Skuz slid the door open and hopped out. "I can't stand this waiting." He flung open the passenger door and dragged Irving out of the van. "Come on, boy. Show your manhood. You want that bottom rocker, don't you? Prove your worth."

"I've got this." Irving took occasional peeks at the house. His hands trembled as he turned to face the building. "I'm ready."

"Good." Garret brushed past him. "Then chamber a round and get ready."

Skuz pushed him forward. "Time to back up that bravado, kid."

Garret hunched over and held the gun in front of him as he approached the building. He put his back to the brick beside the front door. He motioned the two men over.

Skuz and Irving got down on a knee on the other side of the door.

"I hear somebody," Garret said. "It sounds like a woman in there. She might be in trouble." He stood up and faced the door. "Get ready to head in on my signal."

"Wait," Irving said. "What's the signal?" He sniffed the air. "Do you smell that? It smells like-"

Garret unleashed a trio of kicks until the door finally popped open. "That."

Skuz pushed Irving forward through the door frame. "Get in there. I don't care what you smell."

"Come on," Garret said. "Let's make sure he doesn't get himself killed." He stepped through the door with his weapon at the ready. He pointed his weapon toward the nearby door frame to his right. He pointed to the opposite door without a word.

Skuz dragged Irving behind him as he approached the left door. He looked over at Garret.

Garret counted down from three on his hands. Once his hand balled into a fist he crashed the door open with his shoulder. His eyes widened at the sight in front of him.

A man lay on the tile below beside the oven, blood pooling underneath him. A woman stood over the body with a pistol in her hand. She turned to face them, bruises littering her face. "Piss off."

"Drop the weapon or I fire," Garret said. "Don't make me do this."

She turned to face him. "Who the fuck are you?"

Skuz crashed through the other door with Irving hot on his trail. "Do what he says and we-" He looked down at the body. "Oh shit. Is that the guy we're here for?"

"You wanted this wuss?" She kicked the body's ribs. "You're too late."

"Put the goddamn weapon down," Irving stood up, "before I put you down."

"Easy, prospect." Garret held out a hand. "You put yours away, we put ours away. Deal?"

The red-haired woman's eyes scanned all of them before a wry smile made its way to her lips. "Deal. I know when I'm outgunned and outmaneuvered." She holstered her weapon at her side.

"Alright then." Garret placed his weapon back in his shoulder holster. "Put it down, boys."

"I don't like this." Skuz lowered his weapon but did not sheathe it. "This wasn't the plan."

"Tell your purple haired guard dog to relax," the woman said. "I'm only here for this piece of shit."

"Guard dog?" Skuz toward a step forward but was held back by Garret. "This gash better show some manners before I lose my patience."

"Deal with it, pussy," she said. "Now if you boys will excuse me, I need to take care of this mess I made. Judging from your actions, I assume you had a plan for this already?"

"What if we did?" Skuz asked. "You think we're just going to help you out? Why should we?"

"Easy now," Garret said, patting Skuz's shoulder. He turned back to the woman. "What's your name?"

"Call me Ann," she said, brushing a stray strand of red hair out of her face. "You must be the sane one of the three." She extended a hand toward him.

He stepped forward and shook it. "The name's Garret. Garret Price."

"How about it, Mr. Price? Would you help a lady out?"

Garret looked down at the motionless body and back to Ann. "On one condition."

"Name it."

"We take credit for the kill. This was our job."

Ann folded her arms under her petite chest. "Go right ahead. This was personal, not business. I have no vested interest in being associated with this jackass after death."

"Personal?" Irving asked, stepping past Skuz. "This must have been a monumental disagreement."

"You could say that. This cretin was responsible for the death of my charter."

"A drug dealer managed to break up a lady cycling club?" Garret asked. "How does that even happen?"

"He didn't break it up. He killed the members. I'm the only one left alive and free after that poison wave he pushed on them. At first it wasn't noticeable. One girl nodding off at an odd time for example. The shit got real when girls started dropping dead in the clubhouse. It was at that point I began my hunt. He's been on the run for a while. I finally just caught up with him. The rest is self-evident."

"That's rough, Ann," Garret said. "It's a deal. You got your revenge, we've got our man. We know just the place for this waste of life," he looked at Skuz and Irving, "don't we boys?"

"Just out of curiosity's sake, why do you men want him?" Ann asked, shifting her weight and letting her hand fall to her hip.

"Business reasons. You understand," Garret said. He snapped his fingers. "Prospect, signal the van. We have a pick-up ready."

"Right. Does anyone know where the garage is?"

"Over there." Ann pointed at a door to her side.

"Thanks." He stepped over the body and past Ann. He disappeared behind the door, and a loud, constant shuffling of metal could be heard. The sound of a motor vehicle parking met their ears, then ceased.

"You boys want any help? A girl's got to help clean up after herself after all."

"Knock yourself out, toots," Skuz said. "This tub of lard needs at least two people."

"That's good," Garret said. "You, the prospect, and Ann here will make it even easier."

"I knew I shouldn't have said anything," Skuz mumbled.

2

_____

"Why are you coming along?" Skuz asked the woman sitting beside him in the middle. "We don't need help."

"We're all in this together now," Garret said leaning forward, peering at Skuz on the other side. "She probably just wants to be sure this all goes away. I'd do the same thing. Who would trust three random guys to dispose of a body you just dropped?"

"As a wise man once said, 'Trust, but verify'," Ann said. She jabbed a thumb to her left at Garret. "Your friend's right. No offense to you three, but I don't know you." She looked over at the scowling Skuz. "Don't worry so much, Mr. Peacock man."

"What did you call me?"

"You kind of look like you're peacocking, dude," Garret snickered. "Why did you ever color your hair purple anyway? You look like a dumb-ass."

"When I was growing up, purple hair was totally punk. I refuse to let those nerds ruin this majestic style." Skuz ran a hand over the shaved sides of his head.

"Ignoring your friend's crappy hair," Ann said turning to Garret, "where are we dumping this hot potato?"

"We've got a place out of the way. Which reminds me, we're getting close." He leaned forward and tapped the driver's window. "Vinny, take us to plot C. There should be plenty of room there. It's still in the city limits technically."

"You've got it." He looked up into the rear-view mirror. "You're a tall girl, aren't you?"

"Not quite as tall as you, big man." Ann glanced up front. "Vinny, was it? Why? You got a problem with that?"

"Cool it, sister." Vinny's eyes returned to the road. "It was just an observation. What are you, six feet? That's impressive."

"I'm six one, thank you." Ann's eyes scanned the cramped cabin, eventually landing on Garret. "Judging by those patches, I see you're not anything special in the chain. How did you end up leading this band of merry gangsters today?"

"Club business," Garret said out of hand. "You know how it is. I can't say." He snuck a glance at her out of the corner of his eye. "Speaking of which, what are you going to do from now on?"

"Girl business." She smirked at him. "You know how it is. I can't say."

"Clever girl. You don't have to answer, but I'm curious," Garret said, eyeing Ann up and down.

"I'm not interested. I just met you."

"What? No. I was just going to ask what position you held, if any?"

Ann waved her hand in dismissal. "It doesn't matter to me. If you must know, I was the sergeant-at-arms. Don't fuck with me, tall, lean, and handsome."

"You always did like the tough broads, didn't you?" Skuz asked. "If you ask me, give this one a pass."

"I don't recall him asking you, Shrimp." Ann shoved Skuz against the car door with a giggle. She regained her composure. "Still, that is the best idea. After this, we go our separate ways and hold this silence to the grave. That is how you men run your clubs, right?" She tapped her hand on her knee. "You're not thinking of trying something stupid, are you?"

"What does that mean?" Skuz asked. "We haven't survived this long being water-heads."

"That's what I'm concerned with." Her hand fell to her belt line. "Don't try anything funny."

"She thinks we're going to kill her and dump her body along with his." Garret pressed his right shoulder into the seat. His chin jutted out, a smile on his face. His eyes followed her hands as he conversed. "That's why your hand is hovering over your little .22 there. It's smart. Do you know who we are?"

"One of the local charters I'm assuming," Ann said. "If I had to guess, I'd go with the Order of Vengeance. Am I right?"

"You know the local scene. I'm impressed," Garret smirked. "Then you should also know we're a group that keeps our word. After all, if you don't have that, what kind of business can you do on the street?"

"I'll still be on my guard. No amount of smooth talk will change that. This isn't exactly a typical day in the life." She gazed past Garret out the window. "A wooded area. This is starting to make more sense. I hope we have shovels at least."

"We always come prepared, lassie," Skuz said with his

best Scottish accent. "Maybe the girl squad wasn't professional, but we're a different beast altogether."

Ann snarled, turned, and grabbed Skuz's throat all in one motion. She pushed him back against the window. "Say that again why don't you?"

Cold steel on the side of her head along with a click stopped her in her tracks. Garret's voice was low and on edge. "Put him down before I put you down." He pulled back the hammer.

"Easy now." Ann released Skuz whose hands flew to his throat. He doubled over, coughing. "Don't mention my old charter is all I ask."

"Then use your words like a damned adult," Garret said. He pushed the barrel further into her temple. "At least have better impulse control than a toddler." He pulled the weapon back. "Jesus, lady."

"We're nearly there," Vinny said, turning the wheel. "It'll only be a couple of minutes until we're at the end of this trail."

"Face the other window," Garret ordered. "Now."

"Is this really necessary?" Ann asked. She turned to Skuz who was giving her dirty looks as he massaged his larynx.

"It is now after you showed your ass." Garret swiped the weapon in her belt line with his left hand. "At least now we don't have to worry about you having another little bitch fit."

"Whatever makes you happy. Sit there with your .357 if it makes you feel better," Ann said, the corners of her mouth curving upward. "Are we there yet?"

"Actually, yes." Vinny pumped the brakes and the car stopped. He put the car in park and turned around in his seat. "We're ready to get started." He reached over and swatted Irving's shoulder. "What's wrong, kid? You've been quiet."

Irving's eyes stayed glued to the rear-view mirror. "Just watching how things unfold."

"Prudent," Vinny said. "A little cowardly, but smart. Did you learn anything?"

"Don't piss off Garret."

"Cool," Garret said. "Now who's got first shift on digging?"

"Not I," Skuz and Vinny said in unison.

"I guess it'll be me, Irving, and the little lady." Garret's eyes never left Ann. He passed Ann's weapon to Vinny. "Hold onto this for the moment." He looked over at Skuz. "That means you're on lookout duty. Think you can handle that?"

Skuz leveled a dirty look at Ann. "Yeah. I got it."

Garret pulled the sliding door open and climbed out. "Then let's get to work. The longer we sit here, the longer it'll take."

"The sooner I can put this all behind me, the better." Ann followed Garret. "I'm tired of it."

"Who could get tired of this wondrous lifestyle?" Vinny asked. "Blood, guns, drugs, sex, and rock and roll."

"Don't forget the hogs," Skuz said, "or the parties."

"I would have gone with fellowship personally." Ann pulled the van's back doors open.

"With the way you act, that's a shocker to me." Skuz climbed into the back cabin. He passed out the shovels. "I would have thought you'd be the quiet loner who just beats people up."

Ann took the shovel. "Who says I didn't? I just can't stand assholes."

Once everyone had a shovel, Skuz jumped out of the cabin and slammed the doors shut. "Just don't make it a habit. Every woman gets one incident before

I start treating her like a man. You've already used yours."

Ann slung the shovel over her shoulder and walked off from the van. "That was your first mistake. Never assume anyone's abilities until you see them."

Skuz looked at Vinny and Garret. "Can you believe this broad? She's crazy."

"I like her." Garret pushed Skuz away and followed Ann. "Just watch it around her and follow my lead."

"Follow your lead?" Vinny asked. He glanced at Skuz. "What's that mean?"

"We'll see, won't we?"

Two hours later...

"Put your back into it, Scrawny." Ann stood up and wiped her brow. "Where was that fire you had when we started? Don't let a girl outdo you here."

"I think she's enjoying this." Garret hefted another load of dirt over his shoulder. "At least we're almost done."

"I certainly am." Vinny jabbed the shovel into the dirt and kicked. "It's not every day he's quiet."

"Piss off," Skuz scowled. "I'm a rocker, not a ditch digger. Some of us have skill sets beyond moving vast amounts of dirt - like modifying our voice, ripping sweet guitar solos, or working the crowd. The only reason I'm doing this is because the prospect bitched out and complained about his back over there." He pointed toward a nearby tree with Irving sitting under it.

"Yeah, whatever, Mr. Punk Rocker." Ann rolled her eyes. She watched Garret. "What's your story?"

"Nothing special."

"I don't believe that." Ann took a break and sat down in the nearby grass. "What's the matter? Ashamed of it?"

"Has anyone ever told you that you're nosey?" Garret asked.

"They let me get away with it due to my skills. So, I ask again, what's your story?"

"She seems awfully interested, bro." Vinny reached down to his feet and took a swig from the water bottle. "I wonder why."

"You know why," Ann grinned. "I'm going to ride him cross-eyed tonight until I can't walk."

"An attractive proposition." Garret stopped digging. "Unfortunately, it's not all that special of a story. But if you insist...my parents died when I was sixteen in an automobile accident. I went searching for something to grab onto, and I found these jackasses. The rest is history. See? Boring."

"There's got to be more to it than that."

"You need to stop digging," Garret said.

"I was just curious." Ann held both hands up in front of her.

"No, I mean really stop digging. The hole is deep enough now." Garret tossed his shovel aside and his hands fell to his hips. "Finally. Let's finish this. You three, grab the body. I'll get the gasoline and matches ready."

"Come on," Skuz whined. "No rests?"

"It appears not. He's a real workhorse, isn't he?" Ann followed Garret, leaving Vinny and Skuz near the makeshift grave.

"Let's go then." Vinny followed the other two. He stopped and turned back to Skuz. "Come on, you lazy crap. That guy's heavy."

"That fat sack has to easily weigh two hundred eighty."

Skuz trudged back to the van, avoiding Ann and staying between Garret and Vinny. "The slob probably gorged himself to assuage his conscience."

Ann grabbed the body's arm, braced her foot against the back bumper, and pulled. The body slid out of the cabin and flopped onto the ground. "Let's just drag his ass. It's not like he deserves better." She hawked a mouth full of spit onto his face.

"I agree." Vinny reached down and dragged the body toward the hole with Ann. "He doesn't deserve the dignity of being carried."

"I'll get the gas." Garret climbed into the back of the van and picked up the red can. He jumped out and saw Skuz still standing there. He let loose a sharp whistle, causing Skuz to jump. "Get your head in the game. If you don't want to be near her, then go keep lookout."

"Lookout?" Skuz asked. "For what?"

"I don't know. Hikers and shit or something. The last thing we need is for them to stumble across us right now."

Skuz peered over Garret's shoulder at Ann. "Yeah, just so long as I don't have to be near that crazy broad. Be careful around her." He looked back at the trail they had entered and walked. He raised a hand as he walked without looking back. "I don't trust her yet."

Garret turned back to the group. He motioned over at Irving. "Hey, Prospect, come over here and learn something."

Irving pushed himself to his feet and followed behind Garret.

Garret and Irving approached the hole where Vinny and Ann had dumped the body. "Let's clean this up, fill in the hole, and get out of here." He stopped in front of the grave and splashed liquid over the bulbous corpse.

Ann pinched her nose. "Just in time too. He's starting to stink. I never could take the smell of corpses. It always makes me nauseous."

Garret placed the can by his feet and pulled out the match book from his jeans' pocket. "You get used to it. This is what makes a man retch right here." He struck a match against the back of the package, igniting a small flame. "Back up." He took a step back along with everyone else. He tossed the stick into the hole and a strong flame exploded into life. He pulled the prospect closer to the hole. "You see that? That's how you get rid of evidence. After the bodies turn to bone, we crush that and fill in the hole. No one could get any forensics off that, even if they did know it was here."

Skuz's voice cried out over the roaring of the flame. "Hey, we've got a problem here."

Everyone turned their head to see Skuz sprinting toward them in a dead heat. He stopped and panted. "There's a huge formation of bikes coming this way."

"In the middle of this place?" Garret asked. "Did you see who it was?"

"It looked like Baphomet's Knights."

"Oh, fuck me running. They had someone follow us and called it in." Garret hefted the gas can up and emptied the fuel onto the fire. "Get in the van, now. We'll come back and finish this tonight." He tossed Ann her pistol back. "You might need this."

Everyone dashed back to the van and slammed the doors shut.

Garret rolled down the backseat window and poked his head out. He looked behind the van and saw the procession of motorcycles begin turning into the clearing. "Go!"

Vinny stepped on the gas. The van bounced as it took off. "Go where?"

"This path goes through the forest, so keep going." He got onto his knees and peeked over into the back cabin. He nudged Ann's shoulder. "You and Skuz are with me." He climbed over the seat.

"Just when I thought I was getting out of this shit," Ann sighed and followed suit. She looked over her shoulder. "Hurry up, Purple."

"It's just one thing after another." Skuz toppled over the seat and landed on his back with a crack. "Of course my back hurts now."

Ann kicked Skuz in the side. "Get up and get your gun out. We're on interference."

"Here we go." Skuz got into a sitting position and pulled out his automatic pistol. "I'm ready when you are."

"Let's get the drop on them then." Garret scooted along the floor toward the back door. He looked back. "Make sure my head's out of the way before you start shooting."

"If she shoots you, I shoot her." Skuz glared at Ann.

"Whatever. Here we go." Garret kicked open the back doors to see two lines of bikers following behind them. He rolled to the side until he hit the wall. He sat up and leveled his pistol. "Light them up." Muzzle flashes appeared from the end of his weapon. The lead biker veered off after clutching his chest. His bike crashed into a tree. The rest of the men reached into their jackets and pulled out their own pistols.

"Get your heads down up there," Skuz called over his shoulder. The barrel of his gun continued to jump as more and more of their pursuers dropped out of the chase.

Garret stumbled to his knees and placed his elbow on them to steady his aim. "You want some of me?" He squeezed off another round, causing another to fall off his bike. He fell backwards as a mist of red emanated from his hands. "Ah shit." He fell back beside Ann. "The bastard got me in the hand."

Skuz bared his teeth and slid another magazine into his weapon. "You'll pay for that." He swept left and right as he unloaded into the crowd. Halfway into the magazine the group following slowed down and turned around. He pounded on the ceiling. "That's right! You turn around and don't fuck with us."

Ann placed her weapon back down her belt line and grabbed Garret's wounded left hand. She looked over her shoulder, her irate voice overshadowing Skuz's. "Slow this thing down." She looked at Skuz. "And shut the door when they do."

"Who do you think you are?"

"I think I'm probably the only one who knows how to treat that wound your friend has. I need to focus on this."

"It's not that bad," Garret said, gritting his teeth. "They only got me between the thumb and finger. It went right through."

"You're bleeding pretty good." Ann squeezed the hand. "We need to keep the pressure on. Anyone have a clean cloth?" Her neck swiveled back to Skuz. "Don't just sit there. Get me the first aid kit."

"The what?"

"You don't carry a first aid kit? Leave it to men to forget something essential." She released Garret's hand and fell to her belly. She twisted the cloth of her shirt and yanked, eliciting a rip in the fabric. "Just stay still." Her short red hair fell in front of her face as she leaned in toward the wound.

Garret's emerald eyes watched Ann. "Where'd you learn this from?"

"My mother." She wrapped his hand in the cloth and

tied it, holding it in place. "She signed me up for a first aid class when I was a teenager. Aren't you thankful?"

"Remind me to send a thank you card," Garret said. He raised his other fist and banged on the seat he was leaning against. "Get us back to the clubhouse."

"You should just drop me off before you get back." Ann leaned back. "I have no business there."

"That's not a good idea," Irving said from the front, loud enough to be heard.

"What was that pipsqueak?" Ann turned and peered over the seat. "Are you saying I don't have a choice in the matter?"

"He's saying you're a target now," Vinny said. "They saw you here. If we leave you alone, they'll take you out. You're involved now, whether you like it or not."

"I'll pay my respects to your charter, but I'm not staying there for any length of time. Fair?" Ann asked. "I'm trying to get out of this life, not dive back in."

Garret leaned forward and studied the back of her kutte. A winged woman with a spear in one hand and a shield in the other occupied the middle. The word Valkyries was embroidered above it. "You don't have to stay any longer than you want. We're just not stopping until we get back behind our walls. You can do what you like after that. It's a matter of safety. I'm sure you understand as a former sergeant-at-arms."

Ann turned around as Skuz climbed over the seats to her left, leaving just Garret and Ann together. Her back slid down the seat until her legs were straight in front of her. "I was never one for running away."

"Admirable," Garret said. "Foolish, but admirable."

"Then again our rivals never just opened up on us like that shit," Ann sighed. "The most we ever had was a good old-fashioned melee with weapons. What just happened was crazy."

Skuz's head popped up above the seat. "Welcome to the big boys' league. We play for keeps. Street fights are more common, but firefights are never out of the realm of possibility."

"You're at war with them I take it?" Ann asked.

"They killed one of ours a week ago, and now they think we did the same. It'll turn into one soon enough at this rate," Garret cradled his hand and groaned, "if it's not already with this little slaughter."

"We're also going to need to clean this mess up, guys." Irving squeaked out.

Vinny turned off the dirt road and onto the paved road. "We'll have to come back tonight and deal with it. It'll be an all-night job with that many bodies and bikes."

"That's assuming they don't come back for their dead," Skuz said. "First thing's first. We need to get Garret to someone with real medical training. Lucien was a medic in the army. Would he work?"

"It didn't hit bone," Ann stared at the immobile hand, "probably."

"After we get back, we'll figure everything out," Vinny said. "Like the boss says, we need to focus on one thing at a time."

3

"I've seen privates get shot in the dick and survive." Lucien unwrapped the field dressing and leaned in to inspect the wound. "Looks like it went in and out. You'll have a scar, but that's about it - assuming those antibiotics work." He looked up at the group surrounding the seat. His eyebrow raised. "Who's the girl?"

Garret's free hand brought a bottle of whiskey to his lips. "The one who dressed this and helped us survive our little surprise."

Lucien's red face stared at Ann. "Is that right? She probably kept you from a massive infection. Now to make sure." He reached over to the smaller seat with a box atop. He extracted a small brown bottle, undid the top, and poured the contents over the open wound. The liquid bubbled and hissed as Garret winced.

"Get over it, you big sissy." A deep laugh erupted from Vinny a across the table. "It's just a little disinfectant. That's never killed a man before."

"You obviously don't need me anymore." Ann took a step back from the group. "I'll be on my way."

"Before you do," Richard opened the door from the meeting room and stepped out, "I need a word with you four. Prospect, stay out here and clean this place up."

"He's ready." Lucien finished wrapping the wound back up and cut off the remaining wrapping. He stood up with a grunt, running a hand through his whitening hair. He stopped in front of Ann. "Be on your best behavior, little girl. We'll be watching."

Ann watched the old man as he passed by. "I know the rules, old timer."

"I see that by the colors you're wearing. The Valkyries were a strong group. We appreciate you helping patch Garret up. Just remember we do things a bit differently, and mind our rules." He stepped forward, invading her personal space. "Got it?"

"Yeah."

"Good." Lucien strode off and sat at the bar. He grabbed a nearby cup and bottle and set to work filling the glass.

Garret stood up and put on his kutte. "You heard the man. Business doesn't wait."

Skuz stayed at Garret's side, away from Ann. "It's not like the day's over either, with that cleanup waiting on us. At least it was in the forest. Has anything been on the news?"

Lucien pressed the remote at the bar. "Nope. I haven't seen anything, I think you're in the clear for now."

"If you are done," Richard pushed the meeting room door open, "get in here."

The group followed the president into the room and closed the door. The four members pulled out their respective seats while Ann remained standing behind Garret.

Richard pointed to a seat lining the wall, away from the table. "Take a seat."

Ann backed up and lowered herself into the seat.

"Now tell me, what the hell happened out there?" Richard asked. "It was a simple job, and you come back with a bullet hole."

"It didn't go as planned, but it did get done." Garret shifted in his seat. "It got complicated quickly when we found our guest." He jabbed a thumb over his shoulder. "When we finally found the little shit, we found her there having already killed him."

Richard's focus turned from Garret to Ann. "Is that right? Go on."

"So we agreed to take the responsibility and cleanup."

"Uh huh?" Richard's eyes narrowed as he looked at Ann. "Finish your story."

"We drove out to the place, dug the hole, dumped the body, set it ablaze, and then the knights turned up. We ran for the van, opened up the back, and lit them up after they started chasing us. That's pretty much it."

"I see." Richard stood up and moved to the seat beside Ann. "You want to explain why you were there?"

"I already did to your men."

"Humor me."

"Pres, the reason she-" Garret was stopped as Richard lifted a lone finger.

"I want to hear it from her." He lowered his finger. "Go ahead."

"We had history, bad blood you might call it. It was my last remaining duty to kill that roach. Your boys here just caught me afterward. I was standing there contemplating if I should just take off or call in a cleaning crew. Luckily, they were gentlemen."

"Your charter is gone then I gather." Richard looked down and saw the patches. "Sergeant huh? It's starting to make a little more sense. The only thing I'm hung up on is how your charter ended? Don't say drugs. I'm not stupid. Unless you women have different rules, we don't allow men to get addicted to the point they kill themselves. We straighten them out and then kick them out for subsequent offenses. Was your group simply incompetent or addicts?" He tilted his head. "Aw, did I offend you with that question? Tough tits. Answer me."

Ann looked away from Richard and back to the table where everyone was facing her, waiting for an answer in silence. She stared down at the floor. "Fine. I might not have said everything before."

"Here we go," Richard said. "Spill it."

"The Knights of Baphomet have a little sister club. You may have heard of the Dames of Baphomet?"

"Of course, but we never really gave it much mind. Were your two groups beefing?"

"We weren't a big charter to begin with. About like yours, just above six. We were struggling to fill ranks before we disintegrated. The feud didn't help matters. The president took a mortal wound during a fateful melee that broke out early in the war. A fucking knife got jabbed in her throat." She paused, inhaled, and let out a shuddering breath. "From there, things spiraled. Girls started getting high on all manner of substances. I'm not talking a little bud. I mean meth, H, and crack. I tried to hold it together, but eventually some of the girls stopped showing up to church. From there it all fractured until everyone was either dead or junkies. I just eliminated their provider before I left town. Call it a sense of completion. Happy?"

"You said they were all dead before," Garret said.

"I never said all."

Richard took a step back and sat in the seat at the head of the table. "It's beginning to make more sense now. I take it you're planning to run as soon as you leave here and never come back?"

"That was the plan. I don't want to get involved any deeper in this shit."

"Too bad," Richard said. "You made this mess, so you're going to clean it up. We're not going to do your dirty work. You help us clean this up, and you're clear. Deal?"

"Fine."

"Good." He turned back to the men. "How many were there, and how many did you take out?"

"It looked like the entire damned charter." Vinny looked past Richard at the windows covered in blinds. "It had to be at least a couple dozen bastards. We took out maybe five or six."

"They followed us there. They had to have." Skuz shook his head. "There's no other way they'd have known we were there."

"You didn't watch your tail or double back?" Richard asked.

"We made sure no one saw us load up the van." Garret scratched his nose. "It had to be a kid from the neighborhood snitching if you ask me. It would also explain why it took them a couple of hours to mobilize. My worry is the bodies dropped tonight. They might be there to drag their dead back for a decent burial. If nothing else, we need to get back there and finish what we started. The body's burned but we're not done yet."

Vinny nodded. "Filling in the hole will only take about ten minutes. I say we let them deal with their dead while we deal with our business tonight."

"If we run into the Knights?" Garret asked. "What do we do then? I'm not up for another firefight tonight, brother."

"We take another trail. There's more than one way to

get there. I know that place like the back of my hand. I can get us there without prying eyes." Vinny readjusted the sun glasses perched atop his head and turned to Richard. "We need to get that body under the earth. The longer it's out there, the higher the chance a hiker stumbles across it."

"Agreed." Richard looked at Ann. "You're going with them tonight and, no offense, but I hope we never see you again afterward."

"You gentlemen know how to show a girl a good time and how to ask a favor." She stood up. "I'll see myself out and get ready for tonight's exercise." She moved to the door and froze as Garret spoke up.

Garret leaned forward, placing his elbows on the table. "I'm going too."

"With that hand?" Richard asked.

"It's filling in a hole. I can do that one handed, with my foot, or just watch. Either way, I'm going. It was my job, and I'm finishing it."

"Alright, fine. Be a big man." Richard leaned back in the seat and swiveled left and right. A small smile crept its way to his face. "Go and finish your business."

"It'd be best if we kept the numbers down," Vinny said, "just in case the Knights are prowling around. We don't want to make a bunch of noise." He snapped his fingers. "I've got an idea. Why don't we use the prospect's car? You know, that piece of shit electrical powered car. It's silent with that pussy engine."

"I like it." Garret dug a pack of cigarettes out of his shirt pocket and placed one between his lips. "At least it'll be good for something other than getting a bunch of soccer moms wet for once."

"I know it's not my place," Ann's hand wrapped around

the doorknob, "but do you really think he'll just allow his car to be used for club business?"

"He will if he ever wants his bottom rocker." Garret craned his neck to face her.

"If you say so. I'll trust your judgement on that." Ann pushed open the door. "See you in a bit." She stepped out into the main room, shutting the door behind her.

Richard sat up in his chair. "You boys watch her. I don't trust her. Something's off."

"Man, Pres," Vinny started, "you don't trust anyone who's not in the club. She seems alright. Maybe a little feisty, but cool."

"I'm with the President on this one." Skuz frowned from Garret's side. "Appearances are only skin deep. We don't know this chick. I'll keep an eye on her."

"That's the first smart thing you've said yet." Richard stared at Skuz. "You don't like her, do you?"

"They had a bit of a squabble," Garret snickered.

"Yeah," Vinny chuckled, "and he lost."

Richard had an amused look on his face as he turned back to Skuz. He shook his head. "Shame. I wouldn't have thought you'd have had any trouble from a woman."

Skuz glowered at everyone at the tower. "Piss off."

The group erupted into laughter.

"Alright," Richard said, "get out of here and get it done. Go whenever you're ready. Make sure you watch the news before you go. We don't want to get there and find a bunch of news cameras and police. If they do find them, we're going to have to roll the dice. You were using unlicensed guns, right?"

"With the serial number scratched off," Skuz said. "They'll only know the caliber of the bullets."

"No time like the present." Garret stood up and moved to

the windows. "He pried open the curtains to see the orange sunset. "It's getting dark. It's time to move out." He turned back to the table. "The sooner we start, the sooner we get back."

"Before you go hog wild, I want there to be no more bodies tonight. We'll be lucky escaping a war as it is."

After Nightfall...

"Hey, yo." Garret leaned his head in between the two front seats and patted Vinny's shoulder. He pointed out the front toward some lights. "Turn off the lights and engine. We need to figure out who that is first before we get started tonight. Who wants to sneak over there?" He looked to his right at Irving. "I guess that means you're up. Stay low, slow, and quiet. I don't want to have to go rescue your ass. Stick behind bushes and trees if you have to."

"What do I do if it's the cops and they see me?" Irving wiped away some sweat from his brow. "I don't want to be charged, man."

"Don't be a pussy. Think about it, man," Garret said. "If they see you, what are they going to charge you with - hiking at night? Have some sense."

"What you really need to be concerned with is if that's the knights." Ann spoke up from the back beside Garret's seat. "They won't have any due process, and if they recognize you, even without your kutte, you're screwed. They'll be hankering for some revenge."

Irving's hands shook in his lap. His left engulfed his right and held it still. He looked over at Garret and nodded. "I got it."

Garret's eyes noticed the trembling hands before they could be hidden and sighed. "Alright, fine. I'll go with you if it'll make you feel better."

"Bro, you can't." Skuz spoke up from the very back of the cabin. "Your hand's still healing."

"It's a life endangering mission. I can't assign it unless I'm willing to go too. It's called leadership, buddy." He turned to Vinny. "You watch out here, and get out if things turn to shit."

"I'm not just leaving you with those savages. If they catch you, you'll end up six feet deep tonight too."

"Hopefully it won't come to that, but it's better for two to fall than five. Remember that." He fell back into his seat and turned to Skuz. "Let me out."

"Nope."

Garret narrowed his eyes at Skuz who returned the same look in kind. He turned to Ann. "How about you?"

"I have no qualms with you doing this." Ann slid open the door and hopped out. "Just don't get yourself killed."

Garret stepped out onto the dirt path. "I always do my best."

Ann pushed Garret back gently. "And don't let them kill the kid. You watch out for him."

"Easy." Garret pushed off the car. "He's my responsibility, and he'll be just fine."

Ann stood at the open door and watched Garret walk past the front of the car and meet up with a visibly shaking Irving. "I don't like this." Her voice fell to a mere whisper. "Why do I care? It's not my business. It's not the same as last time."

"Did you say something?" Skuz asked. "Get back in here. You're letting the heat out."

She looked at Skuz and slammed the door shut. She

jogged off to catch up with the two. "What am I doing?" She ducked as she approached the two still men in front of her. She whispered as she approached. "Who are we dealing with?" She looked forward and saw two men near the veritable pile of bodies. One lamp illuminated the whole path as one man dragged a body off into the opposite tree line. He reappeared with a hand bracing his arched back as he yawned.

"It looks like a cleanup crew. A cheap one at that. Probably here on orders from the Knights. It makes sense. They wouldn't want to be near this if those bodies become news."

"So we can head back now?" Irving asked.

Garret scratched his chin and pointed over his shoulder. "I suppose so. Go ahead, kid. We'll catch up."

Irving scrambled to his feet and stumbled behind a nearby tree in his haste.

"Did you hear something?" An unfamiliar appalachian voice asked from in front of the two. "It sounded like something moving over there."

"It's probably just a deer or something," another undeniably southern voice answered. "We need to get this all done before dawn. Stop focusing on sounds and focus on the job, boy."

"Man, screw that. I'm going to go check on that. I ain't planning to get mauled by some dumbass bear."

"Have at it, Sampson. Go wrestle you a bear why don't you?"

The pair watched as the farthest of the two workers reached behind him, extracted a pistol, and cocked it. Garret reached for his firearm when Ana's hand grabbed his and held it in place.

"Stay quiet and this might work." Ana pushed Garret onto the cool grass and fell on top of him. She grabbed a bundle of branches that had fallen off a nearby tree and placed it atop her back. Her voice was barely audible. Her hair encompassed his entire view and blocked out all light once her nose was scarcely an inch away. "Stay still."

Heavy footsteps crunching the grass and the symphony of insects was all that could be heard. Garret felt Ann's breath against his mouth suddenly pause as the footsteps ended.

"I could have sworn I heard something. Well tarnation, wouldn't you know it? I think the critter ran off before I got here."

"I'll tell you what you heard. It was a stupid squirrel or raccoon. What were you hoping for? Supper?"

The footsteps began again but were becoming softer with each step. "I thought it might be a complication. In this line of work you never know who's watching. Besides, don't be knocking squirrel stew if you haven't tried it."

The voices were becoming indistinct. Garret reached a hand up and tapped Ann's shoulder. "As much as I enjoy this position, I think the danger's past."

"Oh poo." Ann climbed off Garret but kept her head below the nearby bush. "I was just getting comfortable too." She winked at him.

Garret inched away from the workers along with Ann. "What the hell are you doing here? Not that I'm complaining. You just kept it from popping off."

"One firefight's enough for a day, don't you think?"

"You're not wrong," Garret smirked. The two caught up with Irving outside the car. He stood outside, looking in the passenger front window.

"Where'd they go?" Irving asked. He turned around and faced Garret and Ann. "They're not in there."

"Don't even joke about something like..." Garret swung

the door open and went quiet. "Fucking shit. I guess we're going looking."

"In this humongous forest?" Irving asked. "That's a needle in a proverbial haystack."

"Dumbass." Garret gave a playful shove on Irving's shoulder. "They're probably just over at the body. Let's get on over there and bust their asses for wandering off already." Garret swaggered past Irving toward the grave site, leaving the two behind him. "Come on, prospect. Follow me and learn something."

Ann opened the trunk and reached inside. "Hey, hold up."

Garret turned around and paused. "Yeah?"

"I don't think they're at the body." She hauled out three shovels. "No shovels were missing." She pointed down at the dirt. "See the shoe prints heading in the other direction. It looks like they either left willingly, or someone dragged them away."

"There's no way those two would let themselves get kidnapped," Garret said, taking off ahead.

"I don't know about that," Ann said under her breath, staring at the footprints.

Irving gave a nervous glance at Ann at his side. "Where do you think they went?"

Ann shrugged. "I don't know those two. You'd know better than I. You've been here for a while, right?""

"I've been here ten months thus far. I'm mostly just doing things for the fellas though. I never get the chance to talk too much with all the junk I'm doing. These dudes don't screw around with work, so they're probably just playing a prank. The only thing that concerns me is they follow orders to a 'T'. If Garret said to stay put, they'd stay here unless something happened."

"That's worrying." Ann's gaze focused on Garret's broad back as they walked.

Garret pushed through an especially thick bush and stopped once he'd trudged through. His head scanned left and right.

"They here?" Irving asked, pushing through the foliage.

"They're gone." Garret scampered to the open hole. "The body's still here. Okay, time for a new plan. First we finish here, then we go find Skuz and Vinny. We can't allow this body to be exposed to air any longer. It's just a call to the five-o away from being under investigation." He held up a hand toward Ann. "Toss me one and let's get started."

Ann hefted a shovel underhanded to Garret and another to Irving.

"Before we start, let's do the preliminary work." Garret placed a palm beside the hole and hopped down beside the charred skeleton. He lifted his boot and unleashed a flurry of stomps until the skull eventually crumbled. "Get down here and help. It'll take forever otherwise."

"I think that's on you." Ann pushed Irving closer to the grave. "I'd use the shovel, personally."

"Good looking out." Garret spiked the end of the instrument into the remaining bits of skull, obliterating it." He lifted his foot and stomped where it once was. "She's right. Split it first, then crush it."

"This is disgusting." Irving jabbed the metal tool through the body's leg.

"Just think of it this way," Garret said. "It's necessary to stay out of the pen. You know what twenty-three and one means kid? Because that's what we'd get if we were caught right now, almost guaranteed."

"The number of hours in a day?"

"No, you blithering idiot."

"He's talking about the hole," Ann said. "Prison's jail if you will. You're locked up for twenty-three hours and you get one hour out of your solitary cell."

"One hour?" Irving stepped on the leg bone. "I thought you only went to the hole if you shanked someone or were caught with contraband."

"Normally, yes," Garret said, "In this case, the CO's might have a different plan. I mean, we are mutilating a dead body here. That's probably a pretty high-risk inmate in their minds." He stomped on the ribs. "You don't have to worry. I've been to the pen, kid. I'm not going back. I don't intend on letting any of you go there either. Just stick with me and do what I say. You'll be fine."

"Okay, good." Irving visibly relaxed and even smiled as he crushed assorted skeletal remains.

"I'm more surprised our newest arrival knows about solitary." Garret stuck a shovel through another rib and leaned on it. "What'd you do? Fight over ramen noodles to be thrown in there? Knowing you, I can't imagine it's too bad."

"I introduced my blinkie to my cellmate."

"Uh, what's a blinkie?" Irving asked.

"She flashed a shank and probably scared the bitch." Garret picked the shovel up and resumed the job. "Interesting. Did you use it, or was it an intimidation play? My bet is it was to get a viking out of your cell, right? Wait, are dirty female inmates called vikings or some other name?"

Ann's facial expression turned dour. "With all due respect, that's none of your business."

"Alright now, no need for that tone, darling," Garret said in a suave voice. "I was just interested is all. A guy needs some entertainment in times like this. Especially when his backup has disappeared."

"It's not fun memories. I don't know how you can

remember that misery and not be pissed," Ann growled with her next stomp. "It was a bad time in my life. Let's leave it at that."

"Fair enough. I guess I'll just enlighten the prospect some more." He watched the prospect crush another bone to dust. "After we're done with this, we'll toss some gas to cover the dust. That way it'll be next to impossible to get any evidence off this mess. After all that, we cover it back up. Everyone's got a different way of dealing with bodies, but ours is probably one of the best if I do say so myself."

"It's certainly exhaustive," Ann panted. "Maybe a little overkill, but you can't argue with the results."

"Don't tire yourself too early now, girl," Garret said. "We've got a nice night of hiking ahead of us. We're not leaving this forest until we find Skuz and Vin."

"I know the deal," Ann said. "Just remember, I'm out after this job. That's the deal. I help you find them after filling in this hole, and I'm done."

"Of course. We're gentlemen." He gave a playful slap to Irving's shoulder. "Right, kid?"

"We are? I mean, we are."

"Don't pay attention to the prospect. He's nervous. We always keep our word."

"We'll see. You'd better," Ann muttered under her breath.

"What was that?" Garret asked.

"Nothing. Let's just finish this crushing task."

Irving laughed, causing the two to look at him. "That was pretty good."

A half hour later...

43

"Fricking hell, we're done." Garret tossed the last pile of dirt on the makeshift grave. "Hey, Prospect, catch this and take it back to the car." He threw the digging instrument to Irving who caught it in one hand.

Irving transferred one shovel to his other hand and held out an open hand to Ann. "Come on. I only want to make one trip."

"Yeah." She handed him the tool and watched him sprint back to the vehicle. She turned to Garret. "Any idea how we're going to track these guys in the middle of this forest? Where would they have gone?"

Garret spit on the grass at his feet and looked ahead into the darkness. "They wouldn't have. That's what has me concerned. Don't tell the prospect I said that."

"Always have to have that hard ass image huh?" Ann asked. "Someone might call you boys insecure."

"Someone might say maybe that's why we're still around."

"Low blow."

"You started it, missy."

Irving jogged back. "Alright, they're packed up. Are we going looking now?"

"You know it." Garret reached into his pocket and removed his phone. "Just give me a minute. I don't want us getting lost."

"What's a phone going to do?" Ann asked.

"The wonders of technology are limitless. I found an app where I can record where I am utilizing the gps of my phone. Using that I can save our location and it'll guide us right back here."

"Why do you have that app? Do you get lost often?"

"That's not important right now." Garret took off in a

brisk walk into the night, following the boot prints near the car. "What's important is getting this done. Follow me."

Irving gestured to Ann. "Ladies first."

Ann took off into a run and caught up with Garret. She walked side by side through the brush and tree lines. "You should have gotten an app where you could track your buddies using their phone numbers. At least then we'd know we're making progress, not wandering around in the dark."

"Enough," Garret snapped. "I know. This sucks. You won't get an argument from me. I'm not leaving them behind. You understand me?"

"More than you know." She shoved her hands in her pants pockets and watched the ground turn from grass to a dirt path. "Hold up." She held up her arm and barred Garret's forward progress. "Shine your phone down here."

"What's up?" Garret squatted down and held his phone to the ground, illuminating boot prints. "This could be them or the Knights' cleaners. There's no way to know. Still, it's a lead. Look." He pointed ahead. "They end here. They don't keep going. Where the hell did they go?"

"Those prints look awfully big." Irving placed his hands on his knees and squinted at the footprints. "They don't look like Vinny's."

"You know how big his shoes are?" Garret asked.

"Well, not a hundred percent."

"Then we're checking. If you were lost out here in the middle of the night, would you want us to give up based on some shoe sizes we weren't sure of?"

Irving bit his lip and looked away. "Sorry, I guess not."

"Exactly, we're brothers out here. Start acting like it."

"I don't mean to be the downer here," Ann said, "but I think it's time to start entertaining the idea that they were taken. These look like tire marks here." Ann paced to the left farther down the trail and pointed down at the grooves in the dirt.

"That's bad news for everyone then."

"How so?" Ann asked. "I'm gone after this."

"You're gone after we find them, not a moment before. That was the deal, remember?"

"He has a point," Irving said. "That was what you agreed to."

"Were you a paralegal before you joined, kid?" Ann glared at Irving. "I know what I said."

"Don't bitch at the kid for your laziness," Garret frowned. "We're all tuckered out. Let's just push through this. We still have a lot of land to search before we head back..."

4

"What time is it?" Ann asked from the back seat.

"It's eight a.m." Garret rubbed his eyes as he pulled into the club's parking lot. "I'm not looking forward to this conversation."

"You? I'm the one about to be drafted for an extra few days when I should be a hundred miles away," Ann said.

Garret parked the car. "You're a big girl. You'll deal with it. At least you're not locked up, since we took care of your clean up."

Everyone exited the vehicle and walked toward the clubhouse. Garret and Irving put on their colors during the walk.

"You're assuming I had no clean-up plans of my own. Aren't you wondering why no one's called the police yet? My own cleaner showed up to that house and cleaned up all that blood. She would have gotten rid of the body too."

"Just accept your circumstances." Garret pulled the door open and walked inside. "Hey yo, we need a meeting right now." He looked at Irving. "Stay out here with her, Prospect. We need to show her the utmost courtesy after all." He

47

walked past the pool table. "Come on, boys. Into church. We've got an emergency."

"What now?" Richard asked, hanging up his pool cue. He stomped on the tile below. "Get in there, now."

Lucien and Tony immediately got up from the bar and filed into the meeting room. Garret walked inside shoulder to shoulder with the president and shut the door behind them.

Irving looked up at Ann at his side. "So, can I get you something to drink?"

"I need a place to sleep."

"Uh, Garret normally uses it, but I don't think he'd mind." He pointed down a hallway on the other side of the room. "It's down there, first door on the right."

"If he has a problem, he'll take it up with me," Ann said. She took off down the hallway. "Try and get some rest, kid."

Irving looked over at the closed curtains of the meeting room. "I doubt I'll be so lucky."

"Send Garret my way after he gets out of there." Ann disappeared inside and slammed the door shut behind her.

Irving cast a longing glance back at the meeting room and tiptoed over to the window. He cupped a hand over his ear and leaned against the glass. He could barely make out indistinct voices.

Meeting Room...

"You lost Vinny and Skuz?" Richard rubbed his chest, gliding over the president patch. "How does that even happen?"

"Here's how it went down." Garret leaned forward. "I

brought the prospect with me on a bit of a scouting mission, and by the time we got back the boys were gone. We went out searching for hours, but all we ever found was their boot prints that suddenly ended next to some tire tracks. My best guess is they were kidnapped while we were scouting out the Knights' cleaners."

Tony scratched his beanie clad head. "It had to be the Knights. They had reason to be there, motive, and means. I say we ride over there and get our boys back."

"Without them, we're not even a charter anymore," Lucien said. He shook his head. "We were already dwindling. Losing two more would break us permanently. You need six for a charter. All we have now are at this table and possibly the prospect. That makes four or five, depending. We need to get them back or recruit. Good luck recruiting if this story gets out. No one will join if we don't try and protect our own.

"I know already!" Richard pounded his fist onto the wooden table. "We can't just roll on them and go in guns blazing. We don't have the numbers - and even if we did, it wouldn't be smart. First things first. We need to find where they are. Then we go get them without a mountain of bodies." He looked to Garret. "Get the prospect to go rumor digging on the internet. We need to find out which of their local hangouts have had a lot of recent activity. The rest of us will be doing some good old-fashioned street surveillance. I want teams of two to stake out each of their properties. They're not a huge organization, so if we see any significant numbers, we're on the right track. Garret, you're with me. Tony, you and Lucien start on the east side of town. We'll take the west."

"At least we get the strip clubs," Lucien laughed lasciviously.

"This isn't a pleasure trip," Richard said. "If you do go in, it had better be a quick in and out to look inside. I don't want you in there all day, old man. I've fielded enough phone calls from your old lady over the years wondering where you were. I don't want a repeat of that."

"Fine," Lucien scoffed with a smirk. "I'll find the tykes and be out in a flash if they're in there."

"You watch him," Richard pointed at Tony. "Make sure you two stay on the move. We don't want anyone spotting us and calling in reinforcements in their territory. Remember, gentlemen, a moving target is a harder target to hit or find. They may be using the same strategy. Take note of any vans you see leaving locales and write down their license plate number. They could be using them to transport Skuz and Vinny for all we know."

"Let's go get our brothers back." Richard banged the gavel against the wooden block.

The men stood up from their seats and exited the room. Irving backed away from the windows at the sudden crack and rubbed his elbows as the door opened.

Garret noticed him and stopped. "You get an easier job this time. Don't worry." He pointed at the personal computer in the corner of the room. "Use the satellite imagery app and go to each of the Knight's hangouts. We can only cover so many at a time. If you notice tons of vehicles, ring us and let us know. You got all that?"

"I got it, but Ann wanted to see you after the meeting." He pointed down the hallway she'd left. "She said she needed rest."

Garret sighed. "Women, can you believe it, Prospect? Fine, before I go I'll pay her a visit. Now get to work. If we're lucky you'll find them before I even head out." He trudged down the narrow hallway until he arrived at the first door on his right.

"Open up. We're about to leave." Garret banged on the door, then placed his hand beside the door. He leaned forward against the frame.

The door opened. Ann grumbled and, without further words, moved back to the bed. She fell onto it and waited as she sat.

"I know you're tired, but we're not done yet." Garret stepped inside and closed the door behind him. "What did you need?"

"I might have an idea where they are."

Garret's eyes widened. "What? How?"

"I'll explain later, but for now you have to take me along. I have a good idea where they might be. You probably won't like it though. They won't have them at their hangouts if I'm right."

"How would you know that?"

"One of my former sisters became old lady of their vice-president during our spiral. They're more than likely using one of our old safehouses. They think you'd have no idea about them. Which is precisely why they bought them after we disbanded."

"Damn. That is smart. Alright, you're with me. Come on then."

"But I haven't slept in like twenty hours."

"Suck it up, cupcake. Now come on." He stepped forward, grabbed her hand, and pulled her into a standing position. "We're with the president today, so be on your best behavior; otherwise, you'll tarnish my reputation." He winked with a sly smirk.

"I'll have you know I'm a perfect lady, Mr..." She looked to the side, "What was your last name again?"

"Price," Garret said. "Garret Price."

"Ann Thompson, good to meet you, Mr. Price."

"Don't call me Price, just Garret."

"Are you two done flirting?" Richard's voice asked, "Get your ass out here. It's time to go."

"Time to go." Garret stepped out into the hallway. "We're riding three deep today."

"That wasn't the plan."

"She can help us." Garret checked behind him to indeed see Ann exiting the room. "She can ride with me."

Richard pushed past Garret and looked her up and down. "Just don't try anything."

"Of course, Mr. President."

He turned and walked past Garret. "Get on your chopper," Richard said. "We're not taking a van this time. We need speed for this. If we find them, we'll call the prospect and get him to bring the van."

5

Garret stopped beside Richard's bike and turned off the engine. "See anything?"

"She might be right." Richard dug into a pouch hanging off his hip and pulled out a pair of binoculars. He brought them to his eyes. "There's a lot of activity here. What did you say this was?"

"It was a roller derby rink the last I remember," Ann said from behind Garret. "They've probably retooled it since then though. It'd be a perfect place to hold somebody hostage. I do know it's closed now, so there's no way it could get that kind of traffic without someone pulling some strings."

"Let's see if the other group has any leads." Richard reached into his pants pocket and dialed a number. "Lucien, any luck yet?"

Loud music could be heard amidst Lucien's voice. "Not yet. We're still looking."

"Well, stop looking in the damned strip club. I can hear the music from here."

"Fine, we just checked the vip area anyway. He's not there."

"I'm sure that's a load off your mind." Richard's voice dripped with sarcasm. "Now move to the next place already. We might have a lead here."

"You got it. Hey, Tony, come on. We're leaving. Rich may have a lead where those boys are."

"For real?" He could hear Tony's surprised voice. "Where are they?"

"Head to the old roller derby rink on the west side."

"Isn't that place abandoned?" Lucien asked.

"Not anymore. Get over here." Richard abruptly ended the phone call. He looked back to Garret and Ann. "Any idea how we're going to confirm they're even in there, much less get them out?"

"Give me those for a second." Garret held his hand out until Richard passed him the binoculars. He looked through them at the motorcycles lined up outside the building. "This won't be easy. They're in a defensive formation. We'll have to wait until nightfall at least. There are like twenty dudes in there by my count."

"That makes a frontal assault an impossibility." Richard leaned over the side of his hog and spat on the pavement below. "Are there any other ways in?"

"There was the entrance in the basement, but no one wants to use that way. I guarantee it."

Garret angled his head to look over his shoulder. "Why's that? It sounds perfect."

"It involves going through a manhole cover on the street, hunching down in the sewers, and coming out in the basement. It's smelly, cramped, and dark as night down there."

"How did you find that?" Richard asked. "It's not something a bunch of ladies would know. No offense."

"That's a funny story. We had a kid get into the building one time. We chased him around due to his stink until he left the same way he came. We saw him open the cover and jump out. He never did come back. Still, I know it would work. I even know the way, since I followed the little bastard through the winding passageways. I'm pretty sure I still remember the path anyway."

"Pretty sure? Garret asked. "I don't like the sound of that."

"Sounds like you'd need a flashlight to even think of heading down there," Richard said. "How long would it take if you had one?"

"I'm not sure," Ann said. "If I had to guess, I'd say fifteen minutes. That's allowing me time to get turned around and figure it out."

"I have an idea." Richard grinned. He whipped out his phone and dialed. "Prospect, get to the west side roller derby rink. Drive the van. We're going to need it. What is it? That confirms it. Get over here now."

"What's the news?" Garret asked, resting his foot on the foot peg below.

Richard deposited the phone into his front pants pocket. "Irving hasn't seen any activity at any of their fronts or their clubhouse, which would indicate our newfound associate here is right." He nodded at the faraway building. "They're in there all right."

"Why don't we go buy a cheap flashlight and head inside while the kid's on the way?" Garret asked. "That way we can be ready and not draw attention. We passed a convenience store right near here."

"Good idea," Richard said. "Then when you get under the building, call us, and we'll set the plan in motion."

"Which is?" Ann leaned back away from Garret and planted her hands on the tiny sliver of seat behind her.

"Call for an emergency meet," Richard said. "They're not going to head out there alone. It'll draw a lot of men out of there. Dealing with a handful is better than all of them. Just keep your head down, and don't go crazy in there. I'll also call Lucien and Tony while you're stocking up. We need all hands on deck."

Later, below the streets...

"I forgot how much it stinks in here." Ann covered her entire mouth and nose with a hand. A retching sound penetrated her hand and echoed around the cramped quarters. Her other hand fell to her knees as she continued gagging.

"It's not so bad once you get used to it." Garret slid past her and shone the light ahead through the tight enclosed canals. "It reminds me of the hole. Remember when guys would go crazy and flood the entire block with sewer water from their toilets? This smells like that."

"Were you locked in there with out and out animals?" Ann asked. "Who does that willingly? The worst I ever saw was a crazy bitch flooding the place with sink water."

"Men with nothing to lose and far too much free time on their hands do anything they can." Garret took another hunched step forward. "About like Vinny and Skuz right now. Let's get a move on. The kid should be here soon, and I want to be in position."

"Alright, fine." She regained some composure and pointed over his shoulder. "The first turn, or is it last from this direction?" She brought a hand to her jaw. "I think we go right here. It's hard giving directions backwards."

"Right would make sense considering the building's physically to our right." Garret turned the corner and waited for Ann to catch up.

She turned the corner and pointed ahead. "Next is left."

"Did you ever catch the kid?"

"Does that matter?"

"Call me a curious man. How about it?"

"I poked my head up onto the street and saw him dashing off. He was too fast for me."

Garret came to an intersection and looked over his shoulder. "Kids usually are."

"It should be left here. We shouldn't be far now. Maybe another hundred feet or so. We should come up in the basement. Let's hope they didn't put anything on top of the entrance."

Garret turned the corner to find a long unbending corridor. "I'm not letting a crate stop me from what has to be done."

"It should be straight ahead," Ann said. "I noticed you and Skuz are close. Did you know him before you joined the Order?"

"We grew up next to each other," Garret offered. "I've known him since I can remember."

"That makes sense."

Garret came to the end of the passage and stood up straight. He raised his arms and placed them on the circular cover. "Give me a hand with this."

Ann stood up in the small space. "It feels like a broom closet in here."

"I didn't know girls couldn't handle a little tight quarters." Garret grinned down his nose at her. "I'm disappointed. You strike me as a tough girl."

"I'll show you tight quarters. Let me get at this." She gritted her teeth and the slab of metal above moved to the side with a squeal. "How about that, tough guy?"

"Not bad," Garret smirked. "Next time do it without my help, and I'll be impressed. Now let me call this in, and we'll get started." He fished the phone out, and his finger danced across the surface. He brought it to his ear. "We're in position. Let us know when to go."

"Alright. I'm calling now. Be careful in there, Garret. Let her go first. You never know."

"I got it. I'll hear from you soon." He dumped the device in his pants pocket. "We go when he calls back."

"I'm sure they're fine," Ann said.

Garret's face turned somber. "They better be, or there will be hell to pay. I've gotten him out of worse than this before believe it or not."

"Bullshit."

"No, really. He's been kidnapped twice now. Back in high school he got grabbed up by a local street gang that he'd been smart mouthing off to during school. They had him tied to a chair cutting him up when I got there. Suffice it to say, they never did that again after the boys and I had a word with them."

"Right. This situation is a little different though. We can't just go wild here. Right?"

"We don't want a tri-state beef. We need to do this with as little blood spilled as possible. We're already at the tipping point of an all-out war." Garret felt his pocket vibrate. He checked the screen. "Alright, we're ready to roll out. I'll go first." He climbed up the metal footholds in the wall and into the musty basement filled with crates and various cleaning instruments. The muffled sounds of motorcycles revving up outside the building met their ears.

Ann climbed up. "Now to find them without causing an incident. Did he say how many were still here?"

"Prospect said all but three bikes were leaving."

Ann crept up the stairs in the corner to the door. "Let me lead. I have an idea where they might be keeping them."

"Be my guest." Garret followed and stopped a step behind. He reached down to his pant leg and pulled out Ann's .22 caliber pistol. He handed it to her. "Try not to use it if you can help it."

"That's trusting of you." Her left hand snaked behind her and returned with a second .22. "I never carry just one weapon though. You boys are lazy."

Garret pulled out his own pistol. "Or gentlemen, depending on who you ask."

"Don't get ahead of yourself." Her hand rested on the knob. "You ready?"

"At your leisure." Garret held his .357 at the ready.

Ann opened the door and stepped through. They stepped into a bright hallway illuminated by the artificial light above.

A towering man ahead leaned sideways against a door frame at the end of the hall. His right hand dangled at his side with a lit cigarette burning away. He brought the stick in front of him before billowing clouds of smoke appeared before him. "I don't know why we're even meeting with those bastards. We should roll up on them and unleash holy hell after yesterday."

Another voice from further in the room responded. "We hold all the cards. Why not listen to them grovel over their two members? Besides, we get to unleash all of our rage on them, so it's not a total loss. Why don't you take another turn beating up the purple one?"

"He was already coughing blood. I don't want to break our negotiating chips further. I don't like this," the smoking man's deep voice grumbled.

"You don't like anything when you get outvoted. Come over here and help me with these boxes, and make yourself useful."

Garret took a step forward, his hands balled into fists. He watched the man disappear behind the door frame then felt a hand grab his wrist. He turned to see Ann shaking her head.

"It's not worth it. Let's just look around while they're busy, okay?" She pulled him back.

Garret snarled down the hallway. He yanked his hand free from Ann's hold. "Yeah. I just lost my head there for a second." He looked ahead and nodded toward a nearby door. "Let's start here." He stalked over to a nearby cracked open door on their right.

He pushed it open with a creak, and a voice from inside greeted him. A man sitting with his back to the door was hunched over a lone table with ambient music playing from the boombox on the surface. "Yes? I told you I was cleaning my piece, Earl. What is it now?"

Garret walked up behind him without trying to conceal his presence. "Just one thing, buddy."

He gasped and looked over his shoulder. "Hey, you're n-" The man was caught off guard as he was enveloped in a rear, naked choke hold.

"No, I'm not Earl. Earl is busy. You're going to tell me where your two prisoners are if you want to live through the day. I can snap your neck, slice your neck open, or blow your head off if you don't. What's it going to be?"

"The guy with the dumbass haircut is still here. Head out the door, take a right and it's the second door on your right. Just don't kill me, man."

"The end of the hallway essentially," Garret said with a squeeze of his arms. "Where's the other one?"

"They took him to the meet," he gasped out. "They said they might need leverage when dealing with that sneaky rat Rich."

"You watch your fucking mouth," Garret growled.

"Do it already. Kill me. I tire of this."

"Don't tempt him." Ann came up beside Garret. "Move your head."

Garret moved his head a foot to the left.

Ann's right hand wound up and rocketed into the back of the man's head. He went limp in Garret's grip. "He'll only be out for a few minutes at best. We need to hurry."

"That's one way of ending a conversation." Garret dropped the limp body. "That's better than he deserves." Garret nudged the unconscious man with his toe. He stepped past Ann toward the hallway. "Come on, there's no time to waste."

Garret peeked out the door. The man at the end was no longer there. "This could complicate things," he whispered. "Watch the doorway. I'm going in alone."

"The big guy could be watching your friend."

"Bad news for him if he is." Garret stalked down the hallway without further words.

"Oh no," Ann muttered. She pointed her .22 past Garret at the open doorway.

Garret reached the door and pushed his ear against the frame. He could hear Skuz's voice inside.

"I'm hungry."

"You're lucky you're still in the realm of the living. Don't complain too much," the same smoky voice from before said. "If it was up to me, I'd continue your punishment from before. Lucky for you, you're worth more alive than dead."

"I'll stop asking about food when you bring Vinny back here. How about that?"

A loud crash interrupted the conversation. "Shut up. You'll do what I say."

"Oh, fuck that." Garret stood up and opened the door. He saw Skuz covered in bruises, cuts, and dirt tied to a chair in front of him. The chair was laying on its side on the floor. The tall man from before stood over him. Garret closed the door behind him without a sound.

The man wound up a kick when a click from behind froze him.

"Stop right there," Garret growled through gritted teeth. "You're going to untie him and take his place right now."

"If I don't?"

"Then you get a new venting hole in your head." He stepped forward and shoved the cold end of the gun into the back of his head. Take off those restraints now," Garret said.

"Fine." He circled around Skuz and his hands went to Skuz's hands behind the chair. "You know what this means?" He glared up at Garret, his grey handlebar mustache staring back at the young man.

"Let me guess," Garret said, "War with your whole charter? We may not be as numerous as you boys, but we'll handle it."

"We'll see." The older man finished his task and threw his hands above his head. "What's it going to be? Are you going to kill me here?"

Skuz scampered out of the chair toward Garret and settled in the nearby corner by the door. "Don't do it," he coughed out.

Garret kept the weapon and his eyes pointed at the man. He got to one knee and his left hand reached over to Skuz. "No permanent damage?"

"I'm cool." Skuz staggered to his feet and braced himself against the wall with one hand.

"Does this room have a lock on it?" Garret asked.

"I assume so. They left me in here alone."

"Okay then," Garret smirked, "we can work with that."

He backed up a couple steps and pushed the door open. "Go to the right and meet up with Ann. I'll be right there. We're getting out of here."

"That cunt is still in town?" the old man asked. "I'm surprised, considering."

"Considering what?"

"We strong armed them out of commission. Did you ever wonder how they made their money? They didn't sell cookies."

Garret's eyebrows raised, "You're telling me they used to smuggle people like you?"

"They weren't as good as us of course. They tended to give the cargo box extra furnishings, upping the costs and lowering profits. It was amateur hour. We needed the lion's share of the business, so we came up with a plan to take their slice of the pie. All we needed was an inside woma-"

A deafening crack stopped the man's words as he slumped back against the wall.

"Jesus!" Garret crashed against the wall beside him and covered his ears. He turned around to see Ann pointing her .22. A faint trail of smoke came from the barrel. She leaned out the door and fired off another round. "Time to go."

"What the fuck is going on back there?" an unfamiliar voice asked.

"Mind your own business," Ann squeezed off a couple

more rounds and dragged Garret out of the room by his hand, "if you know what's good for you."

"What the hell are you doing here, Ann?" the male voice asked. "I thought you'd learned your lesson and were leaving town."

Ann yelled over her shoulder as they jogged down the hallway. "Stick to what you boys do best, exploiting women. Thinking never suited you."

They turned the corner. Garret opened the basement door and motioned to Skuz. "Get down here, brother. We're getting out of here."

"In the basement?" Skuz asked.

"Just get in there." Garret shoved Skuz toward the door. He turned to see Ann peeking around the corner. "Let's go."

"I'm out of here, Sir Knight. Have fun cleaning up that body." She fired off one last round around the corner, eliciting a loud scream.

"You whore, you'll pay for that." The voice got quiet. "Oh God, my leg. You think this is over?"

"I expect not," Ann responded. "It'll never be over for me after what you did to my girls."

"Come on already." Garret tugged at Ann's hand. "We need to go now."

"You're lucky. You get to live today. Enjoy it for however long you can."

Ann and Garret followed Skuz down the stairs into the dank and musty basement.

"Tell me we're not going down into that thing," Skuz said, pointing at the open manhole sized opening in the floor. "It stinks like shit."

"How do you think we got in?" Garret asked. "Get in. I don't care what you smell." He raised his view to Ann. "You're next. Go! I'll cover us." He aimed at the door.

She ducked out of his line of fire and climbed down. "He'll never crawl his way over here in time, but knock yourself out." Her head disappeared beneath the horizon of the hole.

"My turn." Garret stepped down onto the first metal bar and looked to his right at the cover. He grabbed it and slid it over. Once the slab of metal got near he descended another step and pushed the cover up as he moved it over the hole until it clicked into place above him. "Done." He looked below and finished his descent.

"Hey, buddy, I appreciate the rescue and all." Skuz held his nose and watched as Ann moved forward on her knees. "Just try not to make me go through the sewers next time, alright?"

"It was the only way." Garret followed Ann. "Just be glad you'll get the prospects ride until we get back to the clubhouse. If we're lucky, the rest of the boys got Vinny back."

Meanwhile with the rest of the club.

"You boys are packing, right?" Lucien asked from the backseat.

"Just relax," Richard said. "I'll be the one talking. Just be ready in case it goes down." He looked to his left at Tony. "That means keeping the van running while the meet's happening. We may need to leave in a hurry."

Lucien rolled down the window in the back and stuck his arm out. "I don't trust them."

"You don't trust anyone outside the club," Tony laughed. "What else is new?"

"I'm more worried about Garret and that girl. I should have sent someone with him at least."

"He'll be okay. Garret's a tough bastard." Tony looked to his right and saw Richard staring at him. "I mean that in the best way."

"Whatever." Richard looked out the front window and saw two vans approaching down the dirt path. "Get ready. Here we go. Lucien, you're with me." He reached over, opened the passenger door, and stepped outside. Lucien stood by his side with his hands near his hips, leaving the van doors open.

Richard raised a hand over his cover and raised his voice. "Howdy, boys. I think you've got something of ours, and we want it back. Let's do it civilized and not escalate this situation. That's not good for business for anybody."

The front van's back doors exploded open with grunts and a puff of dust as a wriggling, blindfolded body flopped on the dirt. Another leather clad figure jumped out behind him and dragged him up to a standing position. "Get over there," he growled.

The blindfolded figure stumbled forward to the front of the van, but was stopped by the man behind with a grip on his shoulder. "That's far enough."

Both vans' doors opened, and more men filed outside.

"I have a bad feeling about this," Richard said, loud enough for Lucien to hear. "They don't need that much manpower for a simple hand off. Be ready."

"You got it, Pres." Lucien's hand gripped the handle of his firearm. His eyes narrowed at the growing mob across the meadow.

"Come on, Enrique. Let's talk about this like grown-ups. There's no need for the show of force."

The front van's door opened, and another man stepped

out. An unmistakably deep voice came from him. "I beg to differ, Rich. You know the rules of the game as well as I do. You kill my men, I kill yours - or I appear weak, and my business fails. I am a businessman, and I'm not about to disappoint my men or my clients." He stood between four of his men on either side.

"You mean ES-15? That's a dangerous gambit even for you. I heard they kill their own if they mess up. I'd hate to see that happen to a nice guy like you."

"Your concern is duly noted," Enrique said with a sarcastic bite. "However, they have taught me tricks on how to deal with annoying pests. Say hello to your old friend Vinny." He walked forward and kicked the back of Vinny's knee causing him to stumble to the ground. He backed up, looked to his left, and nodded.

The man pulled out a handgun and leveled it at the back of Vinny's head.

"Wait!" Richard reached out with his palm out. "We can talk about terms."

"Like you did with my men when your boys killed three of mine and crippled nearly half a dozen? There's nothing to talk about." He glanced at the man on his left. "Do it."

The gun bounced back with a muzzle flash and a crack. Vinny crumpled to the ground and stopped moving.

"You son of a whore!" Richard banged on the door and bared his teeth. "You'll regret that, you piece of shit."

"Kill them all." Enrique ran back behind the van and the men took aim.

"We're leaving." Richard dove back into the van and slammed the door shut. "Get us the fuck out of here and stay down.

Lucien hopped into the front seat and slammed the door shut.

Tony leaned down, stepped on the gas, and rotated the wheel as bullets pierced the windshield. "God damn, man. This is crazy." New cracks stopped appearing. He raised his head and looked out the mirror on his left. "I think we're clear." He looked to his right and glanced over his shoulder. "Is anyone hit?"

"I'm whole." Richard sat with his chin on his chest. His voice was weak and his eyes were downcast.

"I say we kill them all for this.

6

G arret steered his bike into the parking lot. He leaned the bike onto the kickstand and removed his helmet. He saw Skuz pull into the spot next to his and shut off his engine. He climbed off the bike with Ann. "How'd your little drive with the prospect go?"

Skuz reached down and removed the hand clasped around his waist. "Get off of me, you fag." He jumped off the motorcycle. "It's like he's never had to ride bitch before, hugging on me like that."

"Seems like bitch behavior to me," Ann snickered. "Sorry, kid. Next time grab onto the bike below."

Garret and Skuz took off ahead of the other two toward the clubhouse. Garret looked up at the painted skull on the side of the building. "At least one good thing happened today."

Skuz pushed the door open and held it for Garret. "It's good to be home."

"Welcome back." Richard sat at a nearby table. He stared ahead with a blank expression and his voice weary. "It's good to see half the plan worked at least."

"What do you mean half?" Garret asked.

"While you three were sneaking into the Knight's secret hangout, we had our own run in."

"Right," Garret said. "They said they'd taken Vinny with them to the meet."

"That's right," Lucien said from the bar. He poured more alcohol into the shot glass in front of him. He drank all the liquid with a grimace before continuing. "Only they didn't do it as a hostage exchange program."

"You're not saying what I think you are." Skuz leaned against the table and stared at Richard.

"I'm sorry, gentlemen, but Vinny caught a bullet." Richard sighed. "They rolled up, brought him out, and just blew his brains out right there on the spot. I hadn't even gotten a greeting out yet before it all went down."

"They weren't on a mission of peace, that's for sure." Lucien slammed the glass down on the bar.

Garret's voice went low. "That means we need the prospect just to stay whole."

Richard looked up with a nod. "I know." His timid voice became loud. "Meeting in fifteen minutes. Everyone's required to attend, even our newest associate."

"I'll go let them know," Garret said. He poked Skuz's shoulder and pointed at Lucien. "Try to keep him halfway sober before the meeting, okay?"

"Why do I get the shit job right after escaping?"

"You always had a way with the old man. Work your persuasive powers." He exited the building to see both Ann and Irving still near his bike. He shoved a hand inside his pocket and strode toward them. "There's a meeting in fifteen minutes, and you're both required to attend."

"I'll be there. How's Vinny?" Irving asked, staring at Garret's sky-blue eyes. Garret shook his head. "The cowards shot him at the meet with the men. They didn't even get a chance to say anything."

"Oh shit." Irving's eyes widened and then looked down at the concrete. "I'm sorry, man."

"We all are."

"Is it war then?" Ann asked.

Garret glared at her. "We don't know yet. I would guess so after your little outburst back there."

"Her outburst?" Irving looked between them. "What happened over there?"

"You'll see." Garret plucked his cigarette pack out of his plaid shirt pocket and extracted one. He lit it and puffed out a cloud of smoke. "We have a lot to talk about today."

"I was only-" Ann started before she was interrupted.

"Save it," Garret said. "I'm going to go get started on funeral arrangements before the meet. It's the least we can do for his family." He nodded at Irving. "Do you still have the number for Vinny's sister?"

"Yeah, it's inside by the bar." He hopped off the bike. "I'll go get it."

"Thanks, man, and remember to bring your dues when you show up for the meeting. He watched with a tiny smile as Irving's eyes lit up as he took off into a sprint toward the building.

"As for you," Garret said turning back to Ann, his face dour, "I hope it was worth it. Whatever that old dude was about to say better have been worth starting a war over, because you may have just ignited one."

"It was my business, not yours."

"Yeah? Well your business of smuggling may have just fucked my club. You'll understand if I'm pissed." The cigarette danced around Garret's mouth with every word. "I don't care how your club made money, or who turned on

71

you. What I care about is the lives of every man in that building, and you endangered them with this little stunt."

Ann looked to the left toward the open street.

"Nothing to say? I guess not. I wouldn't either. You probably think you'll be free after this meeting. Why should you care? You get to make a new life after this. We're the ones to clean it up for you after all." He took the cancer stick out of his mouth and flicked it to the ground before stepping on it. "I'm heading inside. We'll call for you when we're ready."

Ann watched him disappear inside the graffitied building. Her voice came out a mere whisper. "Kate, you'd better appreciate this."

Ten minutes later, inside the meeting room

"As you all know, we lost Vinny today. Garret got hold of his family, and we're going to take care of the costs." He looked at the sparse table. "We're here not to focus on the past, but the future. We're down to just the five of us: Lucien, Garret, Skuz, Tony, and me. We need one more to stay whole. We need to vote whether to promote Irving or not. Show of hands for inducting the prospect.

Everyone around the table raised their hands.

Richard looked to Tony. "Bring the prospect in." He went to a locker in the corner of the room and extracted two patches before returning to his seat. He kept them under the table.

Tony pushed his chair out and opened the door behind him. "Get in here." He reclaimed his seat and waited.

Irving poked his head inside, then stepped into the room. "Yes?"

"You've been a prospect for nearly a year now. It's time we do something we should have done right from the start," Richard said, his voice firm.

Irving's eyes darted across the room. He backed up a step and bumped into the door. "What?"

Richard's hands appeared above the table and tossed the patches onto the table. "Sew those on. You're a full-fledged member. You do have the dues, right?"

Irving's eyes bugged out. He dug in his pants pockets before withdrawing the necessary money and putting it on the table. "Of course."

Everyone around the table cheered, stood up, and congratulated Irving with pats on the shoulder.

"Take a seat and get sewing, brother." Tony pointed at the empty seat beside his. "He reached up, removed his beanie, and ruffled his short black hair.

"That's right." Richard banged the gavel on the wooden block. "It's a new day for the prospect, but it's still the same for us. For now, Skuz, tell us how this happened."

Everyone settled back in around the table except Irving, who moved to the locker and removed the various supplies needed before taking his seat.

"We were sitting in the van watching the prospect, Garret, and the woman creep through the darkness when we hear a female voice and an unmistakable banging on the window. When I opened the door to see what was going on, I was grabbed. They used a woman as bait for us to get out of the car. They drug off both me and Vinny, and the rest is history."

"We're in a war. The Knights have made that abundantly clear," Richard stated. "We need to finish this quickly. We can't take a prolonged shooting war. Anyone have any ideas?"

"Turtle up," Tony said as Irving took the seat beside him. "Arm up, close the gate to the clubhouse, and don't let anyone in."

"We need to go on the offense." Lucien pounded his fist onto the table. "Defense won't solve this. It'll just make it take longer. We need to strike first, hard, and decisively."

"Assassination's always an option," Garret said. "If we do it right, we could make it devastating and still keep the spotlight off us." He looked at Lucien. "It won't be as fast or flashy as all out assaults, but it does at least offer a chance at success."

"Who the hell would we knock off?" Skuz asked from Garret's side. "If we go after the local charter president, we'll have the rest of the tri-state Knights on our asses. We'd be screwed."

"We don't go after the shot callers with clout," Garret said. "We go after the rank and file. Take their feet out from under them. Without the grunts, they'll either have to cry to the mother charter and look like a bitch, or let this beef go."

Tony elbowed Irving. "What do you think?"

Irving looked up from his sewing and saw everyone around the table looking at him. "I never thought I'd say this, but assassination sounds like the most sensible plan. Make it look like an accident. They won't even know it was us. For example, we could sabotage some of their bikes. We wait, watch them for a bit, and when the coast is clear we go for it."

"It doesn't deliver a message though," Lucien said. "We need to show we're not afraid of these animals. Skulking around the shadows doesn't show that."

"What do you say, Pres?" Garret asked, entwining his hands in front of him.

"We can't win in an all-out war." He looked at Lucien.

"Sorry, old timer." He cleared his throat. "We're not going to hide inside our clubhouse either. Sorry, Tony. I agree with Garret on this one. We do need a vote however. Show of hands, who think we should go with knocking them off one by one?"

Irving, Garret, and Richard raised their hands."

"Who thinks we should hole up in here?"

Skuz and Tony's hands raised.

"That settles it, majority rules. We're going hunting." He banged the gavel down. "We have a couple more things to decide before we head out. We need a new sergeant at arms now that Vinny's gone. Suggestions?"

"Garret," Lucien said.

Richard looked at Garret. "You have a problem with that?"

"Nah, man. I can handle it," Garret said with a cocky grin.

"Show of hands, who votes for Garret to become the new sergeant at arms?"

Every arm, including Irving's, shot up.

"Congratulations," Richard said, tossing the patch in front of Garret. "Now just one last thing to take care of today."

"The woman," Garret spat. "We promised we'd let her go after we found Skuz and Vinny.

"She did help us get Skuz back," Irving said.

"She also was the one who shot one of them during the rescue. She was hiding something," Garret said. "The guy was talking about their smuggling business. He said her club was into that, but they spent too much on amenities."

"And?" Lucien asked.

"And then she blew his brains out. She was covering

something up. I don't know what it is, but I know that much."

"We should kick her ass out. We don't need a loose cannon." Skuz looked over Tony's shoulder at the window. "She's not one of us. We followed through on the deal. It's over."

"Agreed." Lucien ran a hand through his white beard. "It'll be one less thing to worry about."

"She is the only one who knows where any of her old club's fronts are," Garret frowned. "As much as I don't like it, that's where they're likely to be holed up. They won't go back to businesses we know they own in the middle of a war."

"That's true," Tony said. "Can we trust her to not keep shooting the places up? All these bodies dropping are bad for business."

"If she knows where they are, I say we keep her until this is done," Lucien said. "We can't hit them if we don't know where they are. Like it or not, she's our intel."

"I agree," Richard said with a nod. "We're in a war now. The only way to end it is with force. To apply it, we need her knowledge. Garret, go tell our newest guest she'll be our guest until this is all settled."

"She'll love that," Garret said, his voice dripping with sarcasm.

"Who cares?" the President asked. "It's partly her fault anyway for starting this shit. The first step is to scout out our targets." He banged the gavel down. "Meeting adjourned."

All the men, minus Irving, slid their chairs out and filed out of the room.

Garret picked up the patch and a needle and thread and circled around the table to stare over Irving's shoulder. He reached over his shoulder and tapped the bottom of the kutte. "It's off kilter. Lower the right side an inch. Take it off and do it again. That's your bottom rocker, it has to be perfect." He patted him on the shoulder and exited the room. "Oh, and get a map of the city and bring it to me when you're done, would you?"

He scanned the room and saw Ann sitting in a corner, nursing a drink. He swaggered over and pulled out the opposite seat. "You already know why I'm here."

"I'm not done yet, am I?" she asked, bringing the drink up to her mouth. "Is this because of the kill?"

"Yes." Garret took off his kutte and placed it on the table. "We don't need you to go out in the field if you don't want. Just grab a marker and circle all the places they might be."

"You don't want me shooting anyone else without the go ahead. That's what this is."

He sewed the title onto the vest. "That's right."

"I need to be in the field for this one."

"Too bad," Garret said. "I haven't seen where you follow orders yet. That's a liability we're not dealing with."

"You're going after the Knights again. You need my help either way. Guess which option involves me helping you. It's not the one where you dictate terms."

"Is that right?"

Ann jabbed a thumb into her chest. "You need my help for your little war. I know where they're newly acquired properties are. They're off the grid, and it would take you a week or longer to get the list the old-fashioned way. My guess is, you don't have the time or patience for that to work. Am I right? Don't waste both our time with this machismo authority crap."

Garret leaned forward. "You're a handful, aren't you?"

"According to my past boyfriends. I am a confident thirty-four C after all."

"How about a compromise? We bring you along to the locale, but you stay behind. That way we don't have to worry about anymore surprise kills."

"I have to go inside. It's not negotiable."

"Why the fuck not?" Garret growled.

"It's complicated." She looked away at the television mounted in the corner of the room.

"Complicated or not, you'd better explain what that means. Are you trying to protect someone? An old club member maybe? Was she the inside woman the old man was talking about before you killed him?"

"No, that was Sheila. She's become the new old lady of their vice president. I couldn't give less of a shit about her. I'm doing this for Kate."

"Who is Kate?" Garret asked.

"Kate was the last recruit we had. She was inducted about two months before the spiral began. Your prospect, Irving, reminds me a lot of her. You know the type, a good kid, hard worker, always raises the mood."

"What's the story there? Why would she be with them?"

"Sheila and Kate were assigned to do vetting work on one of our newest clients who had to hop the Canadian border. During their investigation, Sheila supposedly lost Kate to a raid by the Knights. I thought it was shady at best, so I did some snooping around."

"What did you find?"

"That she's now an indentured servant of the club. My guess is she was an offering from Sheila to get into the good graces of the club. The only way I know that is by paying random people to look at her picture and go into their club. The last I heard, she was tending bar at one of their night clubs. Who knows where she is now?"

"Things are starting to make sense now." Garret leaned

back in the chair. "I can understand the motivation, but why the secrecy? We don't care what your past is, so long as it doesn't bite us. It could have saved this war if you'd just been honest."

"Would you just tell a bunch of strangers in a one percenter motorcycle club your life story and beg for their help? No, you wouldn't."

"She must be important to you for you to stick around this town. Weren't you wanting to leave after all this? What happened to that? Afraid we'd take a scorched earth policy in our war? Maybe you're just trying to use us as cover and manpower in your little rescue attempt before you ride off into the sunset?"

"I won't deny my looking for her. How about it? Let me join you, and I'll be a good girl until we find Kate."

Garret looked over his shoulder at the rest filing out of the building. "Fine. Let's go. All I ask is no crazy shenanigans when we do find her."

"Great." She jumped out of her seat. "I guess I'll ride with you then. I'll just go."

"Before we get moving," Garret raised his hand, "have you got that map ready?"

"Right here." Irving jogged up to the table and scratched his bald head. "What's it for?"

"For my marking where your rivals are holing up." She looked up at him. "Got a pen?"

Garret dug into his pants pocket and tossed one onto the table. "I'll go show the boys this, and we'll be off."

7

Garret stopped the bike and killed the engine. He reached up and removed the helmet from his head. "You're sure this is the place?"

"That's it all right - the old clubhouse for my club." Ann pointed over his shoulder down the street toward a building behind a red light. "That's where I first ran into the girls when I was eighteen."

"It's a nice recruiting ground." Garret stepped off the motorcycle and placed his helmet on the handlebar. "It's chocked full of hangout spots and restaurants, nice and low key."

"We liked to keep our business to ourselves. No one around here goes prying into another person's business. Mom and pop stores don't generally care so long as no gunshots go off nearby."

"That makes sense." His eyes scoured the busy street.

Ann rubbed the seat Garret had just occupied. "I couldn't help but notice you all formally inducted the kid."

"That's right." Garret raised a hand above his eyes and squinted.

"Do you think he's ready, Mr. Sergeant at Arms? Don't think I didn't notice that promotion either."

"He knew what life he was signing up for the day he showed up at the clubhouse. He's a big boy, mommy." He looked back with a grin.

"You want to tell me the plan? Why did we stop to buy binoculars?"

"Are you my old lady?"

"Hell no."

"Then realize we're following the only plan that makes sense considering the situation. We're not here to start a fire-fight, only to scout out the place. We take the intel back and formulate our next step tonight. Then finally get some sleep."

Ann yawned. "Good, it's been two days for me."

Garret raised the binoculars hanging around his neck and looked at the building. "It's certainly been an exhausting couple of days. It'll all be over soon enough."

"See anything?"

"All I see is a few bikes, nothing definitive."

"This place has plenty of spaces to store loads of weapons. If they're going to hole up anywhere, this is it."

"We're not looking to siege them down. We're looking for that one dumb bastard that gets separated from the pack."

Ann laughed. "Death by a thousand cuts?"

"That's the general idea. Watch the target, memorize their schedule, and snag one before he even knows what's going on. So be on your best behavior. We're just here to observe."

"That's boring."

"Don't complain. It has to be done. Hold up. I see some-one. It looks like someone is exiting the front and starting to patrol alone. We'll see if he does this every hour, and then we might have our first contestant."

"You go ahead and observe." Her eyes fluttered shut. "I'm going to catch up on my beauty sleep." She laid her head down on the seat and curled up.

Garret lowered the binoculars and looked back at the woman lounging in the burning sun. "If you can manage, more power to you." He resumed his scanning.

<hr>

An hour later...

"Wake up," Garret barked.

"This better be good." Ann shot up from Garret's seat and readjusted her crimson hair. "That was a good dream. What is it?"

"That outside patrol is right on the dot. You know what that means?"

"I can go back to sleep again?"

"It means we can plan for it. Wait a minute. A group of four men just exited the building behind him. There's a woman with them. That might be your Kate."

"Kate?" Ann leapt from the seat of the motorcycle and grabbed the binoculars from his grasp. She brought them to her eyes, yanking the cord around Garret's neck toward her. She felt his clean-shaven face pressing against hers as she peered through the lenses. "That's her black hair alright. Oh, sorry about that." She let go of the tool.

Garret coughed and rubbed his neck. "You have a one-track mind. You know that?"

"Where are they taking her?" Ann asked. "Do they just

move her around the different fronts periodically? That would keep people from asking questions."

"Don't even start thinking it."

"I'm just running through the options."

Garret pulled out his phone. "Yeah? I'm just informing my club. Do you think you can sit still for three minutes?" His fingers danced across the number pad and brought the device to his ear. "Yeah, I found our first guest. We just need a van to show him the proper hospitality he deserves."

"You're sure about that?" Richard's voice came from the receiver. "You can get him clean?"

"There's not a doubt in my mind. How's it going on your end?"

"Ah," Richard started, "this place is sealed up tighter than a nun's garments. There's no one here. It looks abandoned. Get back to the club, get to planning, and don't get seen. We'll start this tomorrow."

"Got it. Later, Pres." He ended the call and dropped the phone in his pants pocket. "We can head back now."

"We could totally do it right now you know," Ann said, still staring at the building.

"The plan is to head back, get some rest, plan, and then tomorrow we'll come back." Garret sat down in front of her. "Besides, I'm tired too."

"At least take me home. Don't make me sleep in that crappy room in your clubhouse. It smelled like a college dorm."

"You're our guest. You either get to stay there, or head home with me. Which is it going to be?"

"You have a house?"

"I have an apartment."

"I'll go with you."

"Alright then. Back to the club first, then to my apartment." He revved the motor, causing the deafening engine to roar to life...

8

"What a long day." Garret climbed off the motorcycle and stretched with a grunt.

"At least your meeting was quick." She looked up at the apartment complex towering above her. "You do at least have a couch, right?"

"Don't worry, I'm a perfect gentleman." Garret sauntered forward through the double glass doors ahead and held the door open behind him.

Ann followed. She trailed behind as Garret opened another door leading to a flight of stairs heading up. "My room's on the third floor. Sorry about that. It does help stay in shape though."

They climbed up the cramped stairway side by side. Ann peeked at Garret by her side. "I don't know if I said it before, but I'm sorry about 'Vinny' was it? He didn't deserve that fate. He seemed like a nice enough guy."

"He was." Garret reached the top of the stairs and slung open another door leading into a long hallway lined with doors. "He was always too nice. It's why he died."

"What do you mean?"

Garret fished the key out of his pocket and tossed it into the air before catching it. "Skuz said a woman lured him and Vinny out of the car. My guess? It could have been your girl being forced. I don't know. It would make sense.

"I wouldn't put it above them. They're real pieces of shit," Ann growled.

Garret inserted the key into his lock and pushed the door open. "That they are. Ah, home sweet home." He stepped inside the spacious apartment. He pointed to a sofa in the main room. "That's your bed." He pointed to the left down a hallway. "The bathroom's the first door on the left over there. Any questions?"

"Yeah. What's the plan tomorrow? You never said."

"It's not quite as fancy as the last one. More of a snatch and run. Once we get our man, we're going to make a video of our own and send it to them."

"Going terrorist on them? That'll certainly force things one way or another."

Garret plopped down on one end of the sofa. "How so?"

"Either they'll bend to the pressure or push back twice as hard. Which do you think it'll be?"

"Probably push. Which would make it easier for our next grab to take place. The more they get angry, the more careless they get. Eventually they'll be out of manpower and have to concede."

Ann sat on the other side of the couch. "That, or during their frenzy they'll do some real damage."

"That's the risks we take." Garret picked up the remote control from the arm rest and tossed it underhanded to Ann. "Here." He reached down and untied his dirt encrusted white sneakers. "It's not like we haven't beefed before. It always dies down within a few weeks."

"I hope you have more prospects waiting in the wings then."

Garret sat back up and leveled a glare at her. "We recruit just fine, thanks. Let us worry about club business. Why don't you worry more about your friend? Maybe if we're lucky we can get her back during this little shuffle."

"You mean that?"

"I have no problem going after the men holding her captive. They're worth as much as any man in their organization."

"Truly, you are a regular nobleman. Still, I guess that's as good as I'm going to get."

"I'll tell you what, if we manage to rescue your friend, I'll go to bat for you with the President. That way you two can get out of this whole thing."

"You'd do that?"

"It's better than letting a freeloader stay in my apartment indefinitely without benefits."

"Freeloader? I'll have you know I make a wonderful continental breakfast."

"I'll believe that when I see it." Garret reached his arms above his head and let out a massive yawn. "Let me go get you some pillows and a blanket, then I'm going to turn in." He pushed on his knees to get up and disappeared down the nearest corridor.

Ann reached down and removed her boots.

"Hopefully these will work." Garret reappeared holding a thick sheet under his arm and a pillow dangling from his other hand. "These are all I have for spares. The bachelor life doesn't afford us guys many extra sleeping accessories."

Ann took the items and shoved the pillow onto the armrest. She leaned on it. "It's fine."

"I'm heading to bed then. If you need me, it's down that

same corridor, except it's the door on the right. You're free to anything in the kitchen."

"One more thing before you go."

Garret rubbed one bloodshot eye. "Yeah?"

"What time is this operation tomorrow?"

"Noon. Anything else?"

"Nope. Good night."

"Night."

———

The next day...

Garret leaned forward between the van's two front seats. "How close are we?"

"We'll be there in a few minutes." Irving kept his eyes glued to the road.

"Calm down," Ann said from Garret's left, "I'm sure your little plan will work."

Garret sat back in the seat. He leaned down and picked up the roll of duct tape rolling across the floor. "Don't get too close. We don't want to spook them. Park behind the building. We can drag him back to the van easily enough." He elbowed Skuz at his side. "You're with me when we get out. I'll grab him from behind, and you help me move him."

"Why don't we just knock him out? It'd be easier."

"Have you ever dragged two hundred pounds of dead weight? It's more difficult than if they were awake. We need speed for this to work."

"We're here," Irving said. He raised an arm to look at his watch. "I'll keep the engine running. Be careful."

"I'll open the back door when you get back," Ann vowed.

"That's our cue." Garret slid the back door open and

hopped out. He scampered to the nearby corner and peeked behind. He looked over at the van and motioned Skuz over with his hand.

Skuz followed behind and pressed up against the wall beside Garret. "What are we waiting for?"

Garret held up a lone finger to his lips without replying verbally. He reached down to his belt line with his other hand and removed the knife. His voice was low, almost a ghost of its former self. "He's coming this way."

A bald man wearing the Knights' logo on the back of his vest turned the corner. Before he could do anything, Garret pounced and slammed him against the brick wall. One arm pushed against the man's windpipe. The other pushed the knife against the man's neck. "This can go one of two ways - either I slit your throat here, or you take a ride with us."

Skuz surrounded him on the other side. "You're coming with us." He reached down to the man's belt line and removed a pistol stashed away. He knelt and patted down his boots. "What do we have here?" He extracted another pistol from his socks. "He's clean."

Garret removed the knife and pushed the man off balance toward Skuz. "It's time to move then."

Skuz gripped his neck and held the gun against the small of the man's back. They marched toward the lone black van just up the alley. Ann jumped out of the van, ran around the side, and gripped the back door. "Just get in that van and you won't get a nice lead epidural."

"Hey, come on, man. I didn't do anything to you." The man had sweat pouring down his face. His eyes darted back and forth. "What are you going to do to me?"

Garret caught up with the two and watched him. "That's not up to me. The club decides that."

"You can't just kidnap me and take me God knows

where. Do you know what my club will do to yours? They'll hunt you down like dogs."

Ann threw open the back of the van. "Get in there."

"You boys started this kidnapping business first. Don't bitch to us," Skuz said with a push. The man looked inside at the men staring at him and back down the barrel of Skuz's pistol. He shook his head and climbed inside the cabin toward Tony.

Tony tore off a piece of duct tape. "Show me your hands."

The Knight shook his head.

Tony's leg shot out and connected with his head. It bounced off the side of the vehicle behind him. "That wasn't a suggestion. Give me your hands."

The man's eyes were glazed over, his head drooped, and his hands reached out toward Tony.

Tony began the arduous task of wrapping his hands in duct tape and restraining him. "We're good. Let's go already."

Garret and Skuz climbed into the back with the two men and surrounded him on all sides. They pulled the doors shut.

"Get us out of here," Garret said to the front.

Irving stepped on the gas and the van immediately jerked forward.

"What are we going to do with this little guy?" Tony nudged the man in the rib with the tip of his boot. "Look at him. He looks scared." He leaned forward, his voice low. "You should be."

"You're going to get a taste of our hospitality. It's far more luxurious than your club," Skuz said, baring his teeth. "You best believe that."

A ringing sound came from the front. Irving dug into his pocket and handed the phone back over the seat to Garret.

"Yeah?" Garret answered.

"Everything going as planned?" Richard's voice asked.

Garret looked down at the bound man and rested his foot on his chest. "Yeah. We just finished and are on our way out. We're dropping him off where we agreed. You're meeting us there, right?"

"I'm on my way now. Don't rough him up too much. I want my shot at him too."

"You got it. See you soon." Garret snapped the flip phone shut. "That was the President. He's waiting for us."

"I'm surprised the bitch didn't shoot him," Skuz said. "She seems hell bent on murdering these sad sacks."

"There's a reason for that." Garret gave a light kick to the man's rib cage. "Maybe he can answer that, and we can let her go early."

"Wouldn't that be nice." Ann looked out the side window.

The man on the floor broke his silence with a round of frantic muffled noises.

"What was that?" Garret leaned forward with his hand cupped around his ear. "I didn't quite make that out. Were you trying to tell us something?"

The man nodded without further words.

"I'm going to remove this for just a minute. If you try something, this gets much worse for you. Understand?" He reached down and ripped the tape off the man's lips. "Now what is it?"

"Are you going to kill me?" he asked.

"That's not up to any one of us here," Tony said. "That's a club decision."

"It doesn't look good after the way you offed Vinny though," Skuz spat.

"That was only because of the four men you put down the day before that." The man's wild eyes darted between the cramped space. "Can't we be done with this?"

"Come on, man. Don't beg," Garret said. "It just makes you look pathetic. You joined this life. You knew the risks. It's gang warfare now. It's not called off until it's done. I haven't heard that it was yet," he looked up toward the driver's seat, "have you?"

"Not yet," Irving said.

"So, as you can see, no we can't. Anything else before we put the tape back on?"

"I'll tell you anything you want to know. Just don't kill me."

"Now we're talking. You keep that attitude up, and maybe we might change our mind. Just don't flake out." He bent over and reapplied the tape over his mouth.

9

The gate closed behind the van. Lucien chained it shut. The van came to a stop, and everyone got out.

"It's about time you lazy bums got here." Richard greeted them with open arms inside the walled off compound. "What took you so long?"

Garret gave Richard a light hug and slapped his back. "You know how traffic can be." He took a step back. "Is everything ready here?"

"You know it." Richard walked with Garret around to the back of the van. "Is our boy ready?"

Garret swung the back door open. "The last I remember, the dude was begging like a bitch. He said he was willing to talk, Pres." He climbed into the back and got down on a knee. "Still feel like talking?"

The Knight's head nodded frantically.

"See? He still wants to talk to you." He grabbed the man's leg and dragged him toward the back. He jumped down. "Don't try anything funny. We won't hesitate to end you." He ripped off the tape.

"What did you want to say to me?" Richard's chin angled

up, his chest puffed out. "It's not like it matters. Unless you have some big intel, you're disposable to us."

"No, man, listen. I've got something you'll want to hear. What do you want to know? I know everything about my club."

You're not too brave though," Richard quipped. "Fine. Mark on a map where all of your hideouts are, and maybe we'll think about letting you go." He dug a folded-up map and pencil out of his pocket and tossed it beside the man.

Garret reached behind the man and cut his binds with his knife. "Don't try anything."

The Knight rubbed his wrists and immediately grabbed the pencil and scribbled on the map. "Here they are. I'm in charge of security here." He jabbed the pencil at one circle.

Garret glanced at the map. "That's where we grabbed him."

"Where's the best place to hit?" Richard asked.

"I'd hit here." The Knight pointed to a circle far away from the others, at least thirty miles away. "There's a minimum of guards there. It's mostly just for collecting from the bookies in the area. They get a lot of money moving through."

"We could cut off their money supply."

"The other option is we ransom this helpful guy back to them. It'd buy us some good will." Richard rubbed his chin with his hand. "We could do it at the same time as the raid."

"A little misdirection?" Garret asked. "I like it." He looked at the younger man. "Where's Kate?"

"Kate? How do you know about her?"

Garret looked up and saw Ann peeking around the back seat.

"Answer the question." Garret placed the knife against his throat. "Where is she?"

"Alright, man. Shit. She's here right now." He pointed to the same isolated area. "She's on a schedule. She moves around every few days. She's there for two more days."

Richard snatched the paper and held it above his head. "Irving, get over here."

Irving jogged over and stopped beside the group. "What's up?"

Richard handed the paper over. "Compare this to our other map. See if anybody's lying. Make sure he didn't forget anything."

"Other map?" the Knight asked. "You have another one of us?"

"Maybe." Garret crossed his arms in front of him. "Why? Worried his deal will override yours? I guess you'd better tell us even more to stay ahead in that race."

A ringing came from the man's pants. "Oh crap," he said, fishing the phone out of his pants. "You have to let me answer this."

"I don't have to do anything." Richard stole the device, pressed a button, and brought it to his ears.

"Where the hell are you?" an angry male voice asked.

"We're sorry, but he can't come to the phone. He's a bit tied up."

"What? Who is this? Richard? Is that you?"

"You got it." Richard reached up and fiddled with the bandana tied around his forehead. He leaned against the van as he spoke. "Your boy has been helpful so far. He's a tough cookie to crack, but we'll get him there. Don't you worry."

"My men will never tell your dumbass anything." Enrique said, disdain clear in his voice. "Besides, did you not learn your lesson the other day. You keep fucking with us, and you're going to lose as many men. I happen to know your club can't take it. If you know what's good for you and your boys, you'll let him go. Maybe we won't eradicate you and your families if you do. Do you get me?"

"I don't take threats well, Rico," Richard said through gritted teeth. "We may not have numbers, but I guarantee we're smarter than your tag of hood rats and misfits. Do not ever threaten us again. No one tells the Order of Vengeance what we can do. Not you or anyone else. Do you understand me? Besides, if you want him back you're going to have to deal with me. How bad do you want him?" Richard asked with a growl into the phone.

Irving patted Richard on the back, causing him to turn around. He gave the thumbs up sign.

"You're talking tough. It's been a while," Enrique said. "Normally you dance around everything. You must think you have something to be so confident. No matter, there will be no negotiations. If your ragtag group doesn't immediately disband and release my man, it'll be the end of the Order. You have twenty-four hours until death. Enjoy it while you can, my old rival." The phone clicked and was replaced by the dial tone.

"That sounded heated," Garret said. "What did he say?"

"Lock him in here, and I'll explain the situation." Richard walked off from the van toward the rest of the club a dozen yards away.

"You heard him." Garret retied his hands behind him, placed his palm on the man's chest and pushed him back inside the van.

"No, wait. Don't just leave me in here." Garret slammed the door in his face, silencing further dissent. He sauntered over to the group to hear Richard already talking.

"That was Enrique," Richard said.

"What did our old rival have to say?" Lucien asked. "Nothing cordial I assume."

"The farthest thing from it. It was the usual threats and insults. He seemed worried."

"If he was honest," Garret started, "it's probably because that dude is a head of security. He knows he could sink him if he talked."

"Speaking of which," Richard snapped his fingers and raised his voice, "does that map match?" he asked in an elevated voice.

Irving handed over the two pieces of paper. "They're almost identical. Her map has one more location than his. To me that implies either they're hiding something there, or he's an idiot and forgot. I'm banking on the former."

"Good work," Richard said. He took the papers from Irving's hands and studied them before handing them out to the small group. "The question is, what do we do about it?"

"Do we even know what they're keeping there?" Tony asked, peeking over Skuz's shoulder at the paper.

Ann climbed out of the van's back door. "That was where we prepped our clients before transport. Sorry, I couldn't help but eavesdrop on you boys. I figured you'd need my expertise."

"Didn't that one old man say they were going into the smuggling business before little miss shoot first, ask questions later got ahold of him?" Skuz glared at Ann who stood beside Garret.

"It sounds like we have an opportunity to royally screw one of their businesses if we want." Lucien grinned. "How shall we do it?"

"There's always the option of dropping heat on them," Irving offered. "I know it's not usually our MO but given our manpower, it could be considered justified."

Garret slapped Irving on the back of the head. "We can take care of our own business."

"You never involve them." Lucien spat on the dirt below and placed his boot over the stain. "I say we interrupt their next operation. We know where it is. It won't be hard to throw a wrench in their plan. If we ruin their business reputation, that would do far more damage than a single hit ever could. No one will want to do business if their credibility is tanked. No business means they get no cash. That's how you win a war - by hitting them where it hurts, the wallet."

"I'd be up for a little revenge after what they did to me." Skuz pounded his right fist into his open left hand. "Count me in on whatever the plan is."

"Make that two," Garret said

"If you want to succeed in this, you'll need me too." Ann stepped forward. "I know everything about that place. I can get you in there with no one the wiser. Assuming they're still doing things our way, I have the perfect plan."

Richard scoffed. "We can handle this on our own."

"I wouldn't recommend it," Ann smirked. "Do you know where all the doors inside lead? Do all your men know every passage like the back of their hand? You wouldn't want to get lost and ruin the whole thing. Right?"

"We're going to need speed once we're inside," Garret admitted.

"We don't need more dead bodies from you." Richard glared at Ann.

"Pres, I have an idea," Tony said. He pointed at the van a little distance away. "Why don't we use the guy as bait? We immobilize him, make him visible, and have his club come pick him up."

"There's no guarantee they'll take the bait." Richard shook his head. "If we could, it's a great idea."

"The Knights didn't want their man back? We could always take a play from their book, just not kill him. It'd lull them into thinking we're offering him back under good will." Irving rubbed the top of his bald head and wiped away the sweat forming. "Just take him out into the country and dump him. Set up a camera, take off his gag, and then that'll give us some time. He'll be begging like a toddler."

Richard smiled and laughed. "Now that's sounding better. We get them to go play scavenger hunt. While they're busy, we hit them in the back. I like it."

"It's the same play twice," Lucien said. "Do you think they'll fall for it again? If it was me, I wouldn't be splitting up. Not after last time."

"Then we'll have to sweeten the deal to get them to take it," Richard said.

"We only know of a couple things they want though," Garret said. "They want the coward over there, us dead, and they want her." He nodded to Ann.

"If you give me a bike, or at the very least an escort, I don't mind being bait," Ann said.

"Why would you do that?" Skuz asked with crossed arms in front of his chest. "It makes no sense."

"I'm only here because you all convinced me. I want this done sooner rather than later, plus I'm not scared of these jackasses. I've dealt with them before. I have a score to settle. Besides, if you want more of them to come out, you need me out there. They will come for me, I guarantee it. I know too many of their dirty little trade secrets."

"We can't spare a bike," Richard said. "Anyone want to volunteer to be her escort?" He looked at the small circle of men around him.

Garret stole a glance at Ann out of the corners of his eyes. "It's going to have to be me, isn't it?"

"If you're going, I am too," Skuz said.

"We need as many men as we can get on the main stage," Richard said. "We only need one with her." He glanced at Ann. "Do you mind him being your escort?"

Ann looked at Garret. "It's fine with me. It's better than Skuzzy over there."

Richard snorted. "Alright, watch it now." The rest of the men burst into laughter.

· · ·

A few hours later...

"Don't you just love being bait?" Garret planted the tripod into the soft soil below. He pushed the nearby red button on the camera mounted on top. "The camera works."

"Just let me do the talking when we get ready." Ann leaned against the side of the van. "I know how to rile them up."

"We'll see how it goes." Garret went to the back of the vehicle and threw the doors open. "Rise and shine. It's time to get out of here."

"Where are we?" the man asked.

Garret leaned inside, grabbed the man's ankles, and yanked. "Come find out." He braced his foot against the cabin floor and pulled. The man slid out past Garret and flopped onto the soil beneath.

"The forest? Come on. Don't kill me, man. I did everything you all asked me to. We can work out a deal."

"Get over there." Garret picked him off the earth and pushed him toward Ann. "Follow her lead if you know what's good for you."

"You're over here." Ann grabbed him by the arm and

dragged him in front of the camera. "Stand here, look nervous, and back up what I say. Do you understand?"

"I think I can handle that. Hey, wait a minute. I remember you from somewhere."

"Good." Ann reached into her belt line and removed one of her .22's. "This is just to make sure you stay in character. If you try and make a break for it, I'll just shoot you in the back. It doesn't matter to me." She smiled. "You understand."

"Don't let me slow you down." He looked down at the grass below.

Ann placed the barrel of the pistol against his temple and looked at the camera. "Hello, Enrique. Do you remember me? Because I'll never forget you or your men. I'll always remember what your club did to us. You stole our business, enslaved our members, and sent the rest of us to prison. Did you think we'd just forget that shit? You're not free of me until you kill me. I know you can see this. If you can, track this transmission and come prove me wrong. That is, if your band of monkeys are smart enough to find us. If you can find us in three hours, he lives. If not, I take another piece of trash out, and I still come after you." She looked off camera. "Come over here, darling."

Garret walked onto the screen and stopped at Ann's side. He gave a stern look toward the camera.

"I'm not alone this time." She took a step toward the camera, leaned down, giving the camera a good view down her jacket. "I know everything that can break down your infrastructure. Do not test me. After all, you wouldn't want ES Fifteen mad at your ass for incompetence, would you?" Her hand reached above camera and the feed shut off as she pressed the red button. She turned back to Garret. "Can he still track this if the camera's off?"

Garret approached the camera. He leaned forward, inspecting the assorted buttons on the surface. "The Wifi switch is flipped. If he wants to, he'll find us." He turned back to the man on his knees trying to shuffle away. He jogged over. "Not so fast." He leaned down and grabbed his foot and drug him back toward them. "Where do you think you're going, buddy? You'll miss the party like that." He stood up, took out his phone, and dialed numbers before raising it to his ear. "It's done. Watch them. They'll be scrambling. I'd say they'll be moving within the hour if they care about their man."

"We're moving into position now," Skuz's voice answered. "Just be careful over there. They love using any means necessary. Don't be fooled by any woman. Alright, brother?"

"I get what you're saying." Garret glanced at Ann. "I'll be fine. Just be sure to follow the plan to the T. Otherwise, we'll be left hanging out here with our asses in the air for no reason."

"We're locked and loaded. We'll convince them it's in their best interests to abandon this beef."

"Hopefully this town while you're at it. We need a break, and that's the only way we'll get it. I miss when we were the only outfit in town. Don't you?"

"You're telling me," Skuz said. "Rich's telling me I have to get off the phone. Be careful, bro."

"You too." Garret hung up and shoved the device back in his jeans.

"I wonder how their mission will go." Ann shifted her weight to her right foot. "They are going to the old toy warehouse, right?"

"As you suggested," Garret said.

"You're organizing a raid there?" the still restrained man asked. He fell back onto the grass laughing.

"What's so funny?" Ann asked.

"That place has changed since you were last there, Love. It's not just a staging area for smuggling. It's now the focal point of everything we do here. We cut and package drugs there. It's used as a holding pen for our 'volunteers'."

"You mean slaves." Ann delivered a kick to his solar plexus.

"You're never getting her back, you know that." He got back into a sitting position on the grass with a wheeze. "If you're lucky, they might send her out with their kill squad to fetch me. I doubt it, but they might, given that you're here. I don't think you'll enjoy that very much."

"What does that mean?" Ann asked with clenched teeth and a growl.

"You'll see if she shows up." He laughed again. "You have no idea what you're doing."

"I've heard enough of this," Garret said. "Keep him there. I've got something that'll shut him up in the van." He marched off toward the vehicle, opened the back doors, and climbed inside.

"How did you even hook up with these perennial losers?" he asked, looking at Ann. "Is it one of those birds of a feather flock together things, or more of a desperation play?"

"You've gotten braver since earlier. Is it because there's just two of us now?"

"I just don't care anymore. If you're going to kill me, just do it. Don't pussy around, as hard as that might be for you, lass."

Ann pulled out her .22 and leveled the barrel at him. "Go ahead, keep talking. I kind of want you to."

"Whoa there." Garret hopped out of the back of the van and ran over. He placed his hand on hers and lowered her arm. "We need him alive."

"I was just going to scare him."

"At this point, I welcome the shot. You're going to do it eventually anyway. Get it over with already." He got onto his knees and puffed out his chest.

"You've gotten brave, huh? I can fix that lickety split." He reached behind him and produced his .357, taking aim.

"You're too much of a wuss."

Garret lowered his aim from the man's stomach. "Keep talking, Mr. Newfound big dick. See what happens."

The man's eyes followed his aim down. "Now wait a minute. You don't shoot a man there. You don't do that. Have you no decorum? At least she was going to shoot me in the head."

"You should've been quiet like I said." He squeezed the trigger.

The bullet pierced the man's inner thigh. He folded over with a high-pitched squealing noise. He rolled around on the soil panting incoherent words. Most of which centered around his now wounded manhood.

"Let's get him inside the van. I don't want to listen to this for hours." He grabbed the man by the arm and dragged him.

Ann helped move the now emasculated man. "I thought we weren't killing him."

"He'll live," Garret glanced down at the wound, "more than likely. It looks like I only grazed his leg. He's not bleeding a ton. If not, it's no big loss. He's already served his purpose. I'll take care of the body myself if that happens."

"You just didn't want me to be the one to shoot. Is that it?"

"I did say I'd watch out for you, didn't I?" Garret smirked at her as he threw the rear door of the van open. "I can't let you have all the fun and get all the blame. I wouldn't have much of a job if you did everything, would I? I'm the new sergeant at arms after all."

"Fair enough. Just don't get too gung ho. That'll bite you eventually. Trust me, I know."

"There's a story there," Garret said. The two hefted the groaning man into the vehicle and closed the back doors.

"We do have a few hours, don't we?" Ann asked, slamming the doors shut. "Remember how I said I went to prison before?"

"When you were putting your shoes on over ramen noodles?" Garret snickered and leaned back against the bumper.

"For the last goddamn time, I wasn't fighting over ramen noodles. That was a little payback on Shelia." Ann shook her head, a smile barely constrained. "I got a little too overzealous in my duties on the street prior to that. We were right in the middle of our feud with the Knights. I was on my way over to Kate's house. When I got there, I noticed an extra car parked outside. I snuck up on it and found it was them sitting outside her house, presumably waiting on her to come outside. I ended them right then and there. Unfortunately, a neighbor saw me and called the cops."

"How'd you escape the murder rap?"

"She was convinced to recant her testimony by my sisters. They lost their witness, had no other evidence, and I stayed quiet. They had to let me go after a few months."

"Then when you got out she was already kidnapped?" Garret asked.

"That's about the size of it. I've been spending every day

watching them and planning. You all just happened upon me on the day I put it into motion."

"Just curious, how were you planning on disposing of his body if we hadn't shown up?"

"A pickup truck after dark, a shovel, and a dark country road does wonders for problems."

"True. What was your plan after that kill?"

"What's with you being interested in my plans all of a sudden?" Ann asked.

"I like to know the type of person I'm working with. Are you the type to plan everything out? Maybe you just wing it past a certain point. I need to know these things, especially when I'm in charge of you."

"I was going to continue my plan. Scouting out our various old hangouts using proxies, and paying people to enter bars and tell me if they saw Kate was the only thing even remotely working. Eventually the plan was to get her out and get away from here forever."

"A clean start huh?"

"That's right."

"I can't imagine you going back to being a law-abiding citizen from what I've seen."

"We all have dreams."

"Too bad all your sisters' didn't hold the same ones. Otherwise, this could have all been avoided. What did this Sheila even get for betraying you anyway? Money?"

"She got along with their leadership, which worked fine for communications."

"Until she got a little too chummy, is that it?"

"Something like that. She became Enrique's old lady."

Garret kicked off the van. "Thanks for the history lesson."

"That's it?"

Garret looked over his shoulder at her. "Don't worry, it'll all work out. You watch. We'll get Kate freed, win this war, and you'll get to have your boring life afterward - if that's what you really want."

She watched him stroll to the tree line. She spoke under her breath. "Of course it is." Her eyes wandered down to his posterior. "What else could I want?"

10

"They're leaving now." Richard's voice came from the speaker of Garret's phone. He held it a few feet away from his face. "Get ready, and don't screw this up. Wait a minute now. Irving, give me those." A shuffling noise filled the cabin. "There's a woman with them. It might be your girl."

"Kate?" Ann leaned forward toward the phone.

"I don't know," Richard answered. "How many women would they drag along with them?" He chuckled. "They always did reuse strategies that worked. They're going to try that again it looks like. Be ready. They'll be there inside of fifteen minutes. They're loading into two vans. Don't get your asses shot."

"We're getting into position unless there's something else," Garret said, grasping the door handle.

"Be careful, and stay low." The call ended.

Garret tossed the phone into his pocket. "That's our cue." He pushed open the door to his side and stepped out onto the grass.

"It's now or never I guess," Ann said, following suit.

"If they're using vans, we have the advantage," Garret said, walking to the back of the van. "We have an escape route and can trap this one. It doesn't take much. A few nails or something similar. Now let's check on our favorite prisoner." He grunted as he pulled the doors open. "How are we doing, sunshine?"

"I'm fucking still bleeding. How do you think I'm doing after you tried to shoot my jewels off?" he asked, anger evident in his voice.

"I just shot your thigh. Don't be a drama queen. You'll be fine after a visit to the doctor. Now roll out of the way."

"Why should I?"

"I'll shoot again, and this time it won't just be a flesh wound. Maybe this time I'll choose your right hand. That would be funny, since you wouldn't be able to ride for a few months with that wound." Garret slammed his palms into the cabin floor. "What do you say?"

The man didn't respond in words. He simply kept his legs together and rolled to the side.

"That's right. You can be smart when you want to be." Garret climbed inside and picked up a small box of nails. "You just stay here and say hello to your brothers when they arrive. They'll probably find you. If not, you'll die of dehydration in here, which is a slow, torturous death." He hopped out and slammed the doors shut. He looked over at Ann as they walked toward the trail where they had entered. "I'm sure he'll be fine."

"It's not like I care." She reached inside the box Garret was grasping and removed a handful of nails. "Are we just littering this across the whole trail to pop a few tires?"

"Yep. We can't have them chasing us after we get your girl back, can we?"

"That wasn't your mission, was it?" she asked with an eyebrow arched.

"It may as well be." He tossed a handful down onto the dirt path. "We're here to either kill as many as we can or waste their time. The President never said we couldn't try to get your friend back."

"I appreciate that."

Garret's pocket chimed. He took a break from spreading nails and raised it to his ear. "What's up?"

"As soon as you're done, get moving."

"What about getting Kate back?"

"Kate?" Richard asked. "Who gives a shit about her? She's not our priority. We need you back at the clubhouse now."

Garret snuck a glance at Ann. "We'll be back as soon as we can." He ended the call there.

"That didn't sound promising."

"Don't worry about it. We're still getting her out of this. After all, you did help with Skuz. I can't leave debts unpaid, now can I? It wouldn't be very manly. Besides, they'll be fine without me for an extra fifteen minutes. Now let's focus on our next task. We'll need to separate them when they show up."

"I have an idea." Ann snapped her fingers. "It's rudimentary, but it should work." She reached into her side pants pocket and pulled out a pad of paper. She removed the pen from the spirals to the side and scribbled.

Garret moved behind her, got on his tip toes, and peered down at the paper. "What the hell's a piece of paper going to do?"

"By itself? Nothing." She ripped the paper out of the pad, folded it, and signed Kate's name on the outside. She grabbed a nearby rock and placed the paper under it near the van. "We need to cover all our bases. If they send her alone, she'll pick up this paper. If not," she ripped out another piece of paper and handed him the tools. "they'll read your message. Make it good."

"We could make it a prisoner exchange," Garret said out loud. "Or at least act like it is if they won't bring her out. If this all goes sideways, we're out though. I'm not dying today." He handed the paper to her after writing 'Knights' on the outside of the folded paper.

"Agreed."

Garret turned around and walked toward the van. He spoke over his shoulder as he walked. "In light of that, I'm moving the van so we can get out in a jiffy. No sense having a getaway vehicle that's parked away from the exit and facing the wrong way."

"I'll work on where we'll post up while you do that." She circled around the clearing as the van moved to block the remaining trail out. "There's no good cover here, just old dead trees." She knocked on one and heard a hollow sound. She looked at the other side of the entrance and saw another thicket of trees. "It might be all we have if we want to stay near the car though."

Garret climbed out of the van and walked to her. "Come up with anything yet?"

Ann pointed at the trees on either side of their van. "Those are the best I can come up with given the circumstances." She held up the papers. "As for these, I have the perfect place for them." She reached down to the ground and picked up two decent sized rocks. "I just need a bit of weight for it to work." She walked to the van and placed the two folded up notes on the van's bumper. She laid the rocks on top of the papers.

"What did yours say?" Garret asked.

"To run behind the van and get inside. Yours?"

"Send the girl out and we'll send their boy out. If they shoot, we kill everyone. They're going to be nervous even being in a clearing like this if they can't see anyone. If they're smart, they'll cave."

"I know one thing about these guys," Ann said with a dour face. "They're not always intelligent." She reached over and slapped his shoulder. "Let's get in position. I hear someone coming."

The two jogged toward the vehicle until they split up and took positions on either side of the van behind their respective trees.

A few minutes later...

The rumble of an engine broke the relative silence of the clearing. The gentle chorus of birds was drowned out by the two vans coming to a stop a few feet before the clearing.

Garret peaked out from his cover. He ducked back into cover before shaking his head. "What am I doing?" he muttered to himself.

A door slamming broke his rumination. He snapped to attention as he heard footsteps crunching grass a short distance away.

"There's no one here, sir," an unmistakably feminine voice reported.

"Then look around. They're probably in the van, you idiot," a callous male responded loudly enough to be heard.

He looked over at Ann and saw her sliding around her cover and gazing at the girl wandering into their previous staging area.

"What's this?" The woman bent down and picked up one of the pieces of paper and opened it. Her glance went to the van in front of her. Her eyes scanned the surrounding tree line. Beads of sweat ran down the side of her face. "Is anyone there?" She bit her lip as she inched forward toward the vehicle between them. She approached the van's driver's side nearest Ann and got onto her tip toes. "Hello? Can someone help me? I seem to be a bit lost here? Any assistance would be appreciated."

"You could help me if you wanted." Ann stepped away from her cover so only the woman could see, while still obstructing her form from view of the second vehicle. "If you want out of this shitty life they've forced you into, just circle around the back of the van, get in, and it'll all be over."

"Ann?" Her eyes widened. She glanced over her shoulder at the immobile two vans. "They'll kill us if I do."

"I have backup, honey. No, they won't. This is all planned. Just do what the paper said, and this'll all play out. If you ever trusted me before, trust me now. Play it cool, and act like you're searching the back of the van."

"If you say so," she said in a quiet voice. Her voice grew loud enough to be heard to her captors. "Just come out of the back and I can lead you to a paradise you never knew existed. My sisters will make sure of that."

"What the fuck?" Garret mumbled. "What lame ass line is that? Do they make her say that kind of crap? For that matter, I can't believe Vinny fell for that. Come on, dude." His voice was barely above a whisper.

Kate opened the back door, obscuring her form from her captors a few dozen feet away. A wriggling body got pushed out the back onto the soil below. The doors shut, and she had disappeared inside.

"Time for the show to start." Garret stepped out from his

cover, low to the ground, heading toward the driver's seat with his weapon at the ready.

A crack broke the silence along with a rush of air next to Garret's ear. A cacophony of male voices sounded off. "It's a setup!" one cried.

Garret opened the driver's side door and ducked behind it. He angled his arm around and squeezed off rounds toward the hostile caravan. He looked to his right and saw Ann climb into the passenger's seat. He hopped inside, kept his head low, and turned the key in the ignition. "Hold on and keep low." He stomped on the gas pedal and the van jerked forward.

The voices outside the window grew louder. "They're trying to run. Get in the vans."

Ann chuckled beside him. She watched the mirror outside her window as the men filed into their vehicle. "Just a little closer and we're good."

A loud pop and the brief sound of a car horn blaring caught their attention.

"I think they found our surprise," Garret said with a smile and a turn of the wheel.

"They found more than that." Ann laughed so hard tears formed in her eyes. She wiped the moisture away and peeked over the seat at Kate. "Welcome back to the land of the free," she said to the raven-haired young woman.

"Ann? Is that really you?" She scurried across the floor and came face to face with the tall woman. "I thought I was going to be forced to work for them until they killed me. There were always rumors flying around, but I never actually imagined you'd manage to get me out of there."

"I told you I'd keep you safe when you joined, didn't I? That vow didn't change just because of those pigs. Especially not after how that all played out with Sheila, that whore."

Kate's gaze moved over to the back of Garret's amber hair. "Excuse me, but who is this?"

"You're polite, aren't you? What a welcome change compared to some women," he smirked as he felt Ann give a light jab into his ribs.

"You're with the Order of Vengance."

"Polite, and quick on the uptake." He looked over at Ann. "No wonder you were so adamant on getting her out." He turned to look over his shoulder. "Nice to meet you. I'm Garret." He turned his attention back to the dirt trail and the black pavement in the distance.

Kate looked back at Ann. She threw her arms around her neck and pulled her close. Muffled cries and sniffles were the only sounds in the cabin.

Garret cleared his throat. "Not to break up this touching reunion, but I need to make a call to see what I ditched for this." He brought the van to a stop at the intersection between the dirt trail and the highway. His thumb danced across the number pad and brought the phone to his ear. "We're on our way back."

"What the hell took so long?" Richard's irate voice asked.

"We had to finish up over here. Something important came up I couldn't ignore."

Ann leaned over and planted a chaste kiss on Garret's cheek. A mischievous fire burned in her eyes as he switched the phone to the other hand as he drove.

"What about your group?" Garret asked. "Everything go smoothly?"

"No, everything did not," Richard grumbled. "Which is precisely why I told you to hurry up."

"What happened now?" Garret asked.

"We got the cash. There wasn't but one person in the place. We got rid of him, but there's a catch. I just got a call from our favorite Knight vowing our eventual deaths. We're not sure how he knows, but I'm betting it was because of your fiasco over there. Get back to the clubhouse so we can assess the damage and form a battle plan. This isn't over yet, that's for damned sure."

"You got it, boss." Garret hung up and lay his neck back on the seat behind him. "It's not over yet, ladies."

"Bad news on the club front?" Ann asked. "What happened?"

Garret glanced up into the rear-view mirror and over at Ann. "The raid went fine. The problem is they knew it was us. Retribution is probably in the works."

"I'm sorry." Kate sat on her knees peering over the seats. "It's all my fault."

"Nah." Garret flicked the turn signal. "Don't worry about it, sweet thing. It's our problem. You're just a happy accident. You just focus on what you're going to do after we get back to the clubhouse."

Kate brought both hands up to her reddening face. "Where am I going to live? You're right. Oh gosh, I hadn't even thought of that."

Ann chuckled. "I don't mind if you stay with me until this is all over. Then when you get settled, you can move or what have you. There's just one tiny catch."

"The fact that for the moment you're living in my apartment?" Garret asked. "I don't mind, but someone's going to have to sleep in my old sleeping bag on the floor. That will probably be me."

"Who gets your bed then?" Ann asked.

"Anne!" Kate slapped Ann's shoulder. "You can't ask him

to do that. I'll sleep on the floor. It's only fair after you two saved me from those animals."

"I like her. She has more manners than you." Garret shook his head with a faint smile. "I'll sleep on the floor. Hopefully this arrangement will only last a few days at the most. After we win this war, you both can go about your lives scot free."

"That'll be the day," Ann said.

"Not to be a dick, but do you have any intel that might help us in our little war?" Garret asked. "We're scratching by, but we need a knockout punch. Something to show their higher ups in the cartel that they can't be trusted. You know, make the club implode from the inside. I figured you ladies might have a few ideas where that's concerned."

"The cartel is already peeved at them though." Katie blew a strand of hair out of her face as she leaned on her forearms, looking at Garret. "You didn't know?"

"Tell me more," Garret said. "What did they do? Fuck up a trip?"

"Not exactly. The news has spread fast in this remote part of the country. Everyone in their club is talking about this war. When people start talking in there it inevitably leads to war stories."

"Which leads to the casualty numbers." Garret nodded. "When that news travels up the grapevine, the big shot callers don't like their underlings looking soft. Did I get it right?"

"Mostly."

"Do you know where the cartel's ambassador hangs out?"

"That little tatted up dude that sneers at everyone?" Kate asked. "Sure. I know, but you probably shouldn't mess with him."

"I wouldn't dream of it. The last thing we need is a major player pissed at us. We're only after their vassals if you will. They're the ones who killed our members," he jabbed a finger to his right toward Ann, "ticked off your capable friend, and kidnapped my best friend."

"That's probably because Enrique is on friendly terms with ES-15. He feels protected," Katie mused. "If anything happens, that guy reports it to the higher ups down south of the border. Usually when he does, they send in a group of reinforcements."

"Good to know. We can plan around that. For now, let's get back to the clubhouse and see what happened with the other half of the plan. It didn't sound good over the phone." His face contorted into a scowl.

"You made the right call holding your position." Ann reached over and rubbed his forearm. Her sweet dulcet voice continued, "I'm sure your friends got out fine."

Garret stole a glance out of the corner of his eye. "Let's hope you're right." He bit his lip and kept driving.

11

"Where the hell were you?" Richard yelled as soon as Garret hopped out of the van.

Garret gestured the President over. "Come see. I might have just got us our ace in the hole for this little war of ours - someone who knows everything about them. I'm talking current intel here, not years old." He leaned in close to Richard's ear. "She's also a total hottie."

Richard shook his head with a sigh. "You horndog."

"Here she is now," Garret said, extending his open arm toward Kate circling around the van.

She stopped a few feet away from Garret. She looked down at her shoes and shuffled her feet. Her hands were folded against her chest. "Hello," she stuttered out. "I'm sorry for any trouble I've caused. If there's anything I can do to help, I'll do my best."

Garret turned back to Richard and raised an eyebrow. "What do you say, Pres? Can she help us?"

Richard looked away with a dour look on his face. He reached up and scratched his nose. "I suppose that wouldn't hurt."

Kate hopped in place and clapped her hands. "Oh, thank you so much."

"Now, what happened on your side?" Garret asked.

"I'll tell you inside." His eyes flittered to the two girls at Garret's side. "We'll only be a few minutes. Make yourselves at home." He turned away from the group and disappeared inside the clubhouse.

"Be right back. After this, provided nothing else comes up, we'll get to rest. Then we'll start planning your little revenge. Sound good?"

"Perfect." Ann gave a thumbs up.

"If you'll excuse me." Garret took off to follow Richard.

Kate looked over at Ann. "How did you ever get these guys to help?"

"Most of them aren't so bad. Just watch out for the guy with purple hair and a mohawk. He's a bit of a dick."

Kate brought a hand up and covered her mouth to suppress her snickers. "I remember him. A purple mohawk in this day and age? Oh my God." Her snickers devolved into raucous laughter.

"I don't think I've ever seen you laugh that hard before." Ann blinked a few times.

"It's just nice to finally be able to laugh when I want and not be faced with punishment." She wiped a rogue tear away from her cheek. "You have no idea what it was like in there." She puffed out her chest and her voice got deeper. "Woman, get me a beer." She turned in place. "Woman, be quiet. We're talking here. You'd better not be listening." Her voice and posture returned to normal. "They never were careful either. I couldn't help but hear everything. They were loud, obnoxious drunks."

Ann moved toward Garret's motorcycle and sat on the seat. "What about Sheila? Did you ever see her?"

"Every week or so, depending on her master's schedule, until he eventually dealt with her."

"Explain."

"Did you ever wonder why she was in that jail with you? Enrique figured turnabout was fair play. When she got too uppity, they made sure she paid you a visit in there forcibly."

"That doesn't sound like something she'd put up with."

"You don't understand." Kate shook her head. "At first Enrique treated her as an equal. Over time, she lost that leverage she had. Her standing fell from right hand woman to old lady at best."

"I guess when the war's won, the traitor's just not as useful."

"It probably didn't help that she's just as pushy as ever," Kate's expression darkened, "at least to me."

"You were probably the only one she could boss around. She had to know she didn't have the authority with the guys."

"That didn't help the ridiculous requests she came up with. I'm just glad to be out of there, and it's all thanks to you and," she glanced over at the clubhouse, "and the Order of Vengeance."

"More like one guy. He got a call right before we got you out that ordered him to come back empty handed."

"And he stayed?" Kate's eyes went wide. "Why?"

"Who knows?" Ann shrugged. "Maybe it was my natural charm?"

"I'll have to personally thank him later. Does he like brownies?"

"Idiot, as if I'd know that."

Kate stuck her tongue out. "You're still mean sometimes, you know that?"

"I'm just glad your back."

"Me too."

Inside the clubhouse...

"What exactly happened earlier?" Garret asked the men around him. He glanced around the table. "I see everyone's whole at least."

"By the grace of God only," Lucien scoffed. "It had to be a miracle."

Garret scooted his seat forward. "You've got my interest now." He looked back to Skuz on his right. "Spill it."

"We watched a bunch of them leave, right?" Skuz's hand swept right as he talked. "Well, we went in as a group."

"They weren't all gone," Lucien grunted. "They left four jackasses in there."

"No doubt to watch the fort while they were gone," Irving spoke up from across the table.

"So?" Garret asked. "What was so bad you had to beg for me to come back immediately?"

"The old man here," Skuz nodded toward Lucien, "ain't the most fleet-footed anymore as you know."

"They found us," Lucien said. "I stumbled. Is that what you wanted to hear?"

"You were discovered?" Garret's eyes widened. "It was another firefight, was it?"

"If you want to call that a fight." Tony shook his head. "It was over after the first volley. We caught them while they were sparking up a smoke in the bar."

"What's the problem exactly?"

"The problem, you short sighted ding bat, is that this

was unexpected. It was supposed to be a quiet in and out." Richard stood up and faced the windows behind his seat.

"Yeah, and think about it," Garret started. "They're losing men at an extraordinary rate lately. They're going to go nuts soon. I'd bet within the next week they're going to march on this very clubhouse. It'll probably be in the middle of the night."

"That's not their MO," Lucien said.

"No, but it is ours. They're going to want to give us a taste of our own medicine, mainly because it's been working so well. Their ES-15 overlords are demanding blood. I bet Enrique is trying to hide his recent bout of losses."

"He might try to draw manpower from ES-15 for their little raid," Skuz offered. "I would if I were him."

"Not likely." Richard shook his head, removed his sunglasses, and sat back down at the head of the table. "It would be showing weakness to the higher ups. He'd never ask for their help. If he did, they'd take over the charter. They won't have anyone who can't handle their own business running their local business ventures."

"Their club morale has got to be in the shitter," Irving said. "If he doesn't answer back soon, he's liable to be voted out. If we repel their retort, it could conceivably end this war. Many of their members might straight up leave for their own good."

"Enrique would never allow that," Richard said. "He'd sooner shoot them. The more men he loses, whether that be to death or abdication, the worse he looks."

"I say we take a few days break, come up with a plan with our ace cutie, Kate, and prepare for the end of this beef," Garret said. "With her intel, we could plan a hit on their operation directly. We don't need to take out Enrique himself. All we need to do is get his bosses to do it for us."

"What about if they want retribution against us?" Irving asked. "They're not going to just sit back and let us punk their minions, are they? Surely they'll retaliate. If for nothing else, for their own reputations."

"That is a risk," Garret said, "but it's either that or get into a full-on altercation. We don't have the numbers for that. We're barely whole as it is. We need to recruit more."

"What do we do if they attack us in the meantime?" Lucien asked with a frown. "We'll be separated. It's best to end this as soon as we can. It'd give them less time to respond."

"We don't want to go too fast and end up worse than we are now." Richard shifted his weight onto his elbow. One hand cradled his head. "You know my motto: When it comes to planning, too much is better than too little." His free hand slammed down on the table and his posture straightened as he looked at Garret. "Do you think she'll know their next crossing?"

"I don't know. I'll ask tonight. What are you thinking, Pres?"

"I'm thinking we commission our local friendly bomber and cause an international incident with the Knights at the epicenter. Picture it. We stick it underneath the car they use, follow them to the border, wait until they're right in front of the checkpoint, and boom!" His hands raised up. "They'd have a hell of a time explaining that to the federal government. Not to mention it'd ratchet up the pressure from ES-15."

"Which would either send them underground or after us with a vengeance," Tony added. He scratched his furry chin with his muscled appendage. "That dude's crazy though. Are we sure we can even trust him?"

"Jerry?" Garret asked. "Shit, he owes me from high

school. He'll get it done if I ask him. How big of a boom were you thinking?"

"Big enough to be on the five o'clock news. It must be handheld and remote detonated with a phone. No radio detonators. That crap is too easy to be intercepted or set off early. We can't have that."

"I've got this," Garret said with an arrogant smirk. "As for the next few days, I recommend we stay here and arm up. Close the gates, close the garage, and then only let appointments in. You know, just to be safe. We'll make up the loss in revenue with our new business opportunities after these chuckleheads are gone."

"The Knights do own the biggest market for meth in the tri-state. If we take it over, we're golden," Skuz said with a wide smile. "We'd just need to introduce ourselves to whoever the local dealers kick up their vigs too. I'd volunteer for that job."

"We're getting ahead of ourselves now. First we need to focus on the job at hand. We'll worry about business afterward. We have enough cash from the drug game that we can handle this war. Now let's leverage it and rule this town."

"Hear, hear." Everyone around the table bashed their closed fists against the wood. After the cheer, everyone except Skuz and Irving got up from their seats and made for the exit.

Skuz stood up last, circled around the table, and stopped behind Irving. "Yo, you never got me my weed. What happened with that?"

"Seriously?" he asked. "I thought you were joking."

"You what?"

Irving stood up. His hand dug into his pants pocket and removed a small sandwich bag full of green nugs. "Just kidding. I always get my tasks done on time. It's just been busy the past few days. My bad."

"Let me get in on that." On his way out of the room Garret leaned over and his hand inched toward the bag, only for Skuz's hand to slap his away. "I thought you only smoked at night. Besides, it's not like you need it with two women staying at your place."

"I make exceptions sometimes. Why? Are you jealous? You won't help a brother out? What happened to my infamous wing man? That's not too brotherly."

Irving cleared his throat. "I'll leave you two to it. Just don't expect me to do this all the time now that I'm not a prospect." He followed Lucien out of the door, leaving only Garret and Skuz in the room.

"You're really staying with those two girls? We don't know a thing about them. Do you want me to stay over too? You know, as backup in case shit goes sideways?"

"If you can find a place to sleep, go ahead. I don't mind. As it is, I'll have to sleep in my old sleeping bag. You remember that thing from the scouts?"

"There's no way you're still use that thing."

"I guess you'll see. I'd bring one yourself, unless you fancy sleeping without anything."

"I'll be there tonight. Try not to get yourself in trouble before then."

Garret turned to exit the room. "We'll see."

12

"You're joking," Ann said, following Garret into the apartment. "He's not actually coming over?"

"I'm serious. He wants in on the planning. He might surprise you with his tactical acumen." He went to the right of the room toward the refrigerator. He reached above, opened the cupboard, then opened the appliance. "Anyone want a drink? My treat."

Kate licked her chapped lips and followed Garret. "You don't have to do that."

Garret handed her a filled bottle. "I hope water's fine. I'm not a fancy man." He looked over to Ann. "You?"

She raised a hand. "I'm good. You are talking about the same man? The purple haired, mohawk guy?"

"I've known him since middle school. Don't go bad mouthing him now. He may be a bit of a simpleton sometimes, but I'll vouch for him. Besides, he does occasionally have good ideas too you know."

"I'll believe that when I see it."

"Don't be mean, Anne." Kate frowned and took a swig of water. She took a seat next to Ann on the couch, screwed her bottle shut, and placed it on the small table beside her. "You still have that nasty attitude I see. I'd have thought you'd have grown out of it by now."

"Old habits die hard," she grinned. "You'd better be taking notes. This is how you're supposed to act as a sergeant at Arms."

Kate reached up and pulled a short lock of hair. "Pay her no mind. She has no manners. She always loved using her position to justify it. Thank you for looking out for her."

"That's my line," Ann gently pushed Kate away.

"You two are in high spirits." Garret leaned away from the two women at the end of the sofa. "I wish I could say the same."

The two women's voices became shushed, and they brought their hands up to obfuscate their mouths from view.

Garret looked out of the corner of his eyes. "Are you having fun over there? What are you doing?"

"Girl talk." Kate straightened her posture with a sweet smile on her thin mouth.

"Yeah, whatever." Garret dug the remote control out of the corner beside him and flipped the television on. He used the remote as a pointer and signaled to the left. "In case you're wondering, you'll be sleeping down that hallway at the end." He pointed over his shoulder down a dark corridor near the door. "The bathroom's back there on the left."

The two girls burst into giggles. Kate stood up. "I think I'll go use the bathroom. Save my seat in case that man comes, won't you?"

"Sure thing," Garret said. "He's not fussy."

"You're a proper gentleman, Mr...?"

"Price, but you can just call me Garret. Mr. Price just makes me feel old."

"Thanks for the hospitality, Mr. Garret." She skipped off behind the couch.

"Close enough."

"She's just yanking your chain. She does it to everybody, though not usually this early after meeting them. She must be in a happy mood."

"I'd assume being liberated from a virtual prison has something to do with it."

Ann grunted in affirmation. "Just don't expect too much from her. She was never one for field work. You get me?"

"If I want action, consult you. Got it." Garret smirked in her direction.

"That's ri... wait a minute." She reached over and punched him hard in the shoulder. "Watch your language. I'll have you know I'm a proper lady, Mr. Price."

"Of course. I'd never doubt you on that." He looked away with an amused smile.

"I'm going to have to watch you closer, aren't I?"

"If you want to catch glimpses, it's probably a solid plan."

"You're certainly not lacking confidence."

The sound of rushing water and the door opening did little to disguise Kate's voice from behind them. "I think someone's at the door."

Garret jumped up from the seat and rushed over. Kate stood behind him as he threw open the wooden barrier. "Yo, what took you so fricking long, you slowpoke?"

Skuz stood outside the doorway with one hand behind his back. "Some of us had actual work to do tonight at the club, unlike you," his right hand snaked around and handed over a large piece of paper as he peeked over Garret's shoulder, "you ladies' man."

Garret took a step back. "Then it's time to get down to business." He walked over to the kitchen table and rolled out the paper. "This is blank except for their properties."

"No kidding." Skuz closed the front door and walked over behind Garret. "This is just the blueprint. We need to fill it out first." He pointed over at Kate, who'd wandered over near Ann on the couch. "Which is where our two lovely ladies come in."

"Already?" Ann exhaled.

"We are their guests," Kate mumbled. "We shouldn't be lazy when they're housing us."

"You're too polite for your own good." She glared over at Skuz. "Fine, punk. Let's do this thing now." She pushed herself up and the two girls moved to the table.

Everyone sat on a separate side of the square table. Garret looked to his left and right at Ann and Kate respectively. "So where does Enrique do his planning for his jobs?"

"He moves around daily." Kate bit her lips. "Normally they do their jobs on Saturdays though. Every Friday he and his clique would go to the local pool hall down on Pine Street." She jabbed her finger on the appropriate place on the map. "They have an understanding. Every Friday they close early and let them do their planning or preparing. I never got to be there, so I'm not sure exactly what goes on down there. All I know is they never missed it. Not once."

"So, he's a creature of habit," Garret said. "We can use that to our advantage. Do you have any idea where their caravan left from? Was it the pool hall or a neutral site?"

"I know Enrique always took a car and followed his client until they got to the border."

"It sounds like we could totally scout the place out and tail them from the hall," Skuz grinned.

"We'd have to tail him that night and see where he heads back to. Then someone would have to pull an all-nighter to watch him," Garret said.

"We'd need to follow the smuggling vehicle too, if we're going to booby trap it."

"When he dragged me there one time, I noticed everyone showed up, including the guy they were smuggling. If you watch that meeting, you'll have them all. Do you know where that hall is?"

"We used to go there when we were kids. I always beat him in eight-ball."

"That's not how I remember it," Garret joked. "We'll have to be low key. They're going to be paranoid after everything that's happened this past week."

"We'll need at least another pair of binoculars." Garret rubbed his neck with a glance to his left toward Ann. "We don't want to have any mistaken cases of identity. That'd sour everything before we even started."

"Now that that's settled, who's going to go order us our bomb?" Skuz asked, looking directly at Garret. "I can't stand that dude. He's fricking psycho. I don't want you going to talk to him alone either. Something's not right with that guy. His sister's alright though."

"The dude makes explosive devices - what gave it away?" Garret asked. "Besides, I think he likes you."

Skuz gagged. "Don't remind me. Why me?"

"Now when you say like..." Ann trailed off. "Do you mean admiration?"

"I mean he wants to perform intimate acts with Skuz here. If you catch my drift."

The two girls covered their mouths and laughed unabashedly.

"I don't even know why." Skuz crossed his arms.

"I can tell the story if you want," Garret offered.

"Be quiet."

"So, it was Valentine's day back in '88, right?" Garret noticed Kate's hand flying up. "Uh, yes?"

"Did he still have purple hair then? What grade was this?"

"You're quite the curious one, aren't you? Yes, he did. It was in high school. I want to say tenth grade. Anyway, our Don Juan here came across Jerry in the toilet. He was crying in front of the urinal."

"You should have seen this guy," Skuz said, interrupting Garret. "Tears were streaming down his face as he jiggled his willy back and forth."

"A little less detail please," Ann quipped.

"I tried not to stare as I stood at the opposite end of the facilities. The next thing I know, I hear him muttering to himself. His voice grew in strength as he went on a tirade about the cutest girl in class."

"This should have been when he walked out," Garret chuckled. "He was just too nice for his own good."

"So, I tell him some meaningless platitudes. You know? Like there's countless fish in the sea, crap like that. His face clears up and this tiny smile appeared. It was creepy. He slowly turned to me with this huge grin. All the while his hands were busy, if you catch my drift."

"What'd you do then?" Kate asked, leaning forward toward Skuz.

"Since I was done, I proceeded to go wash my hands, which is where the story takes a turn for the worse. The dude comes up right behind me while I'm getting soap out of the little dispenser and leans down to talk right into my ear. It was the creepiest thing I remember to date. He said, 'Thanks, my dude. I feel better already.'"

"So?" Ann asked.

"So his right hand wasn't idle all the while. It was rubbing my ass. I wheeled around and punched his ass out cold and got the hell out of there. The last I remember of that guy was him out cold on the piss-stained tiles of the high school toilets."

"If that's the last you remember of him, how do you know he creates explosives now?" Kate asked.

"Because I've had to deal with Jerry on previous jobs," Garret said. "He'll still work, but he asks about his flame every time. I had to promise to drag him along next time."

Skuz's eyes widened. "You mean that's the reason you let me over here?"

"Now he gets it." Ann rolled her eyes with a smile.

"There is no way I'm going over there." Skuz shook his head.

"You will for the club, unless you want to explain to the Pres just why you won't." Garret locked eyes with Skuz. A smile appeared on his face. He glanced at both Ann and Kate. "I guess I could be the one to tell him how you're too scared to talk to a guy you knew in high school for the club." He pulled out his phone. "Shall I?"

"Stop that foolishness," Skuz said with a sigh. "Fine, I'll go. It's going to be your fault if he tries something though."

"That guy was a dough ball. You'll be fine. Just remember to be carrying. Besides, we'll be paying the dude, so I don't see why he'd be mad."

"You know damned well why he'd be mad. Don't bullshit now." Skuz pointed at Garret across the table with clenched teeth.

"Ooh," Kate chirped. "I have to hear this. What did you do?"

Skuz crossed his arms and looked away. "I'd rather not say."

"That's no fun." Kate frowned and looked down at the table. "And here I thought you'd be the entertaining one."

Skuz clicked his tongue. "Fine, if it'll make you happy. I might have went to his house once after that and, you know..." He turned his head and trailed off.

"Finish it, or I will," Garret said.

Skuz bit his lips. "I fucked his sister. Alright? It was the only reason I went over there. I went over there under the guise of studying, since Jerry was the class nerd. In my defense, we did do some studying, and as a result I passed that final exam."

"But?" Ann asked.

"But the jerk ends up sneaking into Jerry's sister's room and seduces her straight up. He still won't tell me how he did it."

"Us guys have to have some secrets."

"Okay, Mr. Secretive," Garret kicked back in his chair, "tell us how the story ends then, since you're so proud of your methods."

Skuz's cheeks burned a brilliant red. "The off-kilter jerk just walked right in as we were finishing."

"And?" Kate asked.

"And he stood there and watched like the sick ass he is. We didn't notice until we were done."

"That's disgusting." Ann crinkled her nose and turned away from Skuz.

"That's certainly..." Kate pursed her lips, paused, and looked around the room, "creepy to say the least."

"But he's the best," Garret said. "We have to put up with

it, even if some of us have past histories with him. In fact, maybe you can get us a deal?" He brought a finger up to his cheek. "Maybe just kiss him on the cheek for us? You'll do that for the club, right?" Garret and the two ladies burst into a cackle of laughs.

"Man, forget you. I'm not doing that." Skuz looked away with a pouting face.

"Okay." Garret wiped a tear from his face. "Let's quit joking around and get down to business here."

"Finally," Ann said. "Now who here knows how to actually plant the bomb? Our charter never screwed with explosives."

"Again, since I'm usually the one dealing with Jerry, he's taught me a few things in exchange," Garret said.

"Exchange for what?" Skuz asked.

"Dirty little secrets about his man crush."

"You have to be joking," Skuz said.

"I guess you'll have to find out," Garret laughed. "You want to go along when I commission this tomorrow morning?"

"I would rather overhaul everyone's bike in a single day."

"Aww." Ann tilted her head. "You don't want to go see your long-lost love? I'm disappointed in you. It's not very manly behavior to leave someone hanging."

"Especially for this long," Kate added.

"You two are either evil or certifiable. I'm not sure which yet." Skuz frowned and looked away. "I expect it from Ann." He gestured to her. "She's crazy. Kate though? As a man, I am disappointed."

"Too bad." Kate stuck her tongue out with a whimsical smile. "I'm just having fun. No harm meant."

"Yeah." Skuz's gaze fell to Ann's hip line. His hand reflexively reached up and rubbed his throat. "Just don't turn into her, and we'll be fine."

"They had a bit of a scuffle the first time they met," Garret said.

"That I won." Ann's smile beamed.

"That's debatable," Skuz grumbled.

"No, she did. I had to put a gun to her head, remember?" Garret asked.

"You what?" Kate asked. Her voice steeled as her neck snapped toward Garret. "Why?"

"Easy." Ann placed a hand on Kate's shoulder. "I deserved it that time."

The aggression left her voice. "If you say so." Kate clapped her hands and her frown dissolved into a wide smile. "Now getting off of these awful subjects," she scooted her chair back and stood up, "unless you need me further, I'm going to head to sleep."

"If we have any other questions, we'll ask in the morning. Ann can tell you where you'll be sleeping. Skuz and I will be sleeping in a different room," Garret glared over at Skuz, "and you'd better not go peeping."

"Like I want to tempt the tall devil over there. Next time she'll shoot, knowing my luck."

"It's an old habit." Ann scratched her neck. "You know how it is."

"A little," Garret said. "Now good night, Kate. We'll try not to be too loud."

Kate bowed and kept her hands folded in front of her. "Thank you so much again. Don't worry about the noise. I'm used to sleeping under the bar at a club with the music blaring. I don't have a problem with noise anymore."

Garret whistled. "Damn. They didn't even give you a cushion to sleep on?"

"There was no room under there," Kate said, her voice slipping away.

Ann stood up and took Kate's hand. "Let's get you settled in then and get you used to the real world again." She led her down the hallway and disappeared into the nearby doorway.

"Why doesn't she hate you?" Skuz asked, now that the two men were alone at the kitchen table. "Did you fuck her or something?"

"Probably because I don't take an adversarial tone every single interaction I have with her. I just treat her like a member of the club." His index finger reached up and tapped his own Sergeant at Arms patch. "This was her last job."

"No wonder she's such a hardass."

"Well, if you really want to know, it was actually sof-" He was interrupted by a door slamming and Ann coming toward them out of the darkness. "Never mind."

"She's settled in." Ann sat down and noticed both men staring at her. "What? Is something on my face?"

"No, we were just talking about you," Garret smiled.

"Nothing bad I hope."

"Who do you take me for?" Garret brought a hand to his chest.

"Right," Ann agreed in a bored tone. She pointed at Skuz. "Who's going with you to meet with this infamous 'Jerry'? Since Skuzzie here is too much of a bitch, am I the one going?"

"Watch it," Skuz growled through clenched teeth.

"I choose my words carefully." Ann locked eyes with Skuz. "You heard what I said. Are you going to prove me wrong?"

"Forget that. That dude will kill me if he ever sees me

again. No amount of cajoling will get me to go."

"Do you want to go with me then? I assume you don't want Kate going with me?" Garret asked.

"While she's tough, she's not ready for that quite yet."

"Tough?" Skuz asked. "She seems more like a mild-mannered lamb."

"That's because you've never seen her truly furious. Trust me, you don't want to see that. It's ugly. She's primal, unyielding, and merciless in a fight. I've seen it. She's ripped a guy's neck out with her nails alone. Don't get it twisted. She's every bit as dangerous as me."

"So why didn't she escape on her own?" Skuz fired back.

"She's not as dumb as you. She was surrounded on every side by gangbangers and rapists. You wonder why she didn't just go on a rampage? Are you serious?"

Skuz clicked his lips and looked away with a sour face.

"Are we teamed up again since it looks like my best friend is still frightened of the dude?" Garret asked with a hand extended across the table toward Ann.

Ann looked down at the hand and back up at the rugged face offering it. Her right hand grasped the hand as she nodded her head. "It's fine by me. I prefer working with competent people anyway," she snuck a peek at Skuz, "not amateurs."

"You're lucky I'm such a gentleman that I don't hit women," Skuz said.

"In my experience, the kind of guys who say that usually can't fight worth a damn."

"You'd better watch yourself," Garret interrupted. "He's better at it than me. I'd put my bet on him."

"Is that right?" Ann eyed Skuz up and down. "I don't buy it. You're too skinny to be much of a threat."

"Can we stop the dick waving for just a few minutes?"

Garret asked. "We need to get into the specifics of tomorrow. After we get the device, we're heading straight to their meeting place to get a feel for the place and see where they park their taxi."

"It'll probably be inside, if I had to guess," Skuz said. "They're not going to leave that shit unguarded outside if they have half a brain. Anyone could screw with it."

"That is a decent point." Garret brought a hand to his chin. "There's only one way to combat that, and I know Ann here won't like it." He looked down the hallway Kate had disappeared into.

"You're not thinking of Kate?" Ann asked.

"I'm not insinuating that she would go inside or anything like that," Garret said. "I'm just suggesting she may have ideas on how we could reach it. Let her come along but not go inside. You could call it backup. What do you say, mama bear?" He gave an amused smile toward Ann.

"You are just talking about being on a phone with binoculars a mile away, right? Otherwise, hell no."

"I don't want her hurt any more than you do." Garret's voice turned soothing. "I just don't want to get there with plastique in my hands, only to find out we can't even apply it. I'll be the one to go inside."

"I know you're not trying to leave me behind," Skuz pointed at Garret. "You're hopeless without me watching your back, brother. Leave the two girlies back, and we'll finish this club business."

"This girlie is more competent than you, punk." Ann squinted her eyes in Skuz's direction.

"What was that?" Skuz slid his chair back across the flower printed tile. His hands rested on the wooden surface as he hunched over. "I've had it up to here with you." He raised his right hand to his chin.

"Calm your tits, both of you," Garret sighed with a shake of his head. "I swear, you two fight more than a married couple." A small grin found its way to his stubbled face. "If I didn't know better, I'd guess you two liked each other or something."

"As if." Skuz sat back in the wooden chair and crossed his arms. "Like I'd be interested in her. She pisses me off is all."

"There are far better choices in my life than a purple haired, mohawk punk with delusions of grandeur."

"What was that?"

"Can we focus on what we're here for, children?" Garret asked. He brought a hand up and slid it down his face. "The sooner we get this done, the sooner you two can never see each other again. Is that enough motivation to work together?"

The two gave a faint glance at the other and back to Garret. They both nodded.

"Good. Maybe now we can nail down the specifics." He pointed a finger at the diagram on the paper before them. "We know this is the building he'll be in. The truck will be here." His finger jabbed the side of the building labeled in messy writing 'garage'. Now there's no obvious doors to get inside that won't be locked, seeing as there's only one entrance to it. Skuz, that's where you come in."

"I'm doing what exactly about that? I can't punch through concrete you know. What am I going to do about it?"

"You are going to do what you do best. Scour the internet. Or hell, get Irving to do it if you can manage now that he's not a prospect. Work your magic. Get a floor plan from city hall by sweet talking the pretty secretary, or fucking download the floor plans online. I don't care how you do it -

just get it done by tomorrow. We're going in the next day. After you have them we'll have one more planning meeting with the boys, then we'll be ready."

"Who's going in with you?" Skuz asked, biting his lip. He gave a brief glance toward Ann. "We never decided."

Garret looked between the two. "We'll figure that out tomorrow, kids. Let me sleep on it, and I'll get back to you."

"Hmph," Skuz grunted. "If worst comes to worst, I'll just have to save you two. I can't stand owing anyone."

"You still owe me a dub, you bum." Garret held out his hand with a wide grin.

"What's a dub?" Ann asked with a tilted head.

"I paid you back already, jackass," Skuz fired back with a smile. "Don't try to score more weed for free from me. Besides, didn't Irving get that for you earlier?"

"You can't blame a guy for trying."

"Man, screw you. I'm heading out. It's getting late." He swaggered to the door and flung it open. "Don't do anything I wouldn't do. See you tomorrow." He closed the door, and jogging footsteps were heard for a few seconds before they faded from earshot.

"I think he likes you." Garret locked eyes with Ann. "I can tell."

"Okay, now I know you're lying."

"Maybe a little. He doesn't hate you anymore. At least I don't think so."

"We'll see about that." Ann got up from the table and stepped into the kitchen. She lowered herself and opened a cabinet. "What about you though? You've never really revealed much about yourself. Why did you join a one percenter club?"

"You want my life sob story?" Garret looked over toward the windows lining the wall opposite his front door. "It's not very interesting I'm warning you now. Still want to hear it?"

"I like bedtime stories."

"Well, let's go tuck you in, and I can lull you to sleep then."

"Easy, tiger." Ann shut the cabinet and reappeared above the bar holding a bag of potato chips. She moved to sit beside Garret again.

"Fine, get comfortable." He shifted in his seat. "So, as you know I've known Skuz ever since I was a kid. We weren't always hell raisers believe it or not."

"You mean you were actually a good boy at one point? I find that hard to swallow."

"Good may be overstating it. I wasn't a felon then. Is that better?"

"How did you two become friends?"

"Do you always interrupt and change the focus of the storyteller's tale? Fine. He was getting bullied by a guy I despised at the time. The guy was a total teacher's pet. You know the type, bullies the weaker kids, and then kowtows to the teacher. I watched this for a day or two until I eventually took care of it. Now if I can finally get to my life story you asked about?"

"Don't mind me, I was just curious." Ann leaned forward and rested her chin on her hand. "So why did you join your club? Money? Sex? Come on, tell me."

"Are those the reasons you joined one?" Garret chuckled. "We made a name for ourselves in high school. No one messed with us or our friends. We got into so many detentions and suspensions that they eventually threatened to expel us. After we finally graduated by the skin of our teeth, we became, for lack of a better term, 'hood rats'. You know the type - living on the streets, hustling to make a living by selling what we had to: drugs, weapons, anything really."

"You did that on the Order's turf? I hope you at least asked permission first."

"Do you think my young buck self even thought of that? Hell no. I was going to do what I wanted when I wanted. I had backup in Skuz, and we weren't going to do what anybody told us to."

"Until?"

"Until Vinny came up to us one day after a particularly huge drug deal." Garret looked down at the table. His voice wavered. "As you might remember, he was a huge dude. Bigger than the toothpicks we were back then. We thought we were going to have our legs broken or something."

"What did he say?" Ann asked.

"He threw down some veiled threats, flexed his arms at us, and implied if we didn't stop he'd be back. It was implied he wouldn't be as nice next time."

"You quit?"

"Who do you think you're talking to? Hell no we didn't. We weren't going to let some guy cramp our hustle. We fought back, not literally at first. We went home and spent all night trying to find out who Vinny was. We didn't want to go in blind even then as dumb as we were. We found out he was part of the Order and went to go have a little talk, seeing as we thought we were invincible. This was years back when the club wasn't as small. Can you imagine it? Two young men in leather jackets waltzing into club headquarters with handheld weapons tucked inside their jackets?"

"I'm surprised you're still alive to tell the tale." Her mouth hung agape as the tale continued.

"Well, we got onto the lot and went hunting for Vinny. As you can imagine, we didn't get too far considering the club was about twelve strong back then. We ended up in a dark room that I now know was the supply room. They duct taped us back-to-back in chairs."

"How did you get out of that?"

"We caught a hell of a beating. I'll never forget that day." Garret stopped talking and tapped the table. "After they'd had their fill of giving us bruises and cuts, the President walked in. If you don't know Rich, know this. He's a smooth talker. Don't ever believe everything he says unless you're in the club."

"What did he have to say? Did he make you put in work just to leave alive or something?"

"Ding ding." Garret pointed at Ann. "You've got it. Except, when we were done with collecting debts, he kept giving us jobs. We thought we were going to eventually be done, but it was never enough. Eventually I'd had enough and let Richard know in no uncertain terms."

"I can't imagine that arguing did much good for two young men with pride issues."

"I'm going to be a gentleman and pretend I didn't hear that. Anyway, all he did was laugh. He couldn't believe we went along as far as we did." Garret blew a lock of hair out of his face. "That jackass. After that, we just kind of hung around the club. Eventually we became prospects, and the rest is history. How about you? How does a young, beautiful woman get to be a would-be assassin for a smuggling ring?"

Ann got up from her seat. She turned away, hiding the brilliant red covering her cheeks. "That is a story for another time, maybe tomorrow night. I'm beat. Unless there's something else, I'm heading to bed."

"Are you blushing?" Garret got up and trotted around the table. He buzzed around her. "That's adorable. Are you a pure maiden or something?"

She extended a hand and laid it on his chest. She pushed him, causing Garret to stumble back against the wall, and ran off down the hallway. She slammed the door shut leaving Garret alone with only the television for company.

A mischievous smile adorned Garret's face. "Payback is sweet."

The Next Day...

"Tell me you found something last night," Garret said to the guy beside him in the van. "We need a way in there if we want this to work."

"I've got nothing," Skuz said.

"Fantastic." Garret's foot crashed down on the brake. He took out the key and turned in his seat to face everyone. "We're here. Am I going solo in there?" His focus turned to Skuz. "Or are you going with me, 'sweetie', as he calls you?"

"He what? I'll beat the hell out of him." Skuz flung the door open until Garret reached over and laid a hand on his shoulder. "I'm joking, dude." He paused as Skuz closed the door. "He actually calls you honey bun."

"Damn you."

Kate burst out laughing behind Skuz. She tried to stifle it with her hands but was unsuccessful. "Sorry," she wheezed out. "You two should have been comedians." She wound down until she wiped a tear rolling down her cheek. "I'll go."

Ann's attention snapped to Kate. "No, I'll go. You just-"

Kate's voice turned serious. "Ann, I can take care of myself. You don't have to always coddle me."

Garret nodded with a smile. "I'm fine with it so long as mama bear is too." he looked to Ann. "How about it?'"

"I don't like it," Ann pouted.

"If all else fails, I'll just rip his trachea out." Kate smiled and turned to Garret with a blush. "Your walls are very thin."

"Don't worry, mom." Garret gave a wicked smile. "We'll be fine. I promise to keep us safe."

"Come on, man. Don't leave me with her." Skuz glanced back at Ann in the back.

"You two play nice now. The adults are going to work. Come on, Kate." Garret opened the car door and stepped out onto the pavement. He circled around the van and opened the back door. "Time's wasting, and I don't want to be here any longer than I have to."

"Me either." Kate placed a hand on Garret's shoulder as she stepped down onto the concrete sidewalk. "Be nice, Ann," she said before Garret slid the door shut and they walked off toward the house side by side.

"Don't get too close to this guy," Garret whispered.

"I know I appear gentle, but I assure you I can handle myself." She looked at the lawn of the one floor house. A toppled tricycle among numerous other children's toys littered the grass. "Does this guy have kids or something?"

"That's not what I meant. Just don't say I didn't warn you. And no, I sincerely doubt he has kids. This is just his idea of décor. Hell, maybe he's just lazy. I don't know what he's thinking. Nobody does." He led the pair up the narrow concrete path to the dilapidated porch.

Kate skipped up the brick steps. She looked to the right at the cracked window and litter sitting atop every conceivable surface. "He's not the greatest landscaper, is he?" Her nose crinkled, and she pinched it shut. "What is that vile stench?"

"If I had to make a guess," Garret kicked a large red ball down onto the lawn, adding to the already covered grass, "it's probably his body odor." He gently grabbed Kate's hand and took it off her nose. "Don't let him see you do that. It will set him off, and we can't afford it."

"Are you kidding me? Am I supposed to just hold my breath or something?"

Garret showed a toothy smile. "Show me how tough you really are." He reached up to the doorbell and pushed.

The door opened, revealing a giant of a man. He reached a large hand up to scratch his exposed stomach in his stained wife beater. He flicked his head causing his thin strands of hair to fall to one side. "You again, Garret? I thought I told you that you'd better bring Skuz over?" His eyes fell to Kate behind Garret. "Who's this? Your girlfriend now or something? Nice. She's cute."

"We're work associates, Jerry. I'm here on club business. We need a favor. You know we always pay back our debts." He made a show of sticking his hand into his vests front pocket. "With interest."

Jerry stuck a greasy palm out. "Not interested. Not unless I see him today."

"Seriously? That's it?"

"Yes."

"Cool." Garret turned back to the van and stuck his index finger out. He gestured toward them.

Skuz stuck his head out of the front window.

"There. We have a deal now, right?" Garret asked.

Jerry grunted. "Not good enough."

"Is that right?" Kate stepped past Garret with a soft, "Excuse me, Mr. Price." She stood face to chest to the man.

"Where I come from, men who don't carry through on deals get punished."

"Is that right, little lady? What exactly are you going to do, stomp your little heel into my shoe?"

"If you want to find out, then keep being an asshole," Kate growled, her voice growing rougher.

"We just want a piece of your mastery today. There's no need for this to turn nasty. I'll tell you what. I'll go talk to your man crush and get him to come inside. How about that?"

Jerry glared down at the defiant Kate and then back to Garret. "Fine, but call off your bitch."

"There's no need for that sort of language here." Garret hovered a hand over Kate's elbow before giving a tug to separate the two. "We'll go get him, and you get started."

"Fine. Hurry up and get inside, I don't want people seeing you outside my house all day. I'm trying to keep it low key here, you amateurs." He took a step back and slammed the door in their faces.

"I can't stand that guy." Kate stomped her foot. "God, does he even bathe?" She burst into a coughing fit as she stumbled her way down the few steps onto the concrete path. "How do you even work with that pig?"

"Necessity of the life. You need scumbags of all types sometimes. You just hold your proverbial nose and get it over with. You know that better than any of us I bet. Speaking of which, you're a little firecracker when you're in the free world, aren't you? You remind me of Ann."

"Sorry. I just had that all bottled up from the past few years. I can't stand people that are flagrantly rude for no reason."

"You might want to work on that." Garret slid the back

door open. "We're back, and one of you isn't going to like this."

"Oh God damnit, no," Skuz said. "I know what you're going to say."

"Then get out of the van, you wuss. By the way, he's changed a lot since high school as Kate here will attest."

"What the hell does that mean?" Skuz angled his head around the seat and stared at the smaller girl.

"I don't know what his personality was like, but I don't envy you or Mr. Garret for having to go into his house."

"No kidding. Just look at that lawn," Ann cackled. "Get going, Skuzzie. Your boyfriend looks to be getting impatient." She laughed again and pointed out the front window toward the man standing at the window just staring at the van.

"Shit." Skuz pushed open the door and jumped out. He refused to look in the direction of the house and stayed facing Garret. "Let's do this before I change my mind." He threw the door closed and trudged toward the home with Garret in tow.

"You're making his year by doing this you know."

"Ah, shut the hell up." Skuz stuck his hands in his pockets as he walked up the steps.

Jerry opened the door with an unflinching smile. "Welcome, please come inside." He turned without blinking. "Shut the door when you enter, and lock it. Follow me and tell me what you need, then we can work out the price." He walked down the nearby hallway heading to the right and disappeared into the farthest door.

"I imagined he was going to be clingier." Skuz held his hand under his nose. He looked back to Garret. "How are you not retching right now?"

"You get used to it after a few trips here. You will too." He trotted off behind Jerry. "Come on. I want out of here."

"Amen to that." Skuz caught up and followed Garret into the spacious room filled with tables that were lined with different chemicals and electronics. "This must be your business room then. How long does this normally take per order?"

"It depends on the specifics of the job." Jerry kept his back to the pair and was focusing on the table in front of him. "Anywhere from fifteen minutes to two days. I should have all the boom I need, so it's just a matter of if I have the materials to rig it the way you want." He turned around holding a small electronic chip. "Which I happen to have."

Skuz stood in front of the nearest table and examined without touching all the contents. "How about this one?"

"What does this need to blow up?" Jerry asked.

"A semi, minus the cargo." Garret still stood near the door.

"So you're looking for a controlled explosion. Those are always tricky. You have to get the measurements exactly right. Give me four hours, and I'll have it done."

"Deal," Garret nodded.

"Can I ask a question I've been wondering for years?" Skuz asked, looking at Jerry's bulbous form messing with various components.

"I'll even allow another one," Jerry smirked.

"I don't remember doing anything particularly great. Why the hell do you even like me anyway? The last thing I remember was knocking you out cold. That can't be the reason, unless you're a masochist."

"Since you two are getting along so well, I'll get back to the girls." Garret opened the door and his body disappeared behind it. His head poked around the side. "You two going to be alright?"

"As long as he doesn't touch my tools, it'll be fine."

"So long as he doesn't try anything untoward, he'll be fine." Skuz gave a smug grin and patted his waist line.

"Play nice." Garret's head bobbed behind the door and shut it.

"You want to know why? You're sure?" Jerry kept his focus on the task in front of him.

"Yeah, I want to know why my mere presence is enough payment to commit a felony and possibly be an accessory to murder. That seems like a prudent move. I can only think of a few reasons, and none of them make me feel any better."

"I think you may be misunderstanding something here," Jerry said. He reached over and grabbed another component before continuing working. "Is that why you've been ducking me?"

"Well, the last time we met you watched me screw your sister so..." Skuz trailed off. "I mean, it was really fucking creepy. You have to admit that."

"I had to," Jerry said, barely above a whisper.

"What the hell for?" Skuz asked. "Look, you should know I'm not gay or bisexual. It's not going to happen."

"You're misunderstanding me. I wasn't trying to get my rocks off. I was forced to, you idiot."

"Oh, here we go." Skuz rolled his eyes. "Who in the world would force you to record that? Let me guess, your parents? No, I bet it was the guys from school, right?"

"Good try, but no luck."

"Who then?"

Jerry stopped working and shook his head. "If you really must know, my sister."

"Mitzi," Skuz paused, "got you to record me and her together?"

"That's right. I sure as shit didn't want to." Jerry continued assembling the bomb.

"That doesn't sound like her." Skuz rubbed his chin. "She always struck me as an embarrassed girl."

"You don't know her. In fact, the reason I requested your presence for so long was for her. She's been holding something above my head all this time, and I'll be damned if I let her release it."

"What is that? Maybe I can talk to her and make this all go away?"

"No," Jerry snapped and looked over his shoulder at Skuz with a fire in his eyes. "No, please don't. She'd post that on the world's most famous anonymous message board if I did. It'd be the end of me, both professionally and personally. I'd end up in the pen if the FBI actually did their jobs."

"It can't be that bad." Skuz pulled out one of the chairs and sat down. "What? Does she have you on footage jerking it or something? Everybody does that from time to time."

"That's not it."

"Besides, why would she want that tape? Is she the type to get turned on by watching herself or something?"

"I don't know, and I don't want to know." Jerry made a retching sound. "All I know is her goal is to meet you again. She was just using me to get you in the door, quite literally. In fact, I'm surprised that -" He was interrupted by a knock at the door.

A female voice came through the wood. "I'm coming in. You'd better not be naked, you fat ass." The door opened to show a greasy black-haired woman with bangs covering her eyes. "Wait, what?" Her gaze fell on Skuz. "You're here right now? I'm not ready yet." Her hands covered her eyes and she ran out the door. "Give me just a minute." She slammed the door shut and ran down the hallway.

"As I was going to say, I'm surprised she hadn't come in here yet. Just please don't anger her. Now please, if you'd give me some privacy. This process is delicate, and I need complete concentration unless we all want to go boom. I don't need you peering over my shoulder all the while."

Skuz slowly stood up and kept his eyes glued to Jerry's back. Once he'd gotten to his feet he backed away to the door. "No problem. I guess I can go see what the hell your sister wants."

"Just remember what I said," Jerry called out.

"I got it. By the way, where is her room anyway?"

"Down the hall, next door on the left," Jerry said without looking up.

"Thanks." Skuz pushed the door open and exited before closing it behind him. He walked down the dusty hallway. He coughed, causing a cloud of dust to swirl in front of him. "God, it's like nobody cleans here in the slightest." He waved his hand in front of him. He stopped in front of the door and could hear footsteps inside.

He took a step forward and knocked on the wooden frame.

"Mitzi? Are you in there?"

The door opened to reveal Mitzi with a different, smaller, tube top on. "Where else would I be? This is my room you know."

"Uh huh," Skuz said, scanning the room behind her. "You've still got that old double bed huh?"

She craned her neck and looked behind her. "Yeah, it's still the most comfortable I could find." She stepped to the side and gestured him inside. "Please, come in and sit while my worthless brother does whatever you needed him to do."

"Jerry's an okay guy." Skuz sat down on the bed. "He might need to lose a little weight, but he's not as weird as I remember."

"Enough about him." Mitzi sat down beside Skuz. "It's been a long time since I saw you. Were you avoiding me?"

"Not you," he raised a hand and used his fingertip to brush a strand of dark hair to the side, "more like the guy who filmed us last time."

"You mean a few months ago? That's all? That was nothing big."

"I guess I can see how you would say that considering you were the one who ordered it."

"What?" She brought a hand to her face and gave an indignant look. "I don't know what you're talking about." She leaned over and rested against his shoulder. "I just missed you is all. You never called me. I thought you'd just forgotten me like a used condom."

"Is that how you saw me?" Skuz leaned away for a second with an amused smile. He returned to his sitting position. "No, I thought your brother wanted my junie cakes is all."

"That's what you thought?" Mitzi smiled and shook her head. "I mean, he liked you well enough, but no. I don't think he's gay. I mean if the porn on his pc is anything to go by."

"I'm going to be diplomatic and not ask why exactly you were looking at your brother's porn." He wrapped his hand around her shoulders and pulled her close. "I'll chalk that up to you missing me." He planted a kiss on her forehead. "If you wanted it to be recorded, I would have brought a camcorder."

"You always were arrogant." Mitzi turned her face into

his lithe chest and rubbed. She peeked up at him. "Not entirely wrong though."

He ran a hand through her hair. "I see you're taking my advice. I always loved your hair."

"You're the only guy I know who likes greasy hair. Every other guy thinks it's disgusting."

"They're just not as enlightened as I am." He leaned down and sniffed her hair. "You could have just called me you know. Misunderstandings are cleared up faster that way rather than blackmailing your brother."

"He told you about that?"

"It's a little worrying." He squeezed her to him. "Proper ladies should leave the dirty business to the guy. It's not very ladylike. I've had to deal with a few that loved getting their hands dirty."

"You cheated on me?" Her voice lost its playfulness and she pushed away from him.

"What? Hell no. That bitch put a gun to my head until Garret put one to her temple."

Her eyes shot open and she jumped up. "You should have shot her the next chance you had."

"That was not my decision. That's-"

"- the club's decision," she finished for him. "It's always the same thing. Do you only do what the club says? Why don't we go out on a date like before, or are you too busy with your boys' club?"

"One, it's not a 'boys' club' and two, we're kind of in the middle of a huge war right now. I'd be afraid you'd be caught in the crossfire. I can come back tonight for a date night in though, if you'd like." He flashed a suave smile.

"You always know exactly what to say, don't you?" She angled her head up and captured his lips. Her hands snaked their way behind him and tied his hands together. She pushed him back on the bed and crawled on top of him. "You're not getting away this time."

***

Outside in the van...

"What the hell's taking so long?" Ann tapped the arm rest at her side. "It has to have been at least fifteen minutes already. How long does it take to work out a price? I bet he's just dicking around in there."

"I doubt that sincerely," Kate grumbled. "It's more likely he's in trouble in there."

"He'll be fine." Garret plucked a smoke out of his vest pocket and lit it up before exhaling a puff of smoke out the nearby window. "If I know him, he's probably found out that Jerry's sister still lives there."

"See?" Ann asked. "Like I said, dicking around."

"Or he's getting an earful," Kate said. "It's been months since he's been there you said, right? I'd be pissed if my boyfriend just ditched me and showed up out of the blue."

"Who knows?" Garret shrugged. "I'll give him a few more minutes before I go back in there." He looked over his shoulder. "I don't suppose either of you will go with me?"

"Not I," Kate said immediately.

"Smart girl," Garret said.

"Yeah, sure," Ann said. "What's the worst that could be in there?"

"You poor naïve girl." Kate patted Ann's arm. "You'll see."

"You two are worrying me now."

"There's a reason I don't volunteer that we use Jerry much." Garret took a long drag from his cigarette.

Ann stared out the window at the house. "Did you see that?" She pointed out the window.

"What?" Kate leaned over Ann's lap and looked.

"That window's blinds just closed."

"Let me see." Garret climbed into the passenger's front seat. "That's not Jerry's room. His is on the other side of the house, near the backyard. It looks like we'll be out of here within a few minutes," he laughed.

"Oh my." Kate looked away from the window down at her lap. "You really think he's..."

"If he comes out that door in two minutes, we'll know I was right." Garret moved back to the driver's seat. "He never had endurance when it mattered according to his ex-girl-friends."

"Not like you of course?" Ann asked.

Garret took one last drag before extinguishing the tobacco stick in the car's ashtray. He angled himself to look back at Ann. "Did you want to find out?" His eyebrows raised and a smirk illuminated his face. He glanced over at Kate. "How about you? I'm always up for a challenge."

Ann kicked his seat. "Leave her out of this, you beast."

"I get it. You want all the attention. You're the jealous type. I like that."

"Not to interrupt your emotional foreplay, but it's been three minutes," Kate said.

"Fine." Garret sighed, opened his door, and stepped outside. "I'll go check up on him. I'm not going in that room though."

"You big baby." Ann followed him outside. "I'll do it if you can't handle seeing that."

"That," he glanced at her out of the corner of his eye, "or you're just a peeper."

"How rude to accuse a lady of something so vulgar." Ann

punched his shoulder. "I'll have you know I'm a perfect lady."

Garret jumped up the steps and entered the front door, holding the door open for Ann behind him.

"It smells like extreme body odor in here." Ann covered her mouth. She watched Garret head down the nearby hallway to the right.

"Hey, wait up." Ann coughed and jogged to catch up. She fell into step beside him in the narrow hallway until Garret held out a sinewy arm, stopping her.

"Let's see what the hell's keeping him." He grasped the knob and turned, pulling hard. The door opened.

Jerry's booming voice rang out. "Get out of here already. I need privacy, or we're all going up in flames."

"Tell me where Skuz is, and we're out, man."

"Probably with my sister down the hall. He went to go see her."

"Okay. Good looking out, man. Be careful there." He inched the door closed and let out a huge breath. "I knew it."

Ann grabbed his arm and dragged him down the hall. "Let's go already. I want out of this place."

"Are you that eager for a show? All I have to go on are his stories, but this girl was supposed to be wild. Just warning you."

"I think I'll be fine. Wait." She held her nose and stopped walking. "Do you hear that?"

Garret's brows furrowed. He cupped a hand to his ear and pressed it against the nearest door. He held up an index finger to his lips. He stood up and pointed to it. "Here they are. They sound busy. Go on then. I'll wait over here." He walked a few steps down the hallway, raised his leg up, and placed his heel on the wall.

Ann banged on the door. "We're leaving. You two had better hurry up and finish."

The squeaking from inside stopped. Hushed whispers were heard before rustling of cloth and stomping footsteps approached the door. Mitzi's voice came. "He's indisposed. We made up, and he's staying the night."

"What?" Garret kicked off the wall and stomped over. "Bro, you know what tonight is. We don't have time for this."

"He can make his own decisions, whoever that is. How many of you are there anyway?"

"He can speak for himself. You answer me." Garret pounded on the door again.

A muffled voice could be heard through the door.

"That's it, I'm coming in." Garret backed up from the door and motioned for Ann to move aside. "You'd best open the door or I'm kicking it off the hinges."

"Just wait a minute," Mitzi's frantic voice said. "Fine, you brute." A quiet click emanated through the hallway. The door creaked open to show Mitzi's greasy hair frazzled. She pulled her robe closed by tugging on the sash at her hips.

Garret pushed his way past her and stepped inside the room. "Oh Jesus Christ. Seriously, dude?" He looked down at Skuz's fully clothed from the waist up body tied down to the bed. "At least you still have your undies on. This will have to wait, you two freaks."

"Who the hell do you think you are?" Mitzi's hands fell to her hips. "You can't just come in here and tell me what I can do."

Garret reached down and removed the duct tape from Skuz's mouth. "Maybe not, but I can certainly tell this chucklehead what to do." He turned back to Skuz. "Anything to say for yourself?" He took out his knife and cut away at the gray bonds.

"I did feel the restraints were a bit much." Skuz rubbed his wrists. "I didn't think you were going to go full bondsman on me." He stood up and stretched his arms above his head. "Yeah, I'm ready to go," he said, pulling on his pants and shoes.

"Good," Garret walked back to the door toward Ann. "Hurry up." He disappeared around the corner, leaving Ann shaking her head at Skuz. She had a devious smile as she turned to follow Garret.

Skuz turned back to Mitzi. "I'll be back as soon as I can, baby. Just no more of that tying me up business, okay?"

"Aww, don't be so closed minded."

"I'm glad to hear you say that." He reached up and cupped her cheeks. "What if next time I'm the one who -"

"Anytime now, jackass," Ann's voice called from down the hallway.

"Yeah. Good luck with whatever you're doing. Just don't bring them next time." She rested her hand against Skuz's wiry abs. "And yes, you can be the one tying me up next time," she whispered in a breathy voice.

"Later." Skuz backed up, eying her lithe frame all the way. He blew a kiss and shut the door with a wink.

"God, you are cringe worthy," Ann said, hands folded in front of her. "Come on already, minute man." She exited the building without further word.

"I hate you."

13

"We got the package," Garret told the group of men at the table.

"Good." Richard's chair rotated in place at the head of the table. "Now to just end this war in one stroke. Are we all in agreement on the plan then? Show of hands."

All six hands shot straight up along with a chorus of "Aye".

"Any volunteers for this? I'm not going to lie. It's dangerous."

"No one's going to volunteer for a suicide mission unless we can stack the deck." Lucien slammed his fist on the desk. "There's no way they'll fall for it again though."

"I can do it." Irving pointed to himself using his thumb. "If there's one thing I know, it's how not to be seen."

"Yeah?" Garret asked. "How about planting bombs while staying undetected? You any good at that?"

"Not really."

"Well I am. The question is, 'Am I going alone?'"

"I know you're not about to leave me behind again," Skuz said beside Garret.

"You're not exactly low profile," Irving said. "If nothing else, the purple hair will stand out. If one person catches sight of it, you're in a shootout with dozens of them."

"Then someone else has to go. We can't let him go in without backup. Are you crazy?"

"He's right." Richard stopped swiveling his chair and looked at men on both ends of the table before continuing. "Irving, are you still up for it?"

"If he's going, he's going to the range with me for the rest of the day," Skuz said. "The last time I saw him shoot I had to duck, and I was behind him."

"Yeah, whatever you say. If you want me to beat your high score, I can oblige that tonight." Irving flipped Skuz his middle finger.

"While you two boys are practicing, I'll be calling around the city gathering intel from the street. I'll see if I can gather where they're stationing their soldiers. It might help you find an angle of approach."

"I'll clean all the weapons in storage tonight," Tony said. "Someone has to after all. Leave anything you want cleaned here, and I'll have it done by morning, guaranteed."

"I'll load up the magazines then," Lucien grunted as he leaned forward and placed his elbows on the surface. "What good's a weapon if you have no ammunition?"

"It's settled. Everyone has their jobs. We'll meet back here tomorrow morning and go over the final details." He grabbed the gavel on the table and slammed it onto the wooden piece. "Now get to work, you lazy bums," he said with a wide grin.

Garret stood up from the table along with his five brothers in arms and exited the room into the bar. He saw Ann and Kate sitting alone in the corner of the room at a table. Kate raised her hand and waved him over. He swaggered over. "Ladies? You ready for the big operation tomorrow?"

"Did you all decide how it's going down?" Ann asked.

"It's club business, but yes we did. Don't worry, there are no delays. You'll hopefully only have one more night in my spare bedroom." He leaned down close to Ann's face. "That is, unless you wanted to stay over longer?"

She raised a hand and gripped his chin, pushing him away. "In your wildest dreams. I'm not into precocious pups like you. You wouldn't know how to handle me."

"You never know unless you try."

Kate sighed and stared across the room.

"What's wrong?" Ann followed her friend's gaze to find she was staring at Irving as he stacked boxes near the bar. "Oh, I see." Her lips curved upward. "You like the newly patched in guy, huh?"

"Huh?" Kate snapped out of her reverie. "No, of course not."

"Irving? You could certainly do worse."

"You would talk him up," Ann said. "You're his brother. You're biased."

"Maybe so." Garret looked up at the television in the corner of the room. "I see we're still not on the news. At least there's something going right lately."

"I'd hate to be on there again," Kate said in a sour tone. "Once was enough."

"You all screwed up that bad? Was that what led to your little jailhouse stint that led to that one girl? Sheila was it?"

"You got it." Ann nodded along. "Only it wasn't a job gone awry."

"Snitch?" Garret asked.

"Bingo," Kate said. "Do you want to guess who persuaded our rat to turn?"

"I'm going to go with either ES-15 or the Knights. Am I right?"

"Doubly right."

"So that's why you went after her in the pen. She was the snitch, right?"

"You've unraveled the mystery."

"Did you get her?" Garret asked.

"They never did find out who jabbed her neck fifty times in that prison. It's a real tragic story, isn't it?" Ann sniffed and wiped away an imaginary tear.

"I'll take that as a yes," Garret smirked. "You know how to take care of your business, I've got to give you that." He saw Kate still giving longing glances toward Irving. "I'll tell you what, as thanks for that story I'll do Kate here a solid."

"Oh you don't have to do that."

"Nonsense. I'll have it no other way." He pounded his fist against the table and let out a roar. "Irving, get over here."

"What's up, brother?" Irving ran over. "You ladies need something to drink? Tea? I just went out and got some earlier in case either of you liked it. I've got green tea and mint."

"This girl beside me needs something to drink alright," Ann snickered. "She's as thirsty as can be."

Irving walked over and stood a few feet away from Kate. "What can I get you, cutie?"

"What?" Kate buried her face in her hands. "Mint tea would be delightful."

"It'll be a few minutes. Don't go anywhere." He jogged off and set about preparing the tea.

"Let me give you a piece of advice. That guy? He's a little thick. You're going to need to be a little more forward than that Little Bo Peep routine."

"You're lucky that girl even managed to answer him."

Her eyes snapped open. "Hey, wait a minute. Why didn't he ask me? He only asked her."

"Maybe it's mutual attraction?" Garret asked. "Which means you don't have to be as shy. Trust me, if there's one thing I know about the guy, it's that he won't be cruel when you confess."

"I couldn't do such a thing to a guy I just met. I've never even had a proper conversation with him."

"You're such a prude." Ann slouched down in her seat. "You'll never get laid with that attitude."

"Ann, that's not all there is to romance," Kate sighed. "You call me hopeless, and sometimes I wonder about you. I appreciate the gesture, Mr. Price, but I can handle my own affairs thank you."

"I was just trying to help." Garret raised both hands and placed them behind his head as he leaned the chair back and balanced it on two legs. "I love playing matchmaker after all. It's rare I get to in this life."

"Stick to your day job," Ann said.

"Why don't you go over there and help him before he leaves for the range?" Garret asked. "I'm sure he'd appreciate the help."

Kate clicked her tongue. "What the hell, why not? I like my tea a certain way after all."

"That's the spirit." Garret's eyes followed Kate as she got up and made her way over to the bar.

"What about you?" Ann asked. "Shouldn't you be getting ready for tomorrow? You are the one going in, right? You must be nervous."

"What good will that do? That only holds you back and makes you second guess yourself. In a gun fight, that's fatal."

"Yeah? Well, on a sneaking mission it keeps you alive. Bravery doesn't get you too far when you're full of holes."

"True enough. I'll remember that."

"You're damned right, considering I'm going to be there."

"You'd best go over there and tell Irving that yourself. He's my assigned backup."

"Is that right?" Ann eyed Irving up and down. "He seems like a good kid. There's only one problem."

"If you're trying to convince me to switch him, save your breath. I trust him with my life, and it was already decided. Feel free to talk to Rich or Irving himself."

"Of course, the club's orders are law. I know how it is." She pursed her lips and looked up at the bar. "On second thought, I will go talk to him. I'll give him an earful on forgetting about my drink."

"Good luck. I'll be waiting for when you two are ready to head out. Just come find me. I'll be outside in the garage." He pushed the chair back and stood up. "Just know this is a far more dangerous operation than the previous few. You deserve to know that."

"I can make my own decisions thank you. I'll decide where I go and when I do it."

"Have at it. Just don't expect Rich to change his mind without a hell of an argument to back it up."

"You leave that to me." Ann got out of her seat. "I didn't help lay all this groundwork only to be shut out in the moment of glory." She circled around the round table and came up behind Kate who was sitting on a stool at the end of the bar. Irving worked in front of her with his back to her. She could hear Kate attempting to hold a conversation.

"You have to do something besides club work when you get home, surely?"

"Of course," Irving said, grabbing a mug, "but I doubt it's something you'd be interested in. I'd hate to bore you." He grabbed the teapot atop the nearby stove and poured the drink into the cup. "I'm more interested in your story."

"Me?" she squeaked out.

"Yeah, it's rare we see any women who aren't..." He looked away.

"Sluts?" Kate offered.

"Something like that. They're boring. You know what I mean?"

"My God, talking about vanilla." Ann took the seat beside Kate. "You two need to live a little. Get down and dirty. Trust me, it's more fun."

"I'll be doing enough morally dirty things tomorrow. I don't need to add to it." Irving placed the mug in front of Kate. "I mean, if an international incident doesn't count, what would?"

"Speaking of which, are you sure you're up for it?"

"Ann, don't be rude."

"You're lucky I'm such a nice guy." Irving's eyes narrowed as he looked at Ann. "I'll take that as a slip of the tongue."

"At least you know how to avoid a conversation. We'll see if that skill set transfers to dodging patrols tomorrow. Personally, I doubt it."

"You're treading on thin ice here," Irving said. "How about something to drink before I head out for the night?" He forced a fake smile onto his face.

"At least you're not a meat head who fights at every little provocation like that Skuz ball."

"Just answer me one last question before I head off and let you two flirt unabashed. Did you volunteer for this job, or were you volunteered? Be honest with me."

"I was the first one actually. Does that matter?" He noticed Skuz out of the corner of his eye motioning him over. He raised an index finger.

"Interesting. I didn't think you had it in you. I'll be coming along tomorrow you know."

"I hadn't heard that."

"Now you have." Ann stood up from the stool and backed up a few feet. "I'm not missing the coup de grace on those animals. You'd have to kill me first."

"Ann, don't say such reckless things. It's bad luck." Kate took a sip from her glass and let out a breath. "Don't scare me like that."

"That's the difference between me and you, Kate." Ann patted her shoulder. "I do what comes naturally, and you sit there and think for eternity. You never get anything done that way. Good luck with your preparations, Irving. Try not to get shot by the purple menace over there tonight."

"I heard that, you bloody bitch," Skuz cried out. "Pros-" He caught himself. "Irving, we're heading out now. Stop trying to get laid for a minute, and get ready for the job at hand."

"The nerve of him to say that after today," Kate said under her breath. "I guess he's never heard of self-reflection."

"Him?" Irving chuckled. "You get used to it eventually. You just ignore it after a while."

"I heard that," Skuz said. He stomped over and grabbed Irving's arm. "Come on already, Mr. Volunteer. I need to get you ready in case the shit heads south." He pulled him away and out the club's front door.

"Well, that was rude." Kate took another drink from the mug. "I guess we should be heading out too."

"After one more thing." Ann looked over into the meeting room and saw Richard sitting in there alone. She walked toward the side room. "I'll be right back." She pushed the door open and shut it behind her.

"You're not supposed to be in here. It's club members only." Richard kept his gaze on the table in front of him.

"What's the matter, President? Worried about tomorrow?"

"Of course not." Richard looked up at her with a grin.

"Good, then I suppose you don't mind that I'm going in with Garret and Irving?"

"Come again?" Richard got up and stood toe to toe with her. "That's not your call. You're a loose cannon, and we cannot afford another gaffe."

"You'll have a huge fuck up if you send the new guy in with Garret. Look, he's a great club member, but even I can tell he's shaking nervous."

"Let me guess - you're not?"

Ann pointed up at her 'Sergeant at Arms' patch. "I don't do fear. I have far more experience than your current officer at arms. I want revenge, and I will have it - with or without you. You'd best deal with that reality."

"You have balls, I'll give you that. You want to know what I see from where I'm sitting? He's put out just as much courage as you. What would it look like if I took him off the job and substituted you just because? I can't do it. End of discussion. If you want to be logistics support, go right ahead, but you're not going inside."

Ann took a step forward. "You don't understand. I am going in that damned building one way or the other."

Richard stood nose to nose. "This ain't your women's club anymore. You'd best realize that." He grimaced. "You're here as a courtesy to Garret, nothing more. You'd best get right with that. You have no authority in our operations."

"You pigheaded fool. You'd sooner throw an inexperienced recruit into the grinder than the willing veteran just to please your ego? You're no president. You're a politician in a kutte."

Richard's fists at his side shook. "You'd do well to remember where you're at, little girl, and get out of my face."

"What are you going to do? Hit me? Prove your masculinity by giving me a black eye? You'd throw away your tactical advantage for a little short-term joy? What a strategist you are."

"I didn't get to where I am by throwing temper tantrums, little girl, unlike you. Now if you're done having your little bitch fit, get out." He sat back down and looked away from her. "That means now if you're deaf."

"Whatever you say, 'Pres'," she said with a sarcastic bite. "I'll be a good little girl, don't worry." She curtsied on her way out. She opened the door and threw it closed with a thunderous bang.

"I see that went well," Kate said as Ann approached.

"That man is insufferable."

"You two work everything out?"

"We came to an understanding." Ann nodded toward the exit. "Come on, let's get out of here." She and Kate walked toward the exit. She looked over through the windows and saw Richard watching them. "Tomorrow will be a regular party."

An hour later...

Lucien sat at one table filling the magazines one cartridge at a time. He looked over across the table at Tony. "I should be there tomorrow, not sitting here in the middle of the night and leaving the work for others."

"I know." Tony disassembled another pistol and set about cleaning it with the brass rods and bronze brushes. "We all want to be there. It's a lot harder to remain undetected with a group though. We just need to focus on our job, which is to prepare for the worst case."

"I suppose." Lucien set the magazine over to the right and grabbed another from the pile on his left. He filled the new one as he talked. "We'll be nearby though, right?"

"How would I know? We're nailing that down in the morning. We'd better be."

"Whoever's following the convoy will have to be near if they're to follow it."

"Good point. I'll volunteer for that job. Who would suspect an old man riding in a van?"

"They'll just assume you're a grandpa and not bat an eyelash."

"At least age has some sort of use." A clatter interrupted the men. "Ah shit," he groaned as he leaned down below the table and picked up the wayward magazine. "I was beginning to believe it was all bad, like my back." One of his arms snaked their way behind him and pushed against his lower back.

"You remember when I got patched in?"

"How could I forget that debacle?"

"You were my sponsor though. You set that up, you old goat."

"How was I supposed to know that you had a peanut allergy? You never said anything."

Tony picked up another magazine. "My sister nearly killed you for that."

"At least she was jiggling her assets as she bitched me out. I zoned out after the first sentence."

"You dirty old man," Tony scoffed. "You're lucky she didn't notice. She'd have tried to kick your ass."

"I hear Skuz is into that. Did you hear about it today from Garret?"

"What did that idiot do now?"

"Got totally ruled over by a thin little waif that tied him to the bed. Can you believe that?"

"I've got to get in on that shame game the next time I see him."

"What are you two talking about this late?" Richard emerged from the meeting room and ambled over, taking a seat.

"Just about how much we want to be involved tomorrow, not sitting here," Tony said.

"I know the feeling," Richard said. "Ever since I accepted this patch, all I do is sit in the clubhouse all day."

"That's supposed to be one of the perks of command," Tony said, reassembling the pistol and grabbing another.

"Did Garret head home yet?" Richard asked.

"That was like an hour ago I think," Tony said.

"He took that bitch with him?"

"Are you talking about the redhead?"

"That's the one. She's a real handful."

"She's a tough bird." Lucien stood up, grabbed a nearby bottle, and took a swig. "I know the type."

"Tough or not she's a wild card, and I don't like it. We need to get rid of her soon."

"I think Garret likes her," Tony said. "I also saw Irving get fresh with the quiet one. It might not be so easy to get rid of them at this rate."

Richard shrugged. "So long as they become old ladies I have no problem, but things can't stay as they are. They're too much of a liability. I hate unknowns in the field."

"At least with wild cards there's a chance that you'll get exactly what you need." Lucien sat down, the latest gun reassembled. He grabbed a nearby half amber filled glass and upended it with a grimace.

"It could also end up being a deuce," Tony said.

"We'll see. All we can do is see how tomorrow plays out…"

14

"You got everything ready?" Ann asked the guy beside her.

"I have a bomb of questionable stability on my lap, my .357, and my black attire. I think I'm good to go." Garret pulled a black mask over his face and put on the gloves. "Hopefully they keep it good and dark in there at five am."

"You're going to try planting that in the dark?" Irving's already obscured face asked, shifting his feet. "Isn't that dangerous?"

"According to Jerry, all I have to do is tape it under where I want the boom. It's not a big deal since we'll be triggering it from a distance with a phone call."

Irving looked out the back of the van's window. He squirmed in his position but kept silent all the while.

"Don't worry so much." Ann leaned forward and slapped Irving's knee, causing him to sit up straight for a moment. "It'll all go off without a hitch, and we'll be done with this shit."

"Yeah." Irving refused to meet her gaze and looked at the floor of the cabin. "I know."

"Just stay low and quiet," Kate's quiet voice said from beside Ann. She looked across the cabin at Irving beside Garret. "They're a little hard of hearing from the constant blaring of music, at least the ones I was around."

"He's not a morning person," Skuz said from the row ahead. "Don't pay him any heed, ladies. He's ready. I made sure of it myself. I'm so nice I even brewed him a cup of coffee. Aren't I a nice guy?"

"Considering you drink three cups of that stuff a day, I'd consider that a happy accident from your ass," Richard said.

"I'll bet you the wonder kid ended up being the one getting the coffee if the truth is known." Tony turned the steering wheel. "Old purple hawk back there probably got pissed he took some and is now using it to gain social leverage."

"Ding ding." Irving pointed to his right at Tony. "Except he made decaf. Like that's going to help."

"Someone has to watch your blood pressure today, so you don't stroke out in there."

"Enough joking around," Richard's serious voice said. "We're here. Let's go over this one last time." He turned around in his seat in the front and looked at the packed cabin. "Garret and Irving are going inside and taping our surprise to the undercarriage of their smuggling vehicle."

"What are the rest of us doing?" Lucien asked from the middle row of seats beside Skuz. "I'm not just sitting here while the kids are having all the fun. I prepared their toys, and I want in on some action."

"I'm glad you asked, old man. We're going to be spreading out around the building and reporting back positions of any Knight or ES-15 we see. That way we can get operational support to our infiltration team. All they'll have to worry about are the people inside."

"And if they run into problems?" Tony asked.

"If that happens, we'll regroup outside by picking you up, crash through the garage, and pick up our boys. It'll be hairy. If you do get in trouble, try and find a spot near that, but not in front of it. We won't have to though since Garret won't let them see him. This van's license plates are bogus, we removed the vin tags, it has tinted bullet resistant windows, and the authorities have no idea who is in here. Still, we're going to be dodging a lot of bullets if it comes to that."

"You'd best not let them see you, or we're all in the shit," Skuz said. "Yes, even you ladies."

"So long as you stay behind me, we'll be fine." Garret said to Irving. "Just don't go getting brave in there and try to show off to Kate here. Notoriety only matters if we live to tell about it." He burst into a chortle.

"They grow up so fast." Skuz turned around and looked squarely at Irving. "Why, I remember when you were just a little prospect unclogging toilets, and here you are now."

Richard cleared his throat and quieted everyone down. "Skuz, you'll take the north side near here. Remember, everyone keep your distance and stay inconspicuous. You'd better have your damned binoculars too. I told you to get them. Just act like your bird watching or some shit if anyone asks. Now we can't get too close because it'd be a dead give-away and arouse suspicion. Tony, you're on the south side. We'll drop you off after Skuz gets out. Everyone waits until they get a call saying to go. No one goes early. That's how people get killed. After that, we drop off Lucien on the west side, and finally we need someone for the east road." He scanned the remainder of cabin inhabitants. "Do either of you two want to volunteer?"

"I don't have a phone or I would." Kate looked down at her hands in her lap. "I couldn't actually relay anything."

"Is that all? Give me just a second." Skuz disappeared behind the seat and the rustling of a plastic bag filled the cabin. He reappeared with a pristine cell phone in his hand. He extended it and handed it to Kate. "We always keep a supply of burners. I'm just surprised your counterpart didn't jump for the part. She's usually the outgoing one."

Ann remained quiet and merely replied by giving a silent, dagger filled glance at Skuz.

"It doesn't matter. Does everybody remember their jobs? Once this kicks off there are no reminders, and people's lives are on the line."

No one voiced another concern.

"Alright then. Dealer's choice," Richard said. "Garret, where do you want to be dropped off? Any particular side of the building?"

Ann patted Garret's shoulder, leaned into his side, cupped her hand over her mouth and his ear and whispered.

His eyes widened with a nod. "I'll go with the east side."

Richard frowned. "Any particular reason?"

"Easy," Garret said. "It has the most cover. The north side is just essentially a giant main street. It's too conspicuous. West is no good as it leads to the Knight's primary turf. That's a lot of extra ways to be found. The south has some decent cover but also a lot of pedestrian traffic on foot this time of the morning. Few Knights go east. It has tons of buildings and alleyways, and since it leads out into farmland, most people don't go that way."

"I see you've put a lot of thought into this. As soon as you get inside, send us a text. If shit kicks off, ditto." Richard nodded. "Alright then, let's get this party started. Skuz, you're the first out."

"Be careful, brothers. I'll see you in a little while."

"Good luck, man," Garret called out from the back before the door slammed shut.

"Take us around to the west first," Richard said to Tony. "We'll drop Lucien off next, and then you. I'll take over driving and then swing around east and drop off our last volunteer."

The van backed up and jerked forward.

Fifteen minutes later...

"Alright, you two be careful in there." Richard stopped the vehicle in a nearby alleyway and angled himself to investigate the back.

Garret opened the back doors and jumped out, followed by Kate, Irving, and finally Ann.

"Get the hell back in here, woman," Richard sneered at Ann. "I told you, you're not going."

"I'm just keeping Kate here company." Ann pulled Kate close. "Surely you don't have a problem with that? I mean, what if some shady guy tried something on her? Would you take responsibility?"

"Garret, Irving, don't let that gash anywhere near the building. After all, she's just there for her friend's emotional support, right? Now close the damned door. I need to get in position before you get in there."

"You got it, Pres." Garret closed the doors and the van pulled into traffic and out of sight.

Garret walked down the narrow space between buildings. "You're not here for emotional support," Garret said.

"Was that a question?" Irving asked.

"No, buddy, it wasn't."

"How rude to accuse a lady of lying, Mr. Price," Kate huffed and her voice softened, "even if it is probably true."

"Kate." Ann playfully shoved Kate away. "Speaking of rude, my goodness, I'm trying to keep everyone alive this morning. Is that so bad?"

"You are staying with her, right?" Irving asked.

"You are too naïve." Garret began walking.

"Et tu, Garret?" Ann clutched her heart. "Everyone's so rude to me this morning."

"Then prove us wrong why don't you?"

Ann rushed ahead and stopped at the end of the alley. She turned around. "Irving, I like you, and that's why I'm going to do you a favor."

"Here we go." Garret rolled his eyes. "Wait for it."

"You get to spend the entire morning with a girl crushing on you while you avoid a potentially deadly situation. Aren't I just the best?"

"The kicker being I just have to disobey a direct order?" Irving asked. "No thanks." He turned to Kate. "No matter how lovely the temptation."

Garret was the first to reach Ann and was pushed back. "We don't have time for this."

"Look, this is happening one way or the other. Just accept it."

"Look, Ms..." Irving paused. "What is your last name anyway? I don't think you've ever said."

"Ooh, I know this one." Kate raised her hand and hopped up and down.

"Don't you even dare," Ann said.

"It's Fox."

"Ann Fox?" Irving repeated. Both he and Garret brought a hand up to their mouths to stifle their laughter. "Look, Ms. Fox. I'm sorry, but I have my orders. You understand?"

Ann causally walked over to Irving. "Of course I do. Here's the thing. I either go with you willingly, or I follow behind and try not to get in your way."

"God dammit, fine. We have to get moving. Just don't fall behind." Garret took off into a run across the corner. "Hurry up," he called over his shoulder.

"I'm glad to get that settled. Come on, new guy." Ann followed behind Garret.

Irving gave a brief look toward Kate. "Be careful out here. Bums can sometimes get frisky in this part of town. He pulled out a wrench and handed it to her. "Use that if they try anything, okay?"

"Thank you. I won't tell your boss about Ann going, alright?"

"See you shortly." He took off into a sprint to catch up with the other two and eventually caught up near the alley.

Garret reached out and pulled him into the alley with one hand, his phone resting on his shoulder. "We got Knights coming. Quickly, this way." He dragged him back behind a dumpster where Ann was already waiting. "Skuz said they're coming from the north. They appear to be circling the building, as Lucien saw them before that."

The roar of engines became deafening and then faded out.

"Now we move again." Without warning he ducked out of the cover and jogged again.

"At least we're nearly there," Ann said before taking off after him.

"What have I gotten myself into?" Irving asked himself under his breath before dashing after both. This time he saw them duck behind the building beside their target. He followed them in and saw Ann with her hands on her knees, huffing and puffing for air.

"Don't tell me you're tired already. What happened to that bluster from earlier?" Garret peaked around the corner. "No matter, we're almost there. Now to find a way inside."

"Easier said than done, man. I looked up this place on my map app all night last night," Irving said, putting his back to the brick beside Garret. "All I saw was a stairwell to the side of the garage door that led upstairs above it."

"We can work with that."

"Wait just a minute." Ann recovered and stood upright. "There's a better way in. You're looking at the obvious back-door. Think out of the box for a minute. They're going to have at least one guy posted there as security. Unless you know some secret judo, it's going to be a lot of noise, even if you don't shoot."

"Spit out your idea then. Time's wasting, and we're the ones up right now."

"Take the route they least expect. Did you notice the dead end over there?" She pointed to the building behind her. "The buildings connect there. Here's a tip, Irv. If you're checking for points of entry, always check above and below first. There's around a four feet drop, then we drop in the window above. These guys don't have a window access on their building. Once we're up there, so long as they don't look up we're in the clear."

"There is a rooftop access door and a window up there." Irving's head tilted. "It could work."

"It's a good thing this building is getting renovated." Ann tapped the brick behind her with her knuckles. She led the group along the building away from the garage. She walked up to the door, twisted it open, and ducked inside. The men followed with Garret closing the door behind.

He pushed past the two and rushed up the stairs. "Help me find the right door. There are a lot."

The group split up once they'd reached the top floor and opened doors until Irving found the correct one. "Over here." He hunched over and crept outside, posting up outside the door.

Garret pulled out his .357 and readied it in front of him. He approached the edge and peeked over. "No one's up here. She's right, there's no door on their building."

"How did I not see this?" Irving slapped his forehead.

"Shut up unless you see someone from here on. We can't risk them hearing your bitching. I'm going in. Cover me and follow me once I'm in position at the window." He hopped down onto the roof and got on all fours. He inched forward until he could peek into the spacious chamber below.

Ann went next and came to a stop a few feet to Garret's right. She raised her hand and waved Irving down.

Irving hopped down and crawled forward.

Garret's voice was low, barely audible. "There's only one guy in there that I see." He pointed down into an office with a window, a television, and open blinds. "If he keeps watching tv like a zombie, this'll be easy."

"If he doesn't, this turns bloody in a snap," Ann said in a low husky growl.

"Unless you know mind control, this is as good as it gets." Garret reached into his pants pocket with his left hand and dialed a number. "Quiet."

Richard's voice came on. "You're in position I take it?"

"Just above the garage. I can see the truck."

"Above? Never mind, tell me later. Just be careful. I've got the boys ready. If anything happens we'll rush in and give a little misdirection by attacking from all sides. They won't know what to do."

"Got it." Garret hung up and returned the phone. "It's now or never, girls. See those crates below? When I'm done, I'll climb back up and we'll hightail it out. Stay up here, that includes you, Ann. More people just means more chances to be seen. Your tall frame wouldn't help."

"Just call a girl out won't you? Fine," she readied her own weapon, "just don't make me use this again."

"No promises." Garret reached down and opened the window just far enough to slide inside. He landed on the reinforced wooden cubes with a thud and kept hopping until he was on the concrete floor. He crouched down and scanned the room.

The upper floor consisted of a few tables littered with bottles, cigarette packs, ashtrays, and a lone television nestled in the corner. The television was on, entertaining two men who were chattering away. He descended the stairs, staring at the man in the office the whole time. He reached the bottom floor and made his way to the truck. He got down on all fours and slid underneath the vehicle. He shuffled himself into place and looked to his right. He couldn't see the man due to the tires as he set to work. He reached inside his jacket and produced the roll of tape and device. He ripped off a piece of tape with his mouth and paused when he heard a loud boom.

"You're repairing that if you break it." A disinterested voice drawled on. "What do you need?"

A Spanish accent answered. "Just checking the compartment one last time."

"Worried, new guy? You'd best leave that behind. Border patrol will notice, then you're well and truly fucked."

"A little inspection will give me the peace of mind to do

just that. Being careful is never a bad thing. You should know that."

"Stop lecturing me and go be a bitch somewhere else." The nearby television's volume became blaring.

"Fuck you." Footsteps came closer until the carriage above shook.

Garret quickly stuck the device onto the undercarriage and taped it in place. He heard a loud shuffling noise above and immediately ripped off another two pieces until the noises above stopped. He reinforced his makeshift attempt and put away the tape. More thumping and a wobble, along with footsteps heading toward the office, met his ears. He heard the door slam again and shimmied down until he could roll out between the tires.

He looked up at Ann and Irving and gave a thumbs up. He climbed the stairs, careful to not go too fast. He glanced up and saw Ann raise a palm. He stopped in his tracks until a door closed. She beckoned him to move again.

He raised his leg and hooked it on top of the crate and used the leverage to pull himself up.

"Hurry up," Ann said. She looked to his left as he rushed to climb.

Irving and Ann both reached a hand down.

Garret leapt and grabbed both of their hands. He kicked down on the wall and pulled himself up as he heard yet more voices from below. He pulled his feet out and all three kept still.

"I didn't see anything, but I could have sworn I heard it. It sounded like a grunt." He paused and raised his voice. "Hey, Earl, was that you?"

Garret raised a finger to his lips and slid away from the window along with the other two. He bent over at the waist with a giant exhale. "You'll never believe how that went down. I thought I was dead for a second there." He pulled out his phone and dialed Richard. "It's done." He knelt down and gave Ann a boost back onto the renovated building.

"I never had any doubt. Get out of there and back to Ninth Street. I'll pick you up there, and we can hurry up and wait."

"Sounds like a fun afternoon. We'll be right there." He folded the phone and put it away. "Let's get out of this oily cesspit." He did the same for Irving. He then jumped up and grabbed their hands again. Once all three were back in relative safety they talked on the walk down the stairs and out into the street.

"I thought I was going to have to shoot that guy that stood by the truck until he got in the back." Irving trailed the pack as they headed down the stairs.

"He was just a new guy like you," Garret said. "Except they have him muling their cargo. He's careful, but not enough. It sounded like he gave their compartment a once over and let it go there."

"He should have checked under where you were and the driver's cabin if he was actually smart. He's careful, not smart," Ann chuckled.

"I'm not complaining." Garret pushed open the door at the bottom and walked down the street. He shoved his hands in his pants pockets. "Now the real fun starts, boys and girls."

15

"Check it out." Garret leaned forward and poked Tony's shoulder. "They're getting ready to move."

"Thank Christ." Skuz wiped the sweat out of his face. "I thought we'd be in this furnace all day."

"God is merciful it seems," Richard smirked, watching the garage door open and the truck pull out with its convoy following behind. "Turn the engine on and get ready to follow it from a distance. Pull off before we get to the border. Stay on the left. There's a nice little parking lot up there we can watch from."

Tony twisted the key in the ignition and checked over his right shoulder. "I can't wait to watch this show." He pulled out into traffic and stayed three cars behind.

Richard leaned forward and turned a dial, causing cold air to start blowing. "It's just the beginning. Once they become infamous over here in the states, their benefactors are going to get nervous. They'll try to take over Enrique's turf. That is where the real show starts. It'll be a total implosion is my guess."

"Don't count that horse's ass out," Lucien said. "He'll come at us in his death throes."

"Let me guess. You know his type?" Richard asked.

"That's right. I wasn't always an old man. I was your sponsor after all. Back then we had to deal with even worse monsters than nowadays. Enrique's nothing more than a mentally stunted savage compared to some of the leaders the club's tangled with before. He thinks he's smart. He takes his precautions, but he's young and arrogant." He turned around and rested his wrinkly arm on the seat. "How many men were in there? I bet less than five."

"Three permanently and one walked in."

"I knew it." He slapped the seat and chuckled. "He's about to learn a valuable lesson today."

"He's committed to the crossing now," Tony said. He rotated the wheel left and pulled into an abandoned parking lot overlooking the horde of cars stuck in front of the crossing station.

Everyone filed out of the van. Garret walked up front and hopped onto the hood of the van. He dug a piece of paper out of his hand and handed it off to Richard when he got near. "Here's the number. Call when you're ready for the boom."

"I'll be waiting with bated breath." Richard snatched it and read the paper. "Got it."

Ann circled around the other side of the van and hopped up beside Garret with Kate standing beside her. "It'll be a while. He's back there a ways. My guess is at least ten minutes." She nodded forward. "At this time of the morning it's always hectic. Which is exactly why it's the best time."

"Blending in by hiding in plain sight huh?" Skuz asked

from a few feet ahead of them off to the side. He swiped his purple hair to the side. "I guess that would work."

"I know it does. I used to make the runs myself. Sure, occasionally you'd get some dumbass getting his car searched by dogs in front of you, but so long as they can't find your hidden compartment, you're good. You just act polite, answer their questions, and don't act nervous. Having watched that kid earlier, I guarantee he's going to blow it. You can just tell from the way he carried himself. He has no confidence."

"That's a bold prediction." Garret reclined onto the windshield.

"Not that it matters anyway. As soon as he's half in and half out, he's going bye-bye," Richard said. "I'll make sure of that."

"I almost feel bad for him." Irving kicked a nearby rock out into the grass in front of them. "He'll be there one minute and poof," his arms illustrated a mushroom cloud, "he'll be meeting his maker."

"He deserves it." Lucien spit on the pavement below.

"They're certainly not doing it out of charity or good will," Kate added. "With them it's all about money, favors, and what have you done for me lately? The people they move are scum of the earth."

"How exactly did you keep your operation going if you didn't ask for money?" Irving asked.

"She didn't say we didn't ask for it at all," Ann said. "It just wasn't all about selfishness. Giving discounts in exchange for other favors is how a lot of our opportunities showed themselves. A mother trying to get away from her abusive gangbanger husband, for example, leads to a lot of neighborhood support. They won't call the cops if some-thing happens; and, if they do, they conveniently forget you were there. Of course if the client was a scumbag, they paid over full price and the compartment was somehow always smaller. They always had tough luck."

"No wonder you pissed off the wrong people if that's how you did business." Skuz kicked the front tire. "Does the word 'impartial' mean anything to you?"

"Not everybody deserves the same treatment."

"That's the first thing you've said that I agree with." Richard rested his elbow on the hood beside Garret.

Tony raised the binoculars to his eyes and pointed toward the border with his other hand. "Check it out. He's only a couple of cars back now. You might want to get ready, Rich."

Richard dialed the number and hovered his finger over send. "Just tell me when he stops."

"You boys realize that as soon as this goes off we need to jet," Ann said. "Border patrol is going to swarm all over this area inside of fifteen minutes."

"More than enough time to gloat and get out." Richard took off his glasses and watched the truck move up another ten feet.

"He's almost there. Just one more to go and he'll be ready. He looks like he's sweating bullets in there. He's twitching and looking all over the place."

"Like I said, total amateur hour." Anne hopped off the windshield and grabbed Garret's shoe. She pulled him down causing a loud squeaking sound. "Come on, get ready. I'm not getting pinched after all this because you want to rest in the proverbial red zone." She flung the van's doors open one by one.

Garret slid to the end of the hood and remained on the edge, kicking his feet out in front. "In a minute. I want to see this in all its glory."

"He's there." Tony lowered the lenses.

"Have fun with this fallout." Richard's thumb fell and initiated the phone call. A ring coincided with a humongous shockwave and a multitude of car alarms, horns, and screams going off at the border station. Bits of car rained down in front of them onto the group of commuters' vehicles. Dust obscured any view of the once bustling station. When the dust settled, the once pristine lines of vehicles now resembled a child's playroom. The car behind the truck was sprawled on its side, tilting toward toppling over completely, while other cars behind them backed up into each other to get away.

"Have fun with your overlords paying a visit, Enrique." Richard folded up his phone and moved to get inside the van. "Everyone in. We're getting out while the getting's good."

Everyone hustled inside the vehicle and, without waiting, it made its way back onto the road. Garret climbed in the back along with Ann and Skuz. Richard and Tony sat up front, and Irving, Kate, and Lucien filled the middle row.

"Can you believe that shit? Mexico's government is going to lose it," Skuz cackled.

"The kicker is that the truck had the knight's logo plastered all over it," Garret said. "There's no way they'll be able to explain that away. It was caught on camera, and bombs are homeland security jurisdiction. There's no way for them to talk their way out of it."

"That'll be a fun conversation when the feds show up at the clubhouse."

"Is that before or after the cartel shows up and demands to take over?" Irving asked.

"Hopefully after. They don't give a fuck. They'll shoot

cops, or they'll shoot anyone that gets in the way," Kate said. "I'm just glad no innocents got hurt here."

"Besides some little fender benders and a few cuts anyway," Garret finished.

"There is one other option," Lucien said. "ES-15 doesn't take the bait and cut ties with them. In which case, they're royally hosed. They can't take trying to wage war while under investigation. We'd just have to dot all our 'I's' and cross all our 'T's'. They have nothing on us. It'd be the terrorists' word against ours."

"They'll come up," Kate said, her voice dark. "I guarantee it. Enrique was big money for them. They won't give that up without a fight. I hear they're in their own little turf war down south."

"You got all that from bartending?" Irving asked the woman beside him. "You must have loosened their lips with all that alcohol."

"You learn who likes what drink and how much they can take eventually. From there, it's about not arousing suspicion. Let them talk and show off. They can't help it."

"Regardless of what happens," Richard started, "good job. We dealt a blow to them that won't be forgotten around these parts for a long time. Stay on your toes tonight. If I know Enrique, he'll come at us hard. Probably at our homes. I'd recommend staying at the clubhouse."

"What about us?" Ann asked.

"I'd be for allowing them to stay a night," Irving said.

"Who would have guessed?" Richard asked. "I'm guessing Garret's the same way?"

"I don't care. I just want to rest after today. If I must, I'll sleep on a table in the main room."

"They have helped us. A little hospitality wouldn't hurt," Lucien said.

"Fine, I get it," Richard said. "You can stay in the clubhouse for one night only. After that -"

"We're gone. We get it. Once we're sure this whole thing has blown over, we're out of here anyway."

"We're clear then. We appreciate your service, but you're on your own after this."

Garret leaned over to the preoccupied Ann's ear and whispered in a husky voice with a lick. "Would you like me to show how appreciative I am?"

She squeaked and jumped in her seat, causing everyone up front to look at her, including Kate. "Don't ever do that again."

He wore a devilish grin. "That's your weak spot huh? I'll remember that."

"Keep it in your pants, hotshot," Richard said from in front. "The last thing we need is to catch an indecent exposure charge on our ride back." The whole cabin erupted in laughter as the van continued down the road.

That night...

"Check it out." Irving turned up the television's volume. "Our boy's on the news."

Richard glanced up at the box. "Two killed and five injured. Good job, there were no unnecessary casualties."

"By some miracle." Lucien upended another drink. "We should raise money for the survivors. It'd buy us some positive PR and distance us from this circus."

"I'd kill to be a fly on the wall of Enrique's meeting room tonight." Tony elbowed Lucien in the ribs. "You think he's shot anybody for this yet?"

"We'll make the charity happen in time." Richard got up and walked to the bar and refilled his glass. He walked back to the table. "We'll give it a few days. We can't be too quick."

Garret, Skuz, Ann, Kate, and Irving sat at the neighboring table. Garret extinguished a cigarette in the ash tray. "The next two days will be the last gasp. Those vatos are going to be rushing north. Enrique needs to do something now before they take over. We should set up a guard schedule tonight with rotating shifts to be safe. I'll volunteer for first shift."

"Forget that man." Tony shook his head. "I'll take your shift along with mine. It's not like I was the one going in. I got you, brother. Just get some much-needed rest."

"I'll take a shift." Irving raised a mug in the air.

"I may be old," Lucien grunted, "but I can still stand guard when needed."

"Then I guess Skuz is taking the final watch," Richard laughed. "Thanks for volunteering."

"Fair's fair I guess," Skuz grumbled.

Tony pushed his chair out and moved toward the door. "I guess I should take mine then. Relieve me in four hours, won't you?" He moved over toward the door.

"You got it." Irving looked over at Kate. "What's the matter? Why the long face?"

She shook herself out of her reverie and smiled at him. "It doesn't matter. I'll accompany you on your watch if you'd like tonight."

The other table let loose a chorus of "Ooh".

"Ignore them. Sure, if you don't mind."

"Sounds like you all have it settled." Garret leaned back in his chair with a yawn. "I'm going to hit the bed. You're sure you don't mind taking my shift?"

Tony threw on his jacket and grabbed the knob. "I've got this."

"I'm hitting the sack then. See you in the morning, boys and girls." He rose out of his chair and went down the narrow hallway leading out of the bar, disappearing into the nearby door.

"You'd better go catch up with him quick if you don't want him falling asleep," Skuz winked at Ann. "He falls asleep in minutes. That is, unless you want to sleep on the floor instead of him."

"I'm not sleeping on any floor regardless of the circumstances."

"At least you finally admit you're going to sleep with him. We were beginning to wander if you were..." Skuz trailed off.

"I was what?"

"You know."

"What? A lesbian?"

"You said it, not me."

Ann launched her leg out and connected with Skuz's shin. "No, I'm not. Thanks for finally figuring that out."

"I never heard a denial," Richard chimed in.

"The hell with all of you." Ann stood up and stormed down the hallway.

"Is she..."

She flung the door open and stomped inside.

"Yep," Kate finished. "I think you just got them both laid.

"I must learn to use my powers for good and not for frivolous reasons like this." Skuz pressed his palms in front of his face in a praying motion. "For my next trick, I'll do the same for Irving here. Ow." Skuz jumped in his chair. "Stop doing that."

"I didn't do anything." Irving held his palms up in front of him.

"What? Then," he looked over at Kate who was looking away, "I see."

"You'd best not mess with her." Lucien gave a deep belly laugh. "I know her type, quiet and deadly."

"Of course you do, old man." Skuz took a sip from his drink. He set it down and pulled out his phone. "Ah damn. I forgot to get back over to Mitzi's."

"You're still with that crazy girl?" Lucien asked. "I'm telling you, boy, you need to reconsider that. I know -"

"Her type. Yes, I know you do."

"You mark my words, she's trouble."

"Maybe she is, but I should at least call her." He stood up from the table and stepped outside.

"I'm not looking forward to seeing that fallout." Lucien smiled into his drink.

"She's also dirty," Kate said, fidgeting in her seat.

An uproarious round of laughter erupted. "Say what?" Tony asked, pounding his fists onto the table.

"She's literally dirty. Her hair is all greasy, and the smell in that house is just rancid. I'm still not sure if it was that fat slob's fault or hers. The fact that he wants to go back there is the most troubling thing about his obsession."

"I see you've got some claws on you," Lucien said. "I was beginning to worry you were a pushover. Good to see I was wrong."

"I'd be dead if I was." Kate's joyous demeanor faded to a somber calm.

"Enrique's not gentle I assume," Irving said.

"It wasn't so much him as his men. When a few of them got drunk, they got excited shall we say."

"I'm sorry to hear that," Irving's voice softened.

Richard exhaled. "I can't take this touchy feely shit. I'm going to bed." He stormed off toward the outside door.

"Where's he going?" Kate asked.

"Probably the garage. There's a couch there. Shall I get you a sleeping bag? You should get your rest if you're going to be up later." Irving got up and paused only when her voice interrupted him.

"How about I make myself useful instead of lounging around." She stood beside him. "I need to work, otherwise I start thinking too much."

"I was just going to clean up the bar. Are you -"

"Yes." Kate took off ahead of Irving toward the counter.

"I think we hit a sore spot." Lucien finished the drink and brought the glass over to the counter. "Here you go, darling. I'll get the rest of the glasses before I turn in for the night. He made his way back to the table and motioned Irving over.

"What's up? I can take care of this."

"Be quiet, boy, and listen to me," Lucien spoke in a shushed voice. "You take care of her tonight. She's hurting and, honestly, it's your chance."

"Isn't that like taking advantage of her or something?"

"You'd be surprised how many marriages occur as a result of consoling someone at just the right time. Just listen to me for once if you know what's good for you." He snatched the cup out of Irving's hand. His voice grew louder. "Let me take that and you both can get started doing whatever." He set down the remaining cups on the counter and walked past Irving with a wink and a pat on the shoulder. "Now if you'll excuse me, I have a date with that sleeping bag until someone wakes me. Don't mind me. I can sleep through anything."

"He's not as gruff as he makes himself out to be." Kate's

eyes followed Lucien as he set out his sleeping bag and slid himself in. "If he wasn't so crude, he'd almost be a wise man."

"He's something alright." Irving placed the remaining bottles into the nearby trash can. "He's got a quick temper, but he cares about the club above all else. I'm still not sure if that's a good thing or not."

"Not really, but I understand it." She placed dishes into the sink and turned on the water. "Did I ever tell you about when I was in the Valkyries?"

"I honestly find it hard to believe you were part of a one percenter gang, no offense intended."

"If you'd said that two years ago, I'd have knocked your ass out - or tried anyway."

"Not so much anymore?"

"I relish not being as stubborn and arrogant as I was before. I was a lot like Skuz, minus the dumb leather jacket and purple hair. I knew what I wanted and didn't stop until I got it. It didn't matter what I had to do to find the funding. Smuggling? No problem for the right price. Drugs? Sure, how much? I had connections everywhere that I leveraged for the club." She stopped the flow of water. "Sorry, I shouldn't bore you right before you have guard duty."

"It's better than cleaning in silence, and I was interested anyway."

"What?"

"In the stories."

"Oh. I guess that makes sense." She grabbed a dried plate and put it away above her.

"You're adorable though when washing dishes."

She fumbled with the dish and caught it before it tumbled to the ground. "Don't lie like that to scare me. I nearly did drop it."

Irving stopped behind her, reached above her, and filed away another plate. "Who said I was lying?" he asked before taking a step back.

"You've been trying to learn from Garret I see. You'd be better served acting like you did before, not like his playboy persona."

"You can't blame a guy for trying multiple strategies."

"You do hang out with them all day. I guess it's to be expected you'd pick up some of their mannerisms from time to time. Just don't overdo it."

"What's wrong?"

"Excuse me?"

"I can tell by the look on your face. Your eyes drift when you're thinking of something."

"Is this a new stratagem?"

Irving leaned back against the counter. "No, I'm just being myself again like you suggested. Sorry, I'm nosy sometimes. Get used to it. I normally curb it around the guys here, but you gave me free reign. So, you'd better take responsibility for it."

"I was just wondering about when this is all done. I need to find a place to stay and a job while I'm at it."

"You know what you could do?"

"I am not becoming an old lady. Let me just stop you there. Not yours or anyone's. I've had enough of this filthy life. I don't want to live wondering if the people I care about will come home alive today. I won't put myself through that again."

Irving whistled. "Damn, girl. Shoot me down before I even say anything. You're as brutal as your friend. That wasn't what I was going to say, but it's interesting that's where your mind went. I was going to suggest a job as a bartender. You have plenty of experience, and in a decent joint you'll have bouncers, so you won't have to worry about jackasses causing a scene."

"That is an idea, isn't it?" Kate finished the last plate and closed the cupboard.

"I do have good ones occasionally, despite what Garret and Anne say. You just have to give me a chance."

"It is truly a shame."

"Hm?"

She looked away. "Nothing. I'm going to turn in early. I'm sorry, I won't be able to keep you company tonight. I'm too tired."

"Don't worry about it. Should I get you some tea before bed? It helped my grandma fall asleep. She swore if you put some warm milk in along with some cinnamon, you'd fall asleep inside of two minutes."

"I'm fine." She pushed past him and took a seat at a table in an abandoned corner. Her head fell to the table and stayed there.

"Damn."

Just earlier behind closed doors...

He could hear stomps outside his door. "I'm in no mood for it tonight." Garret removed his shoe and looked up when the door opened to see Ann. "Never mind. I thought you were someone else."

"Scoot over." She flopped down beside him.

Garret laid down and placed his legs on her lap. "Good enough?"

"You've got guts," she grabbed his feet, "laying down when I'm talking to you."

"You'll get over it." Garret arched his back and yawned. "What happened now? You looking for a place to sleep or something? You're welcome here if you like. It's only a twin, but I'm a good bedfellow. I promise."

She lifted his foot up and held it. "After all that bluster earlier, I never imagined you'd be the bashful one."

"I see what's happening here." He pressed his palms onto the mattress and pushed himself into a sitting position.

"I just wanted -" She was interrupted as he pushed her onto her back.

"You've got one more chance to leave," he looked over at the door, "with no hard feelings. What's it going to be?"

"I'm in here aren't I?" she whispered.

"I like a girl who knows what she wants. Now let me review what I've learned over the last few days."

"Just be quiet already and -" She gasped as he dipped his head and nibbled her ear. Her voice grew throaty and desperate. "Do that again."

"You'd best keep your voice down. Your friend's just outside."

"Why don't you make me?"

"Can do." He descended and covered her lips with his. He felt her hand reaching around the back of his head while the other ran down the length of his back. He raised himself up and licked his lips.

16

Garret pushed the door open and shielded his eyes from the light overhead. He looked to his left down the hallway toward the bar and saw Irving walking by. "Hey, did anything happen last night?"

"No attacks or anything, bro. I bet that'll change today."

"No doubt." Garret rubbed his eyes and ambled forward.

Irving held out a cup. "Here, you'll need this. We've got a meeting in a few minutes."

"Thanks, man." He brought the mug to his lips and tasted the piping hot brown nectar. "I won't keep you."

Irving gave a curt nod and continued about his duties behind the bar while Garret took a seat next to Richard at a table. "What's the itinerary looking like today, knowing we have a target on our backs?"

"We're damn sure not about to hide," Richard said. "We still have to vote, but I suggest we go out and do collections and little else. There's no need to push it now that time is on our side."

"That's assuming the two don't unite."

"There's no way. I know Enrique. He'll push back on his

sovereignty. You can count on that. Even if he does somehow put his ego to the side, they're still going to be under the microscope soon enough."

"Hey, listen to this." Skuz stood directly in front of the television and used the remote to raise the volume.

"In more somber news, investigators are now saying that the vehicle which exploded yesterday on the U.S./Mexican border was part of a human smuggling operation. They found a hidden compartment in the back and what remained of its occupant inside. Bomb experts are saying this was blatant, judging by where the device was placed on the truck. There's still no word on who might be responsible."

Richard drew his hand across his neck and Skuz lowered the volume.

"Should we be worried?" Irving asked.

"Jerry knows what he's doing. They won't trace it back to him." Garret took a swig of coffee. "Still, we should distance ourselves from him just in case."

"I know you didn't just say that." Skuz took a seat next to him. "She's already pissed enough at me for not coming back yesterday."

"Let me ask you a question." Richard locked eyes with Skuz. "Which is more important - that woman, or your free-dom? I ask because it could well translate to such a situa-tion. If anyone of us goes back there, and he is under watch, that puts suspicion on the whole club. You are not going back there. Do you understand me?"

"I got it," Skuz said. "I'll invite her out then?"

Garret slapped the back of Skuz's head. "No, dingbat. They'd follow her to you and then, by association, us. Your dick will have to stay dry, at least until the heat dies down. That, or find another woman. One of the two."

"Ignore his whining." Lucien was the last to wake up in the room, and he stumbled from his sleep. He placed a hand on his lower back and arched it with a crack. "That's the last time I sleep on the floor. I'm too old for this." He pulled up another seat at the quickly growing table. "He'll live without his whips and chains for a little while."

"That is not what happened in the least."

"Regardless," Richard interrupted them, "let's focus on business for now." He raised his hand. "Meeting right now. Everyone's required to attend."

The group got up from their table and filed into the room. Irving was the last to enter, closing the door behind him. He took his seat and looked toward Richard.

"We won a major battle yesterday, in no small part thanks to Garret here."

A round of applause and cheering sounded off.

Richard raised his hands with a smile. "Before we get too far ahead of ourselves, let's cross the finish line first. Today will be crucial. If he doesn't fire back, he's done. We're going out in groups of at least two. Three would be better. We're going collecting. If anything even smells funny, I want you to bolt. Let them think you ran. So long as they have no bodies to show off to their Mexican overlords, they're fucked."

"We should keep our ears to the pavement too," Tony said. He raised a muscled arm and pointed out the window nearby. "You never know who has intel that could prove handy. Maybe someone will have heard where they're going to strike. I know a guy who's associated with them but has no real loyalty. I can go get us a lay of the land and see how they're coping."

"You know this guy?" Lucien asked. "Because I don't like it. Those cartel types always get hooks under your skin. He's not into them is he?"

"He's just a dealer of theirs. He kicks up a vig but doesn't care about them in the least. He's just a cog. I've known this guy since I was thirteen."

"It could prove useful," Garret said. "I'll go with you."

"Skuz, how do you feel about you and Irving going out and collecting while they're doing that?" Richard asked.

"I'll go with those two. The owner of the local grocery store hates Skuz. He'll need me to get anything out of the guy without an assault charge."

"I can be subtle. That guy's just insufferable." Skuz crossed his arms. "He ticks me off with the way he talks."

"You mean his lisp?" Lucien asked. "The last time I saw you try, you ended up grabbing the intercom and lisping straight into it for five minutes. No wonder he hates you. If nothing else, send Irv in first. He has some common sense."

"The three of you are going," Richard said, "if there aren't any objections."

No one at the table said anything.

"While you're all out, I'll hold down the fort and coordinate from here. If there's any problems, you call me immediately. Don't try to be a hero on your own. Is there anything else that needs to be brought up today?"

"Yeah." Skuz tapped the wooden table. He turned to Garret. "How was the sex last night?"

"Better than yours with the grease girl."

"What was that?"

"Did you see her hair, man? You're lucky if she showers every week. I hope you wrap up; otherwise, you're likely to get a UTI."

Everyone around the table lost their composure and descended into howls of laughter.

"Laugh it up," Skuz said. "At least I'm getting some on a regular basis, unlike some of you here."

"I'd rather be celibate than touch that," Garret murmured amid fresh laughter.

"Enough." Richard banged the gavel. "Obviously we're done for now, so go get working." He shook his head and banged the gavel again. "Dismissed."

Everyone exited the room and put on their kuttes, grabbing their keys - some even taking last minute drinks.

The door down the hallway opened, revealing a disheveled Ann.

"Morning, sunshine," Garret called out. "You're up late." He straightened out his black leather and tossed his keys up, snatching them from midair.

"Whose fault do you think that is?" Her hand trailed the wall as she walked forward. She blinked and took a seat around the corner at the bar. "Where the hell are you all going so early?"

"Club business."

"I should have figured as much."

Richard came over and stood next to the stool beside Ann. "Go ahead, Garret, and get out of here. I need to talk to Ann here myself."

"This should be fun," Anne mumbled.

"Take it easy now. We'll be back in a bit." Garret turned around and slapped Tony on the back. "You ready?"

"You got it." The pair exited out the door, the group of Irving, Skuz, and Lucien behind them, leaving only Richard, Ann, and the still sleeping Kate in the room.

"I see two choices at this point for you." Richard looked straight ahead. "Either you're gone by tonight..."

"Or?"

"I think you know the second option."

"You're not serious."

"I don't joke around often, especially with non-club

members. You're lucky I've been as accommodating as I have been."

"Yeah, you should work at a five-star hotel, with your customer service."

"If you're going to stick around, you need to decide. I won't ask for your answer now, but you have until tonight." He looked at her with a smirk. "You've apparently already had a taste. The question is, how much do you want to keep it?"

"I'll keep that in mind. My relationships are none of your business."

"Maybe not, but my club is. I can't allow a half in/half out loose cannon to run loose in my clubhouse without some sort of check, can I? That wouldn't be responsible."

"I'll think about it." She stood up. "I'm heading out."

"Coming back?"

"I don't know." She left and headed over toward Kate's corner of the room. She got to a knee and reached out to shake her. "Kate? Wake up. It's morning, and almost everyone's left."

Kate knocked her hand away and rolled over. "Go away."

"Nope." Anne shook her again. "I'm not going away."

Kate rolled over, opened her bloodshot eyes, and sat up. "What?" She asked in a cold voice.

"I think our welcome's pretty much worn out."

"Mine maybe, not yours from what I saw last night."

"What?"

"Nothing." Kate unzipped the cocoon and climbed out. "Just ignore me."

"Who pissed in your sleeping bag?"

"I can't be grumpy in the morning?"

"Fine, don't tell me if you don't want to. I'm heading out today. Are you with me?"

"Yeah. I need to get out of this building. Where are we headed?"

"I'll tell you when we're on our way." Ann looked back at Richard.

"I get it." Kate's hands straightened her hair. "Let's go when you're ready."

"Now you're speaking my language." She craned her neck around to look at Richard. "We're out of here."

"Don't let me keep you." Richard looked down at some paperwork in front of him. "Take the old bike by the entrance. It's small, but you can fit two on it. You'd better bring it back after you get new wheels. Don't say I never did anything for you." He threw a key at her that she snatched out of the air."

"Gee, thanks. Let's get out of here." She led the pair out of the door and into the parking lot. She marched up and handed one of the two hanging helmets over to Kate before securing her own. "Where's the place you wanted to go most over these last few years?"

"Do they still have the old ice cream shop we always went to?" She hopped onto the back of the seat.

"They're still there. After that, we can go apartment hunting."

"Don't you mean job hunting? We can't pay rent without any cash. No one sane would even consider it."

"I have enough cash to cover for at least six months. I figure we can find something by then." She climbed onto the front. "What do you think?"

"I think you never think things through." Her hands fell to the bar behind her and gripped tightly.

"It always works out in the end." Ann kicked up the bar near her feet, engaged the clutch, and pushed the red switch on the handlebar to her right. The engine revved to life.

Putting it into gear, she revved the motor, letting the clutch out slowly until the bike moved forward. She steered them out of the parking lot and into traffic.

Across town...

Garret and Tony stopped their bikes on the side of the road and took off their helmets. Tony looked back at Garret. "This is the place." He pointed to the house a dozen yards up the road. "He works out of his house up here."

Garret hung his helmet on his bikes handlebars and caught up with Tony. They walked side by side down the walkway with their kuttes on full display. "Is this guy usually paranoid?" he asked, looking at the fence ahead which was covered in signs warning would be violators.

"He's always been a little off." Tony opened the gate and stepped through.

"Beautiful." Garret shut the rusting chain link fence behind him. He stepped up the few stairs and stopped on Tony's right.

Tony reached a huge arm up and pressed the button beside the door. A faint chirping could be heard inside along with a voice calling out. "Give me a minute. You're early." The door opened to show a lanky young man with a hoodie on. "Oh shit. Tony, what are you doing here, buddy?" He took a step back as Tony threw the door open and stepped inside.

"Just came to ask some questions, Harry. This is my associate, Mr. Price. I'd recommend showing him the same respect you would me." He jabbed a thumb over his shoulder.

"What's up?" Garret nodded.

"What can I do to help?" Harry asked.

"You heard anything on the street about your overlords lately?"

"You mean the Knights? Those psychos only come over here when they want to collect my hard-earned money. It's not like they let me know what's going on."

Tony took a step forward, closing the distance between the two. "I know you have customers who can't keep their mouths shut. What are they saying?"

"Look, you can't trust what strung out people say. They'll make up any story for a rock. You know that as well as I do."

"What about your high functioning customers?" Garret asked, looking around the small foyer. He looked up at the mini-chandelier. "You must have some in this ritzy neighborhood. What are they saying?"

Harry backed himself against the wall. "One guy I know said they were at war. I assume he meant with your group."

"We need more than that," Tony said. "What about today? Have you heard anything today?"

"I had one guy come in earlier that was claiming he saw a group of motorcycle riders sporting their colors riding through downtown. I assumed it was you guys, since they don't usually do that as much unless they're on cross country runs."

"That means they're mobilizing," Garret said. "Where were they going?"

"He said they were heading toward your turf."

Tony punched the wall beside Harry's head. "You couldn't say that from the start? Anything fucking else you forgot to mention, dipshit?"

"Forget him, bro. We've got to get back." Garret dragged Tony away and out the door back toward their bikes.

"We knew this would happen," Garret said as the two ran in a dead heat.

"I wouldn't have thought they'd do it in the middle of the day though."

"It doesn't matter." Garret threw on his helmet. "We'll figure it out later. I'll lead, you follow me." He surged forward and zoomed through the city with Tony hot on his trail.

17

K ate threw the cup and spoon into the trash and moved back to the picnic table across from Ann. "It's been too long since I've done this."

"Same here." Anne took another bite out of her cone. "I think it was before I got locked up."

Kate stared over Ann's shoulder at the graffiti adorning the back of the ice cream shop. "I try not to remember those days."

"Is that why you snubbed that bald guy last night? Don't lie to me. I can tell by his face and your attitude this morning."

"It's for the best."

"What happened? Did he try to get a bit fresh with you or something? Did the cold night air give him too much confidence?"

"It was nothing he did." She exhaled. "Except maybe come on a little too strong at one point. It's hardly a capital offense, especially with these kinds of men."

"Then again, he doesn't strike me as the regular kind of one percenter."

"Not yet," Kate sighed. "He will in time when he gets his confidence," her voice fell lower, "if he lives that long."

"Don't get all mopey. We lived this long, didn't we?"

"Yeah." Kate's voice was even and without glee. "We're the only two left. What was your point again?"

"You're a glass half empty, girl."

"What about you?" Kate fired back. "Where are you going back to tonight? I assume not to the Orders clubhouse. I know you're not going to be staying at Garret's apartment again."

"I do have my own apartment. You're free to stay there by the way. You are right though. We're free from this motorcycle club drama finally. We should be focusing more on the future, not the past."

"Easier said than done." Kate's ear perked up as a low, familiar roar came closer. "Speaking of motorcycles..."

"Just to be safe, let's get out of here. There's no telling who that is." Anne hurried over to the bike and tossed a helmet to a running Kate. The roar grew louder until the very ground was trembling. "Shit." As soon as Kate and Ann jumped on the bike the exits to the street were blocked off by bikes. She took off her helmet and stepped off the motorcycle. "You boys here for the ice cream? I recommend the rocky road."

"Not quite." The lead rider got off his machine. "We're here for your little friend behind you. You may as well come along too. We could use a window washer for upstairs. None of the other whores are tall enough."

"You must be desperate." Anne's eyes danced between the two groups of men. "Going out in daylight like this is dangerous. There are lots of cameras and civilians walking around who wouldn't think twice about squealing."

"Say what you want," he took a step toward the pair of

women, "but you're coming with us today - either on the back of our bikes, or by trailing behind attached to a chain. "What'll it be? Go ahead and test us. We need some blood after the week we've had." His hand disappeared behind him and produced a chain with a lock attached to it, which he swung around. The men behind him pulled out assorted weapons ranging from wrenches, crowbars, and even firearms. "We're prepared to do this loud, so keep your hands where we can see them, and don't try to be cute."

"Kate, get out of here." She tossed the keys over her shoulder and walked toward the group.

She plucked the key from the air and inserted it into the ignition. She revved the engine and inspected the crowd. She saw that one side only had melee weapons while the group on the right side did have access to firearms. "You're joking. I'm not leaving you. Get on."

"If she moves, my men fire." The ringleader flung around the chain. "For that matter, if the bartender moves, fire. I'm not playing around here." He pointed at Kate. "Get off the bike."

"Head back to the club. It's our only play."

Kate looked between Ann and the armed group. She looked down at the handlebars and back up at the man, her gaze filled with determination and hatred. "Damn it. Fuck you." The bike surged forward and to the left toward the group of men, missing Ann by a matter of feet.

She gripped the bars tightly, lowered her head, and plowed through the group of men.

Men fell left and right, holding their respective limbs. Some men had their feet run over, others had their arm clipped by the sides and drug behind them causing a dislocation. Whatever their injury, they fell to the ground leaving one side open. She zipped onto the road and gained as much distance as she could.

"Hold it right there." The leader marched forward, grabbed Ann's hand, and yanked her forward. "You're lucky we don't shoot you right now, but we need one of you." He hauled her over to his bike. "If you jump off, we're chaining you next time. It's your choice. Now get on."

Ann took a step forward and got on. "Easy. I realize when I'm outmaneuvered. No need for unnecessary bloodshed today."

"In case you get any bright ideas when you're riding, my men are authorized to shoot you if you try anything." He took his place at the helm of the bike and led the caravan out of the parking lot and onto the busy road.

Ann took a glance over her shoulder at the men following behind. "At least it's me this time."

"Shut up back there."

Back at the clubhouse...

Kate pulled up to the Order's clubhouse and into the open parking lot. She threw down her helmet and hopped off. She ran toward the building when she heard more bikes nearing. She looked back at the entrance to the compound and saw two members pulling in. She sprinted over.

"Are they here yet?" Garret jumped up. "We need to shut the gate and get ready for -"

Kate stopped in front of the two. "They took Ann."

"What? I thought they were coming here," Tony asked. "Why would they go after you two?"

"Fuck if I know," Kate said. "All I do know is they nearly

got the both of us. I only got out because I was already on the bike, and she tossed me the keys to get out."

"They must have taken her to be their new slave labor." Garret gripped Kate's shoulders and shook her as he spoke. Where would they have taken her?"

"It sounded like Enrique wanted a word with her. She's probably with him."

"A hostage play gives him needed leverage to get us right where he wants us," Tony said. "He probably wants to lure us over there into a trap to show his bosses he can take care of his own business."

"No kidding." Garret turned around, dug his fingertips into his scalp, looked up into the air, and shook his head. "We've got to get her back."

"I know how you feel, man, but we should bring this up to the club first."

"All three of us know she's not going to do shit they tell her to. What do you think is next on their schedule when they find out she won't play ball?"

"A dirt nap," Kate mumbled. "We can't let that happen. Please, Mr. Price," She pressed her palms together and bent over at the waist, "please help me get her back."

"Bro, we need to at least let Rich know. We can't go cowboy on this. This will have club wide repercussions."

"I'm not leaving her to die!" Garret regained his composure. "Sorry. You go get Irving and send him out here. Then tell Rich, in that order."

"What are you planning?"

"Just trust me."

"I have a bad feeling about this." Tony ran off. "You'd better be here when I get back," he cried over his shoulder. He flung the door open and disappeared inside.

Moments later Irving appeared and took off into a dead

heat toward the pair. "What's up? We just got back, and Tony said this was important."

"Shut up," Garret said. "Ann was taken, and we're getting her back."

"Taken? By ES-15?"

"Who else, jackass? Are you in or not?"

Irving looked over at Kate's quivering lips and back at Garret. "Of course I am. What do you need me to do?"

"We're going to need the other van, some guns, duct tape, a first aid kit, and a few masks. Find those, put them in the back, and meet us there asap."

"Got it." Irving ran into the nearby garage to collected the laundry list of items and transport them to the back of the white van.

"You're coming with us this time. No more sitting on the sidelines," Garret said to Kate. "Are you cool with that?"

"It had to happen eventually," Kate nodded. "Yeah, I'm back in the game."

"Good, we can use your help. You help Irving. As soon as we're ready, we're leaving."

"What about your vote?"

"Better to ask for forgiveness than ask permission. Besides, we have my vote, Skuz's, and I bet the old goat would vote yea. It'll be a fifty-fifty split."

"You hope, otherwise you'll be up shit creek. Still, thanks." She took off after Irving.

Garret approached the van and dug for the keys in the glove compartment. "What am I doing?"

The back doors fluttered open, and Irving dumped two armfuls of supplies into the back cabin. "We're nearly ready, brother. Just another round and we'll be good to go."

"I've got it." Kate threw another round of supplies into

the back and climbed up. "We're ready. We have everything. Now let's not wait for your brothers to stop us."

"Shut the door then." Garret shut the driver's side door and started the engine.

"Oh shit." Irving slammed the back door shut.

"You realize we'll probably be cut out over this," Garret said as they pulled out into traffic. "It's been a fun ride though, eh Irv?"

"Yeah, it's a real shame since I just joined though. Still, better to stand up for what we believe in than live in shame."

"Damn right."

"You two are bloody fools," Kate smiled, "the biggest fools in your club."

"You shouldn't be complaining, sweet thing." Irving said. "If we were sticklers for the rules, we wouldn't be in this life, would we?"

"Do either of you two actually have a plan?" Kate leaned forward between the two seats. "We can't just ride in there guns blazing."

"Just tell me where we're heading first. Where did they take you first?"

"Turn right here." She pointed past Irving. "Wait a second. Do you see that?" She pointed at the sidewalk at a discarded helmet. "That's the same one she was wearing before. They must have gone this way."

"She's leaving bread crumbs," Garret said. "That's a good sign that we're going the right way."

"Turn left about a mile up here when we get past the lights."

Garret pumped the brake and his fingers tapped the wheel. "We won't have a lot of time with her attitude."

"You might be surprised. She sent me to get you. She'll

probably be stalling and playing along if she has any sense," Kate said.

"So, we're winging it with the plan then? We never really fleshed that out," Irving said. "Shall I call the club and try to get backup?"

"Are you brain dead?" Garret asked. "No, idiot. All we can count on right now is the four of us. We'll have to go in quietly and do it like last time."

"You mean like with Skuz? Didn't people get shot that time?"

"They probably will this time too. They won't give her up without a fight. I hope your hand-to-hand game is up to snuff. It's probably going to get down and dirty before it's all said and done."

"Now you're speaking my language." Kate cracked her knuckles. "Just leave it to me once we get inside."

"You would be the one to know where they'd hold her," Garret said.

Irving pointed toward the back past Kate. "Grab a pistol. You might need it. Oh, and grab one for Ann too. She'll probably want one."

"I hate guns, but if I have to." Kate climbed over the seat and fell into the back. "Got one." She shoved it down the front of her pants, grabbed another and tucked it by the first. She returned to the front half of the cabin. "Let's just hope we don't need these." She snapped her fingers. "Turn left."

Garret rotated the wheel, pumped the brakes, and pointed ahead at the faint sight of a group of bikes ahead. "I think we caught up with them."

"Don't get too close. They'll kill her as soon as they're inside if they see us." Kate gripped Irving's shoulder and her nails dug into him.

Irving raised a hand and covered hers. Her grip on him weakened until her palm rested on his wiry frame.

"It looks like they're taking her back to the local underground hangout."

"You know it well?" Irving asked.

"They dragged me there every few months. It's usually a place where the patrons are well behaved due to the amount of muscle around. It hosted a few of their big-wig meetings."

"Then that's where I bet they're going to try and show off their trophy to their cartel bosses." Garret pulled over when he saw a car pull into the parking lot a half-mile ahead. "They'll try to use her as bait for us to expose ourselves and walk right into a trap."

"It doesn't look like they're set up yet." Kate squinted her eyes. "There're even a few peeling out."

"They're keeping who they think they need to keep her under lockdown." Garret ran a hand through his hair. "Now that we're here, does anyone have a plan yet? We can't sit around forever. The longer we wait, the higher the chance that their bosses show up."

"There's always a smash and grab. I know it's not ideal, but what are our options here, really?" Irving asked.

"Something that's not a suicide mission. You just focus on the materials; you suck at plans. Be quiet, and let me think." Garret bit his lip and leaned forward. "It's not connected to any building this time, so that's out. We can't count on the sewers connecting this time." He looked over to Kate. "How would you get in?"

"Me?" She sneered looking back to the building. "Just inside that door is the bar. They're going to be holding her either in the back or at the bar. I still remember the bar's phone number, so I can call and see if they've been fast at deploying her. If she's not there, I say we just ram the goddamn van in the front, throw open the doors, and let hell rain down."

"Damn," Irving said. "Or how about we just sneak in the back?"

"They keep men stationed at the back door twenty-four seven. You'll never get by them without either knocking them out or killing them. You can't go in above or below. There's only one way. Now I won't ask you two to stay, but that's how it is. I'm going either way." She pulled out a phone and dialed. After a moment she hung up. "She's not behind the bar. She's in the back."

"We didn't come all the way over here to give up now. Right, Irv?" Garret asked. "This has to be one of the dumber things I've ever agreed to. If we live through this, we'll have a hell of a story." He pulled out his .357, flicked open the chambers, and re-holstered it down his pants. "Everybody locked and loaded?"

Kate and Irving slid out the magazines and peered inside before reinserting them and pulling down their respective hammers. "Ready as I'll ever be," Irving said.

"We're good." Kate slammed the back of Garret's chair. "Go!"

"Boys and girls, buckle up." Garret reached over his shoulder, grabbed the seatbelt, and looped it over his body, connecting it at his side. "This is going to be a bumpy ride. It also wouldn't hurt to start praying. Keep your doors unlocked. We don't want to be locked in and trapped. We might have to bail and catch another ride home if this crash isn't as controlled as I'll try to make it." He reached his hand back into the back. "Get our masks out and put them on. We can't have traffic cameras catching a shot of our mugs."

Kate climbed over and tossed up two before putting on her own black ski mask.

"Add that to the list of problems I never thought I'd encounter today." Irving finished buckling himself in and putting on his mask. He looked back at Kate. "You ready?"

She clicked her restraint in. "No more stalling."

"Women today." He pulled the fabric over his face, turned the key in the ignition and looked over at Irving, "Can you believe how rude they are when they ask a favor from us gentlemen? It's unreal." He pulled into traffic.

As soon as the last car in front of him turned, they were stopped by a red light fifty feet directly in front of the compound.

"Going full speed from here will do the job, right?" Garret asked.

"Probably." Irving gripped the bottom of his chair. His fingertips dug into the nylon material.

"We won't know if we don't try."

"I think I see why you like her, new guy." The light turned green. "Let's test her theory." His foot fell onto the gas and the van sped forward. He directed the van toward the massive rectangular window. They crashed forward through the brick and glass. The forward windshield cracked in assorted places. The improvised projectile barreled ahead, knocking over tables, and chasing away the men inside. Their forward momentum stopped when the front end of their van met the bar.

"No time to rest." Garret held his ribs. He pulled out his weapon, opened the door, and immediately started firing at the men standing by the wall, stunned.

They seemed to snap out of it after the first shot, but by then one had already fallen forward clutching his stomach and the other was fumbling for his own pistol. Another round cracked off and another went down. He fell forward and collided with the floor.

Irving stumbled out of his side and held his weapon at the ready. "There's no one left."

"You're welcome." Garret pulled out a handful of bullets and flicked his wrist so his cylinder flipped out. He refilled the expended rounds. "Cover me."

Kate climbed out of Irving's side, weapon held out. "Got it." She circled around the van's front and watched the back of the room. A single hallway on the left caught her attention. "Watch the doors on the right."

"I'm on it." Irving aimed down the barrel of his pistol and inched forward, watching the two doors on the right.

"I'm good." Garret closed the cylinder and came up behind Kate. "Where would she be?"

"One of those two rooms, or in the back."

"Then maybe we're lucky. Keep watch on that hallway. Irv, watch the hole we just made while I check the rooms. Call out if you see anything. I don't want surprises." He strafed around the bar and kept his weapon pointing forward. He reached out with his left hand, grabbed the nearest door handle, and pulled. The door creaked open and he peeked inside to see a tiny supply cabinet. "One down, two to go." He sidestepped to the next one and tried his luck there. He opened the door and turned back to the group. "She's in the back."

"Of course she is. She's down the hallway through the door all the way at the end. It's where they send you if you get uppity."

"Sounds like you know from experience," Irving said.

"I don't want to talk about it." Kate inched forward, still pointing her weapon down the darkened hallway.

Garret turned the corner. "Come here, Irv. I don't want us spread too thin. We'll hurry up and be right back."

"You two be careful. I'll guard our exit."

Garret took the lead and creeped down the corridor. "There's bound to be more in here. They're probably entrenched back here. Be ready for anything."

A gunshot caused both to shake involuntarily.

"Hurry up, they're starting to get back," Irving's voice called out. "More are coming judging by that formation coming down the street."

"Fuck." Garret's stalking turned into a rushed run. "Keep up. We're out of time." He barreled ahead until they came to the door. He slid to a stop in front of the lone door at the end of the hallway. He tried the handle, only to find it wouldn't budge. "Of course, it's locked." He backed up a step and launched a kick into the frame, only for it to stand its ground.

"Let me help." Kate lined up beside Garret and timed her kick with his. The door launched open. "Oh no." Kate lowered her weapon and rushed forward to Ann who slouched in the chair in front of them. She pressed her fingers against her neck. "She's still alive. Let's get her out of here." Her hands whirred around ripping off bits of tape here and there while Garret did the same on the other side.

"I'll carry her. Just keep us covered." Garret lifted one of Ann's arms over his shoulder and lifted her unconscious body out of the seat. His right hand dug out his .357 and held it with an unsteady aim. "Now for the hard part, getting out alive." He looked down the hallway. "How's our exit looking?"

"Doubtful. They've arrived and are parked outside." A deafening crack interrupted Irving. "We're now officially pinned down out here. Tell me we have an alternative exit plan."

"There's always the side exit, but there's no telling how many are waiting for us out there," Kate said.

"We'll have to risk it. Where is it?"

"Right behind Irving. That door we walked past to get here leads outside, but it's normally guarded."

"Fantastic. That means we'll have to get creative." He cupped his hands around his mouth. "Get back behind the door frame, kid. We've got a plan."

Irving scurried across the ground and ducked behind the frame. He angled his arm around and fired off another round. "You're not getting in here without another suck hole."

"You're not getting out of this alive," another unfamiliar male voice came from inside the bar room.

Kate took the lead, stayed low to the ground, and stopped beside the door in question. She kept her weapon trained through the door Irving was peeking around until Garret stopped beside her.

"We'll secure our exit. Just keep them in that room until we do." Garret leaned against the wall facing the door and readied his weapon.

"It's not like I have much choice." Irving slid in a new magazine and cocked the hammer.

Kate sidestepped and stood up to look out the nearby window. "I've got this. Plug your ears." She pointed her weapon at the man standing outside staring at the door and squeezed the trigger. The glass splintered, cracking in front of her, as the man outside stumbled back, grasping his gut. "That's one down. Be careful of the other." She got to a knee and reached for the knob before looking at Garret.

He nodded.

She twisted the knob and threw the door open.

Garret fired two shots until a gurgling sound came from outside. "That's our cue, boys. It's time to get out of here."

He resumed carrying Ann and led the group outside, keeping his weapon at the ready in case of further surprises.

"That means you too." Kate reached forward and grabbed Irving's cuff.

"I'm right behind you." Irving fired off one last round into the spacious totaled room. He slammed the door shut once they were all outside. He kept one hand planted on her shoulder as he watched over his and kept his pistol trained on the window. She yanked him around the corner, and they ran for a few more minutes until the sound of sirens made themselves known.

"Out in just the nick of time." Garret holstered his weapon along with the other two. "Now to just get home."

"What about the van, man?" Irving asked. "Won't that be traced back to the club?"

"No, you idiot. We always replace the vin tags and license plates after every job that we use it. Lucien doesn't mess around. He always gets it done."

"I'm just saying. I'll be surprised if I don't end up behind bars for this stunt."

"At least if you do I can teach you how to survive in there." Garret started moving down the alleyway toward the bustling street. "I'll tell you one thing. I'm not looking forward to walking back to the clubhouse." He looked over his shoulder at the other two walking shoulder to shoulder. "Maybe you are though," he mumbled under his breath. He looked over at Ann's unconscious face. "Maybe it won't be so bad."

"Are you hurt?" Irving asked. "That was a rough ride."

"My shoulder's killing me, my ears are ringing, and I'm on a battle high," Kate rattled off. She looked at Ann in front. "I'm just peachy."

"It's nice to see a smile on that face again. I was beginning to miss it." Irving reached an index finger over and poked the corner of her mouth, barely masking his own smile.

"How about we focus on completing our escape before we focus on flirting? Especially since we're still in Knight's territory. We can't just walk out of here with them on high alert now. We need a car of some kind."

"A little grand theft auto in the morning?" Irving asked. "As if we hadn't done enough."

"It's either that or try to sneak back in the middle of the day with an unconscious woman while the cops are patrolling the streets. How's that going to look?"

"Just as bad as stealing a vehicle I'd think. I say we take our chances," Irving said.

Garret stopped and peeked around the brick corner. "That may just work actually." A flurry of flashing red and blue lights zoomed past. "The cops are here, which means the Knights won't be sending out search squads until they're gone. We'll be long gone by then."

"We could always call and get a ride from the other van."

"I think I'll wait on having that conversation, at least until we're on our own turf." Garret set Ann down on the ground with her back to the wall. He squatted down. He gave a light slap to her face. "Come on, wake up."

"She's out cold," Kate said. "No amount of love taps will wake her."

"You've never had my love taps then obviously." Garret continued the slaps until a low groaning escaped Ann's mouth.

"Stop it, jerk." She swatted his hand away. "Hey," she slurred, "I can move my hands again." She blinked her eyes rapidly. "I'm either dead, dreaming, or I missed something."

"I think it was that third one." Garret extended a hand

which she accepted. He pulled her up into a standing position and held her steady by holding her shoulders. "Whoa there. Take it easy, you were out cold until just a minute ago."

"How did I get out of there?" Her head rolled to the side and looked at Kate. "I assume I have you to thank for these two?"

"Don't look at me," Irving said. "The mastermind was your friend here."

"That doesn't surprise me," Ann grunted. "She never knew when to call it quits."

"If you have energy to blame, you must be fine," Garret said. "Ready for a walk back to the clubhouse?"

"You're shitting me. You didn't bring a vehicle to ride back?"

"It's indisposed after our entrance," Kate said.

"What does that mean?" Ann looked between the three but no answers came. "Whatever. Let's get going then. I don't want to stay in this grime encrusted alleyway any longer." She took a wobbly step forward and stumbled until Garret caught her.

"Careful now."

"This will never happen again once I recover."

"I'm sure." He took a step forward. "Now let's head home."

Kate and Irving trailed behind, talking the whole walk home. Irving occasionally peeked over his shoulder until Kate would poke his arm and bring his attention back. "Sorry, I just keep imagining more pissed off outlaws are behind us."

"A not entirely unfounded fear," Kate said. She took a step closer to him at her side. "I just wanted to say thank you."

"She's my friend, the same as you. I couldn't just leave her there, now could I?" Irving smiled down at her. "She might not be a part of the club, but we never leave anyone behind. That's day one stuff right there."

"It just comes naturally to you, doesn't it?" She leaned her head on his arm and entwined their arms. "You're quite the dangerous man. If you're not careful, you could turn into a lady killer."

Garret looked behind him. "At least she's in a better mood now."

Ann snuck a glance. "I don't think I've ever seen her so close to a guy before," she whispered just loud enough for Garret to hear.

"It comes with a price you know." They trudged ahead. "We weren't really authorized to come here."

"You what? You mean to tell me that you three disobeyed orders to bail me out?" She poked his Sergeant at Arms patch. "You won't be Sergeant for too much longer then. Are you okay with that?"

"That could depend on you."

"Pardon me? I'm sure not going to shit talk you after all you've done."

"You don't catch my meaning. You will later I trust."

Ann shook herself free from the man beside her. "I'm just glad to be out of that room. They dragged me back there and stood there telling me I was going to be a drink girl."

"I'm assuming you weren't enthusiastic."

"That's why they left me back there. I was supposed to yell when I was ready to listen."

"You'd have died of dehydration first, if I know you," Garret laughed. "I assume they would have killed you if you disobeyed."

"They would have after a few days," Kate interrupted

from behind them. "They give every girl a chance to play nice for a few days before they dispose of her. They have no need for untamable fillies."

"Which is why we hurried over," Irving finished.

"I was done with those chuckle heads, but now it's personal." Ann pounded a fist into her open palm. "If they think they can kidnap and hold me, they're crazy. I'm just wondering why they went after us, and not one of you."

"No offense, but apparently you two were easier targets. Where were you when they caught up with you?"

Ann looked back at Kate, then back at Garret. "That's not important right now. We were revisiting old memories is all."

"Right." He stopped by the street side and threw his arm up. "Taxi!" A yellow car stopped beside the group. "Let's give those legs a rest."

18

———

"**G**et ready for the inquisition, kid, because we're in for it." Garret reached forward, handing a wad of bills to the driver. He looked out the window at the row of men lined up outside. "Just leave the talking to me."

They got out of the vehicle and approached as a group.

"I heard you boys had yourselves a little adventure." Richard strode forward, hand on his chin. "I heard you went to one of our rival charter's bars."

"We got it done."

"I know you did. The whole damned city knows someone just crashed a van into their building and skedaddled, leaving a pile of bodies. I just put two and two together. Does your majesty intend to grace the rest of us as to why you two just went wild?"

Garret overlooked the rest of the club beside and behind Richard. "You know why already."

"You're right. Tony did say. I just wanted to hear it from you two."

"Me?" Ann asked. "What about me?"

"You were kidnapped I heard. Now I know Garret

wouldn't just disobey the club on a whim. Which then made it all clear to me." He stepped forward and paced left and right. "I still don't like it, mind you, but at least it makes sense to me now." He stopped in front of Ann. "You either have something on him or..." he looked over at Garret. "Never mind." He walked over and stopped in front of Irving. "As for you, what do you have to say for yourself?"

"This was my idea, Pres."

Richard held up a hand, stopping Garret in his tracks. "Why did you go along with this? You're not an adrenaline junkie." His eyes fell and saw where Kate was hanging onto his arm. "Of course. You two are worse than rutting rhinos." He stormed off toward the clubhouse. "Am I surrounded by sex addicts here?" He stopped by the door and pointed back. "This isn't finished." He slammed the door shut with his exit.

"I know I said to go for it, but fricking hell, boy." Lucien shook his head and wandered off into the nearby garage.

"You did all of this for her?" Skuz stepped forward and glanced over at Ann. "I'll never understand you. I hope it was worth it."

"I'm sorry, man," Tony said. "I tried to explain it to Rich, but he wasn't trying to hear any of it."

"Don't worry about it. It's my shit to deal with," Garret said. "I'll pay you back for this solid."

"I've got to get back to work. Let me know if something happens." Tony gestured to the garage.

"Was it worth it?" Skuz asked the remaining four. "You've just stirred this to the boiling point. Are you ready for that? The targets are painted on us now. You just gave Enrique the enemy to point to."

"We did what we had to. Let it go."

"Fine. Don't say I didn't try." Skuz turned his back and followed the others into the garage.

"That went better than I expected," Irving said.

"That's because the shit show hasn't even started yet. When it does, we'll be paying this back with interest. In the meantime, let's prepare for that."

"I guess that's our cue to leave then?" Ann backed up.

"If you fancy your chances against them again. Just know they will come back. I'd rather you not get caught again."

"If you keep that up, I might start thinking you care."

Garret pulled out a cigarette and lighter. After lighting up, he inhaled deeply, then released a cloud of smoke. "As far as those lowlifes are concerned, you're our old ladies. You two do realize that, right?"

"That's the reason you two haven't gotten straight up expelled?"

"A man that can't protect his woman is not a man at all. It's the code we live by. They might not like what we did, but they really don't want to call this out. They know someday they might be in the same position." Garret flicked the expended butt to the ground. "Still, we'll probably get some hellish job and a lot of flak for this."

"I guess we'll just have to make it up to you two then." Kate's honeyed voice whispered into Irving's arm.

"Nothing like an armed assault to bring people together," Garret wrapped his arm around Ann, "wouldn't you say, dear?"

"You are the only guy to ever do that for me." She clasped onto his arm. "Ah hell, why not give it a shot?"

"That's the spirit." Garret noticed Richard peeking out the curtains. "We'd better get to work before he really flips his lid, Irv."

"Now don't go getting yourself into trouble again." Irving traced down her nose and poked the end.

The two men jogged into the bustling building leaving the two women alone outside.

"Are we old ladies now? That happened fast," Anne said.

"I think I'll try a page out of your book for once," Kate said. "Being impulsive has its merits every once in a while."

"How did you even get them to do this anyway?"

"I just told them you were taken. The rest just kind of happened in a flash. He was furious when he heard. He started barking orders, we grabbed a van and some supplies, and we were off in a jiffy."

"It's nice to have backup." Ann showed a toothy grin. She leaned against the nearby building. "Sorry to have forced you to go through that."

"I owed you one. I think we're even now." Kate stared at her shoes. "Did they say anything when they took you back there?"

"Just a lot of threats and vivid descriptions of what they'd do to me later tonight. Trust me, you don't want to know. Then they left me in that room to bake in the heat. I thought I'd dehydrate, and then I heard an earth-shattering quake. I assume that was you. Whose dumbass plan was that? Irving's I bet."

"Not really."

"Jesus, seriously?"

"I was flustered. Okay?" Kate stomped her foot, and the two broke into a fit of giggles.

"So, you recommended they crash a car into a building? There wasn't a better option? At least when I rescued you, we did it on the down low."

"It wasn't' exactly an option this time. We worked with what we had."

The clubhouse door opened, and Richard appeared. "If you two are staying, get in here and make yourselves useful." He closed the door without further notice.

"I guess that's our cue to stop loitering." Kate took a few steps forward.

"A girl can't even get rest after being kidnapped around here." She followed behind Kate into the building.

"We aren't members anymore. We're just old ladies. There's a new set of rules at play here. I recommend you learn them."

Later that night...

The phone at the bar rang while a crowd of four stood around the nearby billiard's table. Kate placed the mug down and answered. "Hello?"

"Who the hell? I remember that voice. Is that you, bartender?" a deep voice asked. "You've shacked up with the Order now? Bad choice in allies, especially after today."

"Did you call for a reason, gutter breath, or did you just want to impotently rage?"

"You little harlot. Put that sniveling Richard on right now. That's an order."

"I don't take orders from you. Say please first."

"Fuck you."

"I guess you don't really need to talk to him. Have fun with your cartel bosses finding out you can't even get a phone call with the man. You're going to look like a bitch. Are they standing over your shoulder now? Hi, boys."

Enrique's voice turned sharp and dangerous. "Woman, put him on the phone, or I swear to God..."

"Gee, I would, but what with that whole kidnapping me and my friend business, I can't in all good faith accommodate you today, sir. Have a nice day." She hung up and saw the group facing her.

"Tell me that wasn't Enrique." Tony chalked the end of his cue.

"He'll call back, don't worry." As if on cue, the phone rang again. "I'll let you answer this time. I don't want to get in the way."

Tony walked over and picked up the receiver. "Yeah?"

"Get me Rich, right now."

Tony pressed the phone against his shoulder and shouted. "Rich! Phone call for you."

"Who is it?" Richard walked into the room from the meeting room.

"It's Enrique, and he sounds pissed." Tony handed off the phone and returned to the table.

"Yeah, Enrique, let me cut you off before you even start. Today wasn't sanctioned."

"You expect me to believe that bullshit? We're at war, and you tell me you didn't order my club ruined, my men killed, and my prisoner taken? You must think I'm one stupid son of a bitch."

"There's no need to state the obvious now."

"Enough of your wise ass quips. I'm calling because this has gone far enough."

"I agree. Let's end this pointless war."

"It'll end alright. Check the news after this phone call if you don't believe me. You've fucked with the wrong people this time, Rich. It's not just me you're facing now." The line clicked, leaving only a dial tone.

"What does that even mean?" Richard slammed the phone down and picked up the nearby remote control. He flipped the control on and changed it to the news. "Be quiet," he called out as he approached the corner of the room near the television.

"Excuse me, ladies and gentlemen, we have breaking news," the well-kept news anchor said. "I'm getting reports of an explosion downtown. Here's a picture now." A square appeared over his shoulder showing a massive cloud of smoke above an apartment complex. "We don't know much so far, but what we do know is that this originated in an apartment inside. There's no reports on casualties so far, but we'll keep you updated as the story progresses."

"That's my apartment." Garret's mouth hung agape. He slammed the pool cue on the ground. "Those savages went after my home?"

"That's what he meant," Richard said. "He hinted that he wasn't alone. I guess that means the cartel finally crossed the border and are operating up here."

"What's the plan?" Tony asked. "We can't just wait for the police to handle this. They're coming at us and our families. I'm not going to let them go after my sister."

"Bring her into the clubhouse. Bring a sleeping bag. She'll bitch about it, but we'll keep her safe. Take someone with you to get her. I don't want anyone riding solo for the foreseeable future."

"I'll go with you." Lucien leaned his pool stick against the wall.

"Anyone else need to go get someone? Now's the time."

"My family's out of state," Irving shrugged.

"You boys are my family," Lucien grunted. "So, no."

"Now's the time. After tonight it'll be too late. Go get them, and be careful. Take no chances. Go on the main streets, and don't duck through their turf. Stick to the basics as best you can. Tony, I know your sister lives near their turf.

236

I'd recommend going in a van. Choppers are going to draw too much attention."

"Good thinking, Pres." He tossed a set of keys up before catching them. "Unless there's anything else, we're heading out."

"Go ahead." Richard watched the two exit. "Garret, Irving, and you two," he pointed at Kate and Ann, "private meeting, right now." He went into the meeting room and sat down at the head of the table, leaving the door open.

The four followed. Garret took his seat while the two women stood. Kate closed the door behind them.

"He cited you four for this."

"I'm sure he did," Kate said. "He never did take responsibility for anything since I've known him."

"Be that as it may, it presents a certain problem for us. We're now dealing with the full might of ES-15 along with a pissed off charter. They're going after us at home now. These cartel types have no sets of rules. They'll rape your grandma and burn her in an oil drum afterward for fun."

"Is there a point to this beyond blaming us?" Ann asked. "Maybe coming up with a plan would be a better use of time?"

"Stay quiet," Richard growled. "I'm trying to think of a way out of this. I'm up to listening to your ideas if you have any, since you did cause this."

"How about we get a backer ourselves?" Garret asked.

"It's a short-term answer with long term consequences. I'm not sacrificing our sovereignty to fix this mess. Besides, no one wants to work with us. We're too hot right now."

"There's always the obvious," Ann said. "Wait until they get caught. If there's one thing these cartel types always do, it's get themselves arrested eventually."

"Usually after they've completed their mission of killing

whoever," Garret said. "The pen's like retirement for them. It's not a deterrent."

"What's left then?" Irving asked. "We can't just wait. They'll keep going after us at home, in the middle of the night. If they don't go after us, it'll be our families. They don't care how far they have to go. They'll go across the country if it means killing our loved ones."

"I'm aware of how far they're willing to go." Richard bit off a chunk of his thumb nail and spat it out on the floor.

"I'm guessing making peace wouldn't fly at this point?" Irving asked. "That'd be too easy."

"These savages don't make peace. They force it through blood." Richard tapped his foot against the tile below.

"Then how about a peace offering? Show our deference to their superior force?" Irving suggested. "Play up to their arrogance. Then when the moment is right, hit back hard."

"You're suggesting that we try and contact them, offer a gift, and then backstab an organized criminal syndicate with thousands of men across the country?" Garret looked over at Irving. "Were you dropped on your head as a child or something? They'd overrun the town with sheer numbers if we take any of them out."

"It sounds like we're fucked sideways then." Ann shifted her weight and leaned on Garret's shoulders.

"He's onto something. Force won't win us anything here. That's what they excel in." Richard said. "Subterfuge is the only hope. We just need to figure out the right play."

"The only way out of this that I see," Garret leaned forward and laid his arm on the table, "is if they don't know it was us. Who are they at war with down south?"

"A rival cartel native to Mexico City. What does that have to do with anything?"

"So, we don't hit them. They do. Frame them, and maybe

they'll think twice about bringing the war over the border if they think their rivals are up here."

"It could ignite an even bigger war if they find out we dragged them into this."

"Do you have a better idea?" Garret asked. "Because I don't, aside from offering up me or Irv as a sacrificial lamb to satiate their blood lust."

"That's not an option," Richard immediately fired back.

"Or we could just get in contact with them and ask," Irving said.

Everyone turned to look at him.

"What? They can't be that hard to find. At least that way we'd have permission, and we could possibly work together, not as allies, but as business associates."

"I've always tried to avoid the big-time organizations. Once you get in with them, it's hard to get out." Richard spun in his chair. "Still, we're no worse off if they say no. Plus, they want to hurt ES-15 so they might actually say yes. I'll just have to make it clear that we're not looking for a master. We'd be working together purely for mutual benefit."

"It sounds like something they'd go for if you ask me," Garret said.

"If you do this, I'd recommend offering an incentive." Kate spoke from behind Irving's chair. "I remember Enrique complaining about how greedy they were back when the two groups were working together. They're huge sticklers for respect being shown. It might give you the edge in the negotiations."

"I'll keep that in mind." Richard pulled out his phone. "Now you two ladies leave, and send the rest of the guys in. We need to figure this all out and vote."

The two women exited the room and left the door open.

Soon the remaining men filled the seats.

"What are we going to do, boys?" Skuz asked. "We do have a plan, right?"

"We came up with an idea." Garret looked over at Richard.

"We know ES-15 is in the middle of a war with their one-time allies in Mexico City. They're not on good terms now. I propose that we enter a temporary truce with their rivals. We offer a gift in good faith and gain a temporary ally."

"What could they do from down south? That would just drag us deeper into the shit," Lucien said.

"It'd give them pause on going wild on us," Garret said, "if they thought we were under their enemy's protection. They could attack their operations down south and inter-rupt their logistics. There's tons they could do. I'm not saying they necessarily would, but they could."

"With the price tag of being a vassal club, no doubt."

"Do you have a better plan, old man?" Garret asked. "The only other thing I can think of involves sending me or Irv over gift wrapped as an apology. That probably wouldn't satisfy them, and you'd be a man down."

"Just because I don't have a better plan doesn't make this a good one."

"Maybe not," Richard said, "but we need a plan of action now. We can't sit on our collective asses anymore and wait to see what will happen."

"Why not offer an appeasement?" Tony asked. "I know it's not usually my style, but what if we're looking at this the wrong way? We can't out-muscle those guys, so play to their egos."

"Then we'd be stuck doing so every single month. They'd come after us if we missed a payment, essentially just putting this off."

"With no guarantee they'd live up to any deal,' Garret said. "They'd be more likely to take the payment and blow us away for having caused this whole thing."

"That's not happening." Richard leaned back in his chair and pointed at Garret. "It sounds like we have a few options. We either pseudo-ally ourselves with their rivals, or two," he held up his index and middle fingers, "the option we all know of but don't want to say."

"You're not serious?" Skuz asked.

"It disgusts me too, but who's powerful enough to take them on? Think about it. An organization that has thousands in manpower, the weapons to take them on, and the means to put them away?"

"You're talking about snitching, Rich?" Garret asked with a sneer. "I don't know, man. No one would work with us, for good reason."

"It'd ruin the club's good name." Lucien shook his head. "No, that's not even on the table. All we have is our reputation around here."

"What's that going to accomplish?" Richard asked. "It's not like we're beloved by the community. Do you see people lining up outside and offering to help us fight? No. This is about survival, old man. Now I don't like it any more than you all do. Tell me what other good choices we have. I'm open to any and all."

Everyone around the table exchanged glances.

"How about if we take a little from column A, and a little from column B?" Irving asked.

"Explain yourself before I slap you." Skuz raised a hand.

"We give them an appeasement gift with an extra special surprise inside. I'm not talking a bomb or anything, but something with a gps. A burner phone or something. We make an anonymous call from a payphone across town to the FBI, or whoever, and tell them where we left it. Tell them we saw a group of guys with guns or something. It gums up their plans, keeps our name's out of it, and actually has a chance to work."

"Assuming you could set up a drop that they would go to," Tony said. "These guys are more than likely to ignore a material drop. They're too careful."

"Then say it's to make peace or some shit. They'll probably send an army of goons, and then they'll be right there wrapped in a bow for their future prison cells."

"That's god damned crazy enough to maybe work."

"It still requires them to show up."

"They'll show up," Rich chuckled. "I'll give them too good of a target to pass up. All we have to do is say we're giving them a dozen or so ounces of crystal, hand delivered by yours truly."

"Are you actually going to go?" Irving asked.

Richard nodded at Skuz who slapped Irving on the back of his head.

"No, dumbass. We'll hire that job out."

"You lost me."

"Hey, Garret, do you still know that drama guy you talked about when you first joined up?"

Garret's face lit up. "You mean Frank? The last I heard he was scraping a living doing late night infomercials. He's not usually into dangerous jobs though."

"Even if the price is right?"

"I can ask him."

"Or just don't mention the details." Lucien retrieved a hard candy from his pocket and opened it before popping it into his mouth. "He doesn't need to know. By the time he knows what's happening, the police will be rolling up."

"I thought you hated involving the police?" Irving asked.

"I hate snitching. This isn't snitching - it's framing those bastards up good and tall. I'm all for that."

"Knowing Frank, he could talk his way out even if the police were late. That dude knows some mad Spanish."

"Wouldn't we be framing him with the meth too?" Irving scratched his head.

"I realize it's hard to keep up, but I'm pretty sure we wouldn't actually be trying to send Garret's friend away for the rest of his life. We'll put the box in the back, and that's it. Just tell the guy not to touch the contents of the truck and not to say jack about the job. Call it his payment for his discretion."

"We're not monsters. We just can't be directly involved. Besides, he needs the money. The cartel may be brutes, but they're not going to kill a random guy."

"You hope," Lucien croaked.

"Let's put it up for a vote. Who thinks framing up our new local ES-15 neighbors with the help of Frank is a good idea?" Richard raised his hand.

Garret raised his and looked to his right at Skuz who had his raised.

Lucien and Tony turned their thumbs upside down.

"Irv? It's all on you. What's your vote?" Richard asked.

"What alternative do we have?" He raised his right hand.

Richard banged the gavel. "The plan passes four to two."

"Let's just hope your scapegoat doesn't get himself killed," Lucien sneered. "You're all betting with his life instead of our own."

"If he doesn't want the job, he won't take it." Garret stood up from his seat. "I'll tell you one thing though. Even if he doesn't, I guarantee there will be a line of young men who want a ten-thousand-dollar payday just to sit in a car and take a little ride in a police cruiser for a little silence."

"Especially if it gains them any favor with us," Skuz grinned. "We need to garner some extra support anyway. Our ranks are wearing a little thin."

"We'll deal with that if Frank doesn't want the job." Garret pulled out his phone. "Now should I go set this up?"

"Go for it," Richard nodded.

"Wish me luck." Garret exited the room.

"I hope you four know what you're doing," Lucien said.

"I don't feel right about this, Pres," Tony said. "It should be one of us in there. That way no innocents would be in danger."

"That's not an option, Tony. We don't sacrifice one of our own to those animals."

"Just an actor. That's okay though," Lucien tilted his head and let spittle fly from his mouth with his next words, "isn't it?"

"The matter's closed. The club has spoken. Wet your panties all you want." Richard pushed his seat back. "Desperate times call for desperate measures after all." He left, leaving only Tony and Lucien looking at each other.

"I guess we'll just have to be sure he'll be safe then." Tony stood up and brushed off his lap.

"If such a thing is even possible with those savages. You've never dealt with the hombres down south, have you?"

"I try to avoid them generally."

"A wise policy," Lucien grunted, getting out of his seat. "All they care about is money. Brotherhood, honor, and respect mean little to them. All that matters is whether you can enrich them."

"I'm sure Garret has a plan. He's known Frank forever."

"I'd hope so."

19

Garret lifted his leg over his bike and stepped off. He placed his helmet on the seat. Skuz passed by on his bike before stopping on the side of the street a few yards ahead. He readjusted his kutte.

"How exactly are you planning on selling this, brother?" Skuz dropped his helmet on his seat. "He's not going to be dumb enough to accept it if you tell him who'll be meeting him."

"Leave that to me." Garret walked past him toward a white house and a picket fence.

"He's doing well for himself. He even looks like he mows the lawn regularly."

"Only you would be amazed at such a simple thing." Garret pushed the flimsy gate open and strode forward toward the two-level building. He skipped a step and hopped up in front of the front door. He rang the doorbell and waited.

"He might not be home. It is the middle of the day," Skuz said from over his shoulder. "Most people aren't free during the day."

"I'm not giving up yet." Garret pushed past Skuz. "Let's check the backyard first before we head back."

"Why not?" Skuz followed Garret around the house. He stopped in front of a massive hedge. "Is this a privacy hedge? How old fashioned is this guy? Why does he even have this?" He looked over his shoulder. "The wooden fence has got to be ten feet tall."

"What are you, a landscaper now?" Garret turned the corner without looking back and came into a wide-open back yard. A shed was nestled in the corner next to another fence, this time chain link.

"Do you know where he works if he isn't here?"

"Either trying to find a gig or at the bookies is my guess. He used to have a little gambling problem." Garret pressed his hands to the side of his head and pressed his face forward onto the window. He went up to the back door and pounded on it. "Frank? It's me, Garret. Open up. We have a job offer for you - a lucrative one at that."

His offer was met with total silence.

Skuz tapped Garret's shoulder. "I'm pretty sure he's not home."

"Maybe you're right." He nodded toward the road. "Let's get out of here. At least we tried."

The two men began the trek back to the road when the back door opened and a loud voice stopped them in their tracks. "Did I hear something about a job?"

Garret stopped in his tracks and let a wide smile cover his face. "It took you long enough. We thought you weren't home and were about to go find another aspiring thespian."

"I was busy in the bathroom. Sorry about that." He stepped to the side and gestured inside. "Please come inside. Get out of this oppressive heat and get yourselves a drink."

"Nothing alcoholic." Garret stepped past him. "We still need to drive."

"Of course." He shut the door once both were inside. He led them toward the living room in the front of the house. "Just take a seat anywhere," he gestured toward the sofa, "and we'll get to discussing this lucrative job."

"You're not in trouble again are you, Frank?" Garret walked through the kitchen and took a seat on one of the two sofas facing each other in the living room. He sat on one end while Skuz took a seat on the other. "You still like betting on the dogs, right? How are they treating you?"

"You know how it is." Frank placed cups of water in front of both men and took a seat on the opposite couch. "It has its ups and downs."

"How about the job search?" Skuz asked, grabbing the cup of water and taking a swig. "I've seen you on a few commercials from time to time."

"I'm making it work. Enough about me. What about this job?"

"It's not your typical job." Garret leaned forward and rested his elbows on his knees. "It pays well though."

"You've got me interested now. Go on."

"Do you still know Spanish worth a damn?"

"Si, habla Ingles y Espanol."

"Good. All we want you to do is go wait at a certain place in a van."

"And?"

Garret leaned back. "That's it. Eventually some folks will show up and the police will follow. You'll stay deadly silent. You'll take a little ride and get out the same day ten thousand richer."

"The fucking police are going to show up? I can't get involved with that. I have a public image to maintain.

Besides, it sounds dangerous. Who the hell's showing up anyway?"

"You wouldn't be paid to ask questions, merely to sit in the van and wait. You're seriously turning this opportunity down? If you do this for us, we'd have even better paying jobs next time."

"All it takes is some courage." Skuz reached a finger into his ear and flicked the gunk off. "I would think someone in acting would have plenty of that. After all, what's the success rate in that industry? Something in the single digits the last I heard. This is your big chance. Your foot in the door, if you will. If you help us with this, we won't forget it."

Frank looked away and tapped his chin with his index finger. "Twenty thousand and it's a deal."

"You must have picked a few losers lately," Garret grinned. He glanced over at Skuz. "What do you think? Should we pay for his expertise and discretion or offer it to the next young talent?"

"So long as he doesn't ask too many questions, I don't see why not. He is a professional after all."

"It's settled then." Garret clapped. "Congratulations, Frank, you've got the job." He dug into his pocket and retrieved a crumpled piece of paper, throwing it on the table between them. "I'll call you with the location. Make sure you pick up the phone, so get up bright and early. Be ready for work, and don't tell anybody else anything. If you do, the contract's void, and you'll have pissed us off."

"I know how it goes," Frank said.

"Do you?" Skuz asked. "If you do tell anyone, we'll have to tie up that loose end. We don't want that."

"Jesus."

"Easy, buddy." Garret waved Skuz off. "Just remember this

is on the down low, and we'll have no problems. That means no bragging to the bookie, your girl, or your parents about your big new payday. We're business associates, nothing more. Think of it like a casting call. You don't tell the world what goes on in there, even though we know what happens."

"Good point. At least this pays more than peanuts for the work done."

"Smart man." Garret straightened up. "Then that brings us to the end of this conversation. You'd best brush up on your Spanish and start planning out where you'll spend your pay then." He stood up and straightened out his black vest. "We'll take our leave now. Make sure to get some rest tonight. You've got a full day tomorrow."

Skuz followed suit. "I don't think I have to say this, but I will for safety's sake. Don't bring anything that will catch a charge tomorrow. You understand?"

"I get it."

"Good." Garret reached out a hand across the table.

Frank stood up, reached over, and grasped it. "It's settled."

"Then we'll get out of your hair," Garret said. He and Skuz walked around the couch and stopped at the front door. "See you tomorrow bright and early." They closed the door behind them.

"I hope we're doing the right thing," Skuz said. He jumped down the two steps onto the grass below. "All we need to do is time this right."

"It won't be our fault if something does happen. He accepted a dubious, under the table job. He knows the risks."

"That's cold, man." Skuz threw the helmet on and secured it. "You're not wrong, but damn."

"We do what we have to," Garret sat on his bike, "no more and no less." He started the engine.

Back at the Clubhouse...

Garret pushed the door open. "He said he'd do it."

"Was that before or after you threatened him?" Lucien jabbed the pool cue into the floor, the corners of his mouth descending. "Does he even know the shit he just jumped into?"

"It's not his business to know ours." Garret walked past the billiards table and took a seat at the bar beside Richard. "What's important is that we just need to set the rest of it up."

"That's where I come in." Richard pulled out his phone and dialed.

An unfamiliar, unmistakably Hispanic voice answered. "What the hell do you want?"

"Who is this?"

"Your worst nightmare. You'd best get talking, gringo. My patience is running out."

"There's no need for hostility here. This is a call to make peace."

"It's too late for peace after the shit you've pulled."

Richard's eye twitched. "Not even if I bring a big gift with me to prove our intentions?"

"I'll tell you what," the voice started. "You deliver it personally, and we'll see. How's that for a deal?"

"Deal. Meet us at -"

"Easy there. We'll set the location. I'll call you tonight and set the place and time, or there's no deal."

"We can work with that. Just let us know."

The line went dead without further words.

"How did it go?" Garret asked.

"He wants to set the time and place. We may need to reschedule with Frank."

"I doubt he'll mind. Just let me know when so I can let him know."

"So he can be ready for the slaughter they're bringing?" Lucien asked.

"Enough already." Richard's voice turned to steel. "We voted. This is what we're doing. You'd best get with the program, old man."

"This won't end well." Lucien hung up his pool cue and barged his way past Tony. "Mark my words." He pushed the door open and headed outside.

"Ignoring him, is everything else set up?"

"As soon as we have the time of the meet we can deliver the tip to the pigs, and everything will be done," Irving said from behind the bar. "All we'll have to do then is watch the proceedings."

"Not that I'm complaining," Richard started, "but where are the girls?"

"They're in the back rooms somewhere. I think they were tidying up last I saw."

"Right. They're probably wondering where they'll stay tonight since Garret's apartment went up in flames."

"Who knows what women talk about?" Garret asked. "It's best not to even guess. We'll just end up wrong anyway."

"That's true." Richard turned around on the stool, leaned his elbows back on the bar, and sighed. "Tomorrow's going to be a hell of a day."

"We always get out of it somehow. This time will be no different I bet," Garret said.

The door opened again, and this time Skuz entered. "Hopefully we won't have to stay here after tonight. I miss my own bed."

"My back agrees with you." Richard arched his back with a groan of pain. "Still, it's better to be safe than wake up to a Sicario over your bed in the middle of the night."

"That's why you keep a pistol under your pillow," Skuz laughed.

"It'd be a little too late at that point, moron." Garret tossed an ice cube at Skuz. "He'd blast you before you could move two inches."

Skuz patted down his shirt when a buzzing sound interrupted him. He pulled out his phone. "Again?"

"Who is it?" Garret walked over and peered over his shoulder. "Sweet Mary. She sent you thirty messages over the course of the last hour? Bro, that's some dangerous territory you're treading in."

"She's just worried I bet."

"Just make sure you keep her on the leash and not the other way around," Richard said. "We don't need any more surprises around here."

"I'll take care of her. Don't worry." Skuz's thumb flew across the screen.

"While you do that, I'll take first shift tonight." Richard pushed himself off the bar. "I can't take that being woke up business. Who's after me tonight?"

"I've got it," Irving said. "I've got to get out from behind this thing." He banged on the bar with his fist.

"Fair enough." Richard went over to the door and grabbed his coat from the nearby rack, slipping it on over his shoulders. "Get plenty of rest tonight, gentlemen." He zipped up the apparel and disappeared outside.

"Maybe tonight you can actually make some progress." Garret grabbed a nearby bottle. "I heard you got cock blocked last time."

"Something like that," Irving said.

"Look, you want my advice?" He untwisted the cap and poured the bottle into a nearby mug. "Just say what you mean. If you do that, everything will work out."

"Thanks, man." He pointed down the hallway. "Ann said she wanted to talk to you earlier. She said it was no big rush, so just whenever you get time."

"Now let's see if my own advice will help me." He brought the mug up, gulped down the contents, stood up, and moved toward the hallway. "Wish me luck."

"Anybody home?" Garret knocked on the wooden door. He opened the door and poked his head inside. "You wanted to see me?"

Ann sat on the lone bed. She laid back on the mattress. Beads of sweat peppered her bright red face. "I just got done cleaning this disaster zone. Do none of you guys know how to tidy up?"

"It's not usually the most pressing issue, considering it's supposed to be a temporary lodgings kind of thing." He took a seat beside her laying form.

"What are you planning on doing after this - buy a house this time or rent another apartment?"

"I hadn't really thought that far ahead." Garret took off his vest, draped it over the bed post, and fell back. "What about you?"

"I'm still figuring that out. I've got options. It really depends on how this all plays out."

"You mean if we all get out of this alive?"

"It's hard to make plans when everything's up in the air. I'll probably lay low and let it all settle down before I make my next move."

Garret rolled to face her. "You mean to stay around here?"

"Maybe." Ann looked up at the ceiling. "Who knows?"

His index finger traced her jaw and tilted her head to face him. "We could give things a shot and see where this goes."

"That is an option." She stared at his bare chest. "Things certainly would never be boring."

"You'd never want for companionship," he moved his head to her ear and whispered, "or safety with me at your side."

"I believe that after that stunt you pulled earlier." She reached up with a hand and covered his ear. She crawled on top of him. "I'd have to make sure you didn't get yourself killed if this happened. You know I'm not going to be a regular old lady?"

"Far be it from me to imagine you being normal at anything." His face rose up, his lips hovering mere millimeters under hers. "That's what drove me toward you in the first place."

She placed a palm on his chest and pushed him back down to the mattress. "Then let me show you a reason to stay then."

———

Late that night...

Irving shut the last cabinet. "That's about everything. It's time to head outside." He walked over to the door and picked up his coat.

"Are you heading outside?" Kate stepped out into the dimly lit hallway and rushed toward him. "It's awfully cold outside."

"It's my turn to stand watch next. I should go relieve him as soon as possible, or I'll get an ear full."

"Let me accompany you this time."

"You don't have to -"

"I want to."

"Alright then." Irving tossed Kate her jacket. "Make sure to bundle up. We don't want you catching a cold."

"Thanks." She wrapped it around herself and pushed the door open. She stepped outside and held it open.

"It's just over here." He pointed near the entrance to the lot toward the closed chain link fence. A large tower stood over top with two chairs nestled up top where Richard was sitting. He looked back when the door closed and climbed down. "It's about time. At least you two can keep each other warm. If anything happens, come get me up." He brushed past the pair and continued inside.

"Ladies first." Irving nodded toward the ladder.

"How chivalrous." She lifted a leg onto the rung and climbed up. She reached the top and sat on the chair to the right. "Come on up. The view's great."

"It's about as good as you get around here." He grunted in exertion as he climbed up. "Just be glad it's not raining tonight." He pulled himself up and took the seat beside her.

"What do we do now? I've never been on watch duty before. We never had need of it. Then again, we didn't piss off huge criminal syndicates either. We were a bit more delicate."

Irving laughed and rubbed his shoulders. "I can't say you're wrong."

"Can I ask you a personal question?" Kate asked.

"You can ask me anything you want." He peered through the binoculars hanging from his neck down at the darkened cityscape.

"You seem like a resourceful guy. What made you join this filthy lifestyle? Was it quick cash?"

"You really want to know?" He asked. "You're going to be disappointed."

"Now I'm even more interested."

"Would you believe me if I said initially I was drawn in because of my love of motorcycles? Not the guys riding down the street in their colors and their chins angled up. I knew they were trouble right from the start."

"Yet here you are."

"That's right. You want to know what changed my mind? It was a combination of a few things. You were partially right. It was quick cash. See, I was raised by my grandma. By the time I was eighteen, she was already in the later stages of breast cancer."

"Didn't you just get patched in recently?"

"You're putting things together I see. You're right. I wasn't getting paid for the jobs they were pulling off while I was prospecting."

Kate reached over and gave a light push to Irving's arm. "Then where did you get the money?"

"That goes back a bit further. My late grandpa knew Lucien."

"You mean...?"

"Yeah, he was a member too. Lucien helped us pay the bills and gave me a sympathetic ear when I needed it most while he was in the hospital. He'd come over almost every day and just talk to both me and grandma. Ever since, I'd wanted to join the club. It sounds like childish naivete' now that I say it out loud, but I wanted to do the same for somebody one day."

"You're right," she said. "It does." She scooted her chair over and leaned against his side. "That doesn't make it bad."

"Yeah. I remember he used to come over every Sunday for dinner and the table just lit up. It was like night and day when he and Lucien started talking. They wouldn't ever talk club business, but that didn't stop me from asking and getting shot down in no uncertain terms."

"Your granddad didn't want you joining I assume?" She asked into his arm.

"That's an understatement. He wanted me to go to college and work in an office somewhere. He used to say, "Irv, you're a smart young man. Don't follow in my footsteps. Make something respectable of yourself." I thought I understood what he meant at the time, but fast forward to now and I wonder what he'd say."

"You want the truth or a comforting lie?"

"You don't hold back, do you?"

She wrapped her arm around his and nuzzled into his side. "He'd be proud of the man you've become, but probably disappointed in your life choices."

"That's fair." A razor thin smile appeared on his face. He kept his eyes on the dark landscape ahead while his left hand snaked around and brushed a lock a hair out of her eyes. "What about you? Fair's fair."

"I guess you deserve to know." Her voice went flat. "You'll probably think differently of me though."

"That boat already sailed when you insisted we ram a car through a building, so go for it."

"It wasn't anything as good natured as you. You've probably guessed by now that I wasn't always so even tempered."

"You got into a lot of trouble growing up, did you?"

"I was always fighting in school. Most girls learn the secret art of talking behind each other's back, but I didn't. I always opted for direct confrontation. This led to me being ostracized by most of my peers."

"That usually doesn't end up going anywhere good."

Kate's hand gave a slap to his arm. "It's not polite to interrupt a lady when she's spilling her soul."

"Sorry about that."

"Anyway," she sniffed, "that continued throughout high school until one fateful day when I got expelled for forgetting to remove one thing from my back pack. Care to take a guess what it was?"

"Let's see," Irving held up a finger for each thing he listed off, "a teenager constantly fighting, a social outcast, and she gets expelled. I'm going to guess you forgot to remove a razor or something?"

"You're closer than I thought. It was a swiss army knife."

"They thought you were going to stab someone?"

"Apparently. I was in a huge argument with the prom queen. She probably squealed. The next day they checked my person, and there it fell onto the ground."

"Damn."

"Yeah. So after I got expelled I was kicked out of my home by my parents as soon as I hit eighteen. I needed to make ends meet, so I wandered all over town looking for odd jobs. That's when I found Ann. She offered me a simple job that ended up taking over my life. You know the rest of the story."

"Then I suppose you were wrong?"

"Excuse me?" She tilted her face up to look at him.

"I don't think worse of you."

"You really are an idiot."

"With that kind of attitude, no wonder you got into fights all the time." He smiled. His eyes widened and he brought the binoculars up again.

"What is it? See something?"

He pointed to the left of the gate. "I see a van about a block up that stopped. It could be nothing, but I don't like it. Nobody ever parks there at night."

"Where?" She picked her head off his shoulder and peeked around him. "Are you sure that's not someone coming home from work late?"

"They didn't park there last night, not to mention this isn't a residential district. There're no houses on this block. Something doesn't smell right."

"I think you're over thinking it. I'm not seeing a group of hitmen file out. It's probably just someone who is sleep deprived, so they pulled over and fell asleep in the back."

"That is one possibility. The other is the cartel has eyes on us right now. Wait a minute." He looked through the lenses again. "Someone got out and went across the street. They're carrying a briefcase? What the hell? No one's open this late."

"We should get down from here." She got up and tugged on his arm.

"Yeah okay." He lowered the spying tool. "You go first. I'll be right behind you."

She lowered herself onto the ladder and scurried down as fast as she could. "Your turn. Hurry up."

He took a step onto the steel and jumped down once he'd descended a few rungs. "You think that was a sniper or something?"

"It fits the profile. They see the gate closed with fences

259

all around and a guard tower. They'd want to send a message that nowhere is safe. A sniper is perfect for such a job. That briefcase wasn't small and could fit a disassembled rifle in there. It's the middle of the night. A single gunshot wouldn't wake people up; and even if it did, they'd mistake it as a backfire and not get out of bed, much less call the police."

"I see you've thought this through." He grabbed her hand and dragged her toward the clubhouse. "We need to report this. We'll catch shit for waking them up, but they need to know."

He burst into the building. "We've got company outside."

"Be quiet." Richard rolled over in his sleeping bag.

"I'm serious. I think ES-15 is outside."

Richard sat up immediately and climbed out of his cocoon. "I swear, if you're making this up you're on toilet clean-up duty for a week." He brushed his hair with his bare hands and threw on his coat. "Now what did you see?"

"A guy with a large briefcase exiting a suspicious van a block up, carrying it into the building across the street. We thought it could be a sniper or assassin. I didn't really want to sit up there and find out."

"It's certainly in their MO." Richard clicked his tongue. "You're talking about the three story office building?"

"Yeah."

"That means if we go outside, and we're not near the barrier, we'll be in a shooting gallery - if you're right."

"That's assuming they're not sending a group besides him to climb over." Kate poked her head around Irving. "I would. It'd flush the targets out into the open."

"Or the two of you are paranoid. That's always a possibility. I can't ask you to go back up there, but we need to confirm it before we mobilize. We need our rest for tomorrow. We can't pull an all-nighter if this is just a false alarm."

"What do you want us to do?"

"We can't just sit in here all night. We're sitting ducks. We need the sight lines outside. The longer we're cooped up in here, the longer this possible sniper has to get setup. He's probably in his perch now, just waiting for us to go outside. There's only one option. We go out the back and circle around from behind."

"If they are cartel? We do what? Blow them away on the street and wake everyone up? We know they won't go away if we just ask."

"What do you suggest? We give up sovereignty in our own clubhouse?"

"You don't need to at all." Kate giggled. "I have a great plan, but it might result in someone getting a disturbing the peace charge. They're not going to stick around if we cause a ruckus, right? How many illegal weapons do you have in storage here?"

"None here," Richard said. "They're all in separate storage locations. All we have here are legal firearms."

"Perfect. Get someone who doesn't have a record to duck out the back and start firing repeatedly at anything, preferably not the air. That could result in an involuntary manslaughter charge."

"That would attract cops eventually. It'd also chase away the would-be assassins."

"Does that mean I should head out the back then?" Irving asked. "I don't have anything on my record yet."

"Do it. Head through the back across that street and fire into a dumpster in an alley. We can't have it being on the premises with tomorrow happening, but it should still be close enough to chase away any sicarios."

"You got it. I'll just go grab some ammunition." He ran off down the hallway and ducked into the storage closet.

Kate watched Irving until he disappeared and glanced at Richard. "I'm going with him, and don't even try and stop me."

"There's safety in numbers," Richard shrugged. "Besides, I don't mess with my member's old ladies no matter how I dislike them, unless they're a direct danger to the club. You keep him safe, and I have no problem with you."

"Fair enough." She jogged off and waited near the back door. She kept her hand on the knob and tapped her foot until the storage closet opened. Irving walked toward her and shoved a few magazines down into his pants pocket. "I'm ready. You're not going surely?"

"Just try and stop me. Someone's got to watch your back."

"I've learned enough at this point to not try and change your mind. Just try to stay behind me if something happens."

"It's nice to see chivalry isn't dead yet, but sorry. I aim best when not obstructed by misguided macho men."

"You can be quite vicious when you try." Irving patted her on the head. "I like that."

"Don't pet me," she pushed open the door, "at least not right now."

"I heard that." Irving went outside first into the alley. "Now follow me."

She closed the door and stayed close behind. She back-stepped, keeping her head low and her weapon ready, until she bumped into Irving behind her. "Why'd you stop?"

"I need to move this if we want to get out from this side. Just cover me. I can handle this." He moved to one side of the brown dumpster and pushed it to the side, revealing a hole in the chain link fence. "You're sure I can't talk you out of this?"

She responded only with a kick to his rear, causing him to stumble through the newfound opening. "You only get to give me orders if we get married, so get used to it. Now stay quiet." She ducked down and passed through onto the open street beside Irving. She pointed across the street. "Those dumpsters between the buildings would work." She checked both sides and dragged Irving behind her.

"Keep watch here. I'll be right back." He pulled out his pistol and ventured into the dark space. He stopped a few yards in front of the metal waste bins. He stepped past the corner and raised his weapon.

His finger hovered over the trigger until a Spanish accented voice stopped him. "Put it down, or I paint this alley gray."

He felt cold steel pressing against his left temple. "Alright, guys. You win." He dropped the weapon by his feet. He turned to face his aggressor and saw a group of three obviously armed men covered in tribal tattoos, numbers, and tear drops. He took a step back.

"You almost had us." The young man stepped forward, reestablishing contact between the barrel of his automatic pistol and Irving's head. "You're just too loud. You two go find her. I'll take care of him."

The two men behind him turned the corner. They stayed back-to-back as they sidestepped onto the main street. The taller one spoke up. "I don't see anybody here."

"Then split up and check each side then," the leader said.

Irving looked over his shoulder and down to the ground. He kicked the firearm behind the man while they were talking.

He turned back to Irving. "Now where do you want it? Head?" He pressed Irving's head back against the cold brick then traced the gun from his neck down to his chest. "Or would you rather have an open casket?"

"I could ask you the same question," Kate said. "If you move a muscle, I end you. Do not test me. I am tired of your entire god-damn syndicate."

"Who the fuck do you think you ar-" He whirled around in the blink of an eye, only for a flash to illuminate his front. He stumbled beside Irving and dropped his weapon.

Irving dropped down and grabbed the weapon, pointing it behind Kate. "Watch the entrance. They have us surrounded."

"I said not to move." She raised her aim and unloaded another shot between his eyes. She took cover behind the corner with Irving at her side. "Sorry I made a mess."

"Better him than me." He fired down the narrow space. "Get down." He used his free hand to press her head down.

Shots ricocheted off the nearby wall accompanied by a spark. A hiss escaped Irving's lips as he tumbled to the ground. A speck of blood appeared in his jeans. "Shit." He kept his aim poised down the narrow alleyway. He saw a silhouette and fired, causing it to stumble to the ground. He squeezed off another two rounds. "He's down."

Kate ducked back behind cover. "I'm out."

Irving handed her his weapon and all his spare magazines. "Take them. I need to get ahead of this." He slid down the wall, took off his shirt, and wrapped it around the wound on his upper thigh.

The spent magazine tumbled near his boot and another shuffled into place. Kate waited until the latest volley of bullets ended and a click rang out. She rotated around the corner and didn't hesitate.

"Fuck this!" the last one yelled. Rapid footsteps could be heard fading into the distance.

"I think he ran. I'll go check the other side." She squatted down and laid a hand on his shoulder. "Can you stand?"

"I guess we'll see." He reached up and pressed a palm on her shoulder to steady himself, then pushed himself up. He grit his teeth and placed a majority of his weight on her shoulder. "If you're good with this, yeah. I think I can manage."

The pair hobbled around the building, only to hear a pair of familiar voices nearby.

"Kate?" Ann asked. "You'd better answer me."

"Irv? You're not dead are you? You'd better not be dead."

"I'm going to guess the guy's not still there," Kate said with a dry tone.

They turned the corner to be rushed by Garret and Ann.

"We heard the shots and got here as soon as we could." Garret looked down. "You got winged?" He got to one knee. "That needs looked at. Here." He looped Irving's other hand over his shoulder. "I've got him."

"No, you clean up the mess in the alley before the authorities get here. You're probably going to need your van. I can carry him." Kate nodded back to the opening between the buildings behind them. "Who's your medical guy?"

"Wake Lucien up. He can get him a makeshift patch job. As for the mess, I'll do what I can." He ran to the entrance between the buildings. "Damn. Kate, go melt those weapons after you finish moving him. I'll pick up these casings. We need to stay clear. At least he's not bleeding down his pants leg yet. Get him moving before he does. We can't have his DNA here."

"On my way." Kate and Irving stumbled back into the opening.

"What about these guys?" Ann asked.

"So long as we get rid of any evidence we were here, they might suspect us but will have nothing. We'll deal with that when the time comes. Now come help me before the cops get here." He dashed down the passageway, picked up the bullet casings, and stuffed them into his pockets.

"Got them over here. Let's get out of here." Ann trotted to the secret opening. "We might even have time to dump the bodies. It doesn't sound like any cops are coming yet."

"One thing at a time. We're not taking risks tonight."

A piercing siren met their ears.

"Cancel that," Garret said. "We'll have to deal with that fallout if it happens. We can't have them catch us tampering with the crime scene."

"I don't think a self-defense charge is your guy's worst problem right now."

"Exactly."

20

"Hold still, boy," Lucien said. "I've almost got the last fragment out." He yanked the tweezers free of the wound. "Stop bitching. It wasn't even a full bullet." He dumped it in the nearby alcohol. "It must have been a ricochet. You don't see those too often. You're lucky this is all you got if you were between buildings. You two were in a major kill zone."

Irving took a swig from a brown bottle on the table. "I think the only thing that saved us was that it was dark in there. Not many rooms had their lights on."

"Whatever the case, you're out of commission for a few weeks. This isn't some flesh wound. You're going to be limping around for a while." He dug out the last fragment and plopped it in the liquid beside him on the table. "Now to patch you up. I wish I had some antibiotics to give you. If this gets infected, it'll be trouble."

"There's always the black market. You mean to tell me you never stocked up?" Irving asked.

"I'm not a doctor. I don't make a living treating wounds. Why would I?"

"Jesus, what happened out there?" Richard came out of the double doors and pulled up a seat across the table. "Are you good?"

"He will be." Lucien splashed more anti-bacterial liquid onto the open wound. "We just need to stitch his leg up and hope he doesn't get infected."

"It was a feint," Irving said. "I think they knew we were watching the front. They caught us in the alley and opened up on us."

"They gave us a show and went around the back. I should have seen it coming." Richard kicked the table causing Irving's leg to wobble.

"They sound as devious as you." Lucien gave a wry chuckle. He stood up and pinned Irving's leg to the table. "Not to mention the meet tomorrow is as good as canceled."

"You let me worry about that." Richard looked back to Irving. "How many of them were there?"

"We managed to put down two when they started firing, but the last one ran away, probably to report back to the bosses."

"He's as good as dead," Lucien grunted. "They don't take cowardice lightly."

"With the cops a few blocks away, they won't be back tonight." Richard wiped away a bead of sweat from his forehead. "That's another thing we'll have to deal with tomorrow morning - cops poking their noses around here. Just what we need."

"My bad, Pres."

"It's not your fault. We're just glad you're relatively in one piece. You just focus on resting until you're back up and at them. We'll focus on the savages that did this."

"We're going to war with the cartel now?" Lucien asked. "Does it ever end?"

"We have to answer back; otherwise, he's just the beginning - and we both know it, old man."

"If we answer back, they'll send thousands over the border to crush us. They have their names to defend as much as we do. Don't get hot-headed now."

Richard bit his lips and glared at Lucien. "I hate it when you're right."

"I usually am." Lucien pulled the needle through the flesh and tied off the end. "There we go." He slapped Irving's leg. "All stitched up. Don't move around too much, or I'll have to redo it. You don't want that."

"I got it. Have either of you two seen Kate?"

"Worried about her?" Lucien smiled. "The last I saw her she was in the garage using the torch. Try and keep the weight off your leg if you decide to head out there."

"I have to make sure she's alright." Irving hopped out of his seat and over to the door on one leg.

"The boy's not the brightest," Richard said loud enough for only Lucien to hear, "but I wouldn't trade him for anyone."

"Yeah. He's got a good heart." Lucien watched Irving struggle to open the door before bashing it open with his shoulder. "He also knows when to take my advice."

"Don't start again, old man. I hear your pleas." He whipped out his phone and looked at the old man across from him packing up his medical supplies. "What would you say to them if you were in my position?"

"It might be too late for that. We've spilled their blood."

"Let's assume it's not too late."

"Then I would try and ascertain whether tomorrow is still on. They'll probably take you for a blooming moron. Just act like you're sure this was someone else nearby. That will make them overconfident, and they might underestimate you. In war it's not about who's more powerful, but who can outwit their opponent. That's assuming they're not as cunning, which they probably are."

"You're a barrel of laughs." Richard stood up and walked to the window overlooking the parking lot. He saw Irving halfway across the lot hopping toward the garage. He brought the phone up and hit numbers when a gunshot broke his concentration. He saw Irving fall forwards onto the pavement. "Sniper!" He ducked below the window. "The fucker stayed with the police near?"

Lucien threw himself under the table. "They don't care about getting caught. This was a message."

"God damnit." He looked down at his phone as the sirens blared to life and rotated around the building. "He needs an ambulance."

"If they see those gunshot wounds that's going to open a can of worms that we won't be able to close," Lucien said.

"I'm not leaving him to die out there without a fight." He raised the phone up to his ear.

"This night's gone to shit."

Outside...

"You can't go out there." Garret held Kate back using his arm.

"Get off of me." She clawed at his arm. "We can't just sit here."

"He wouldn't want you to get your head shot off either. Think about it. Listen. The cops are circling around."

A loudspeaker interrupted them. "We have you

surrounded. Put down the weapon and come outside with your hands above your head."

"Help me with something, and we can get him out of the line of fire." Garret ran over to a nearby shelf. "Are you familiar with smoke bombs?"

"No."

"Then go get me some sugar and baking soda."

"What?"

"Do it." Garret stomped his foot. "I have the saltpeter here. Just hurry up. There should be some in the office. It's like a mini-kitchen in there with all those cabinets." He grabbed the nearby torch, a small strand of string, and a metal bucket.

Kate yanked open the cabinets inside the small windowed room and threw assorted things over her shoulder until she found the necessary objects. She rushed back. She dumped them on the nearby work bench. "What now?"

"Now I work my magic before he bleeds out, which probably won't be all that long considering he lost a lot of blood with Lucien digging out the fragments."

"Hurry up then."

"I'm trying. Hand me that paper towel roll and remove the paper towels."

She removed the white paper and handed him the brown tube. "What's this for?"

"I need something to put this in when I'm done." He poured the salt peter, along with a larger amount of sugar, into the bucket and stirred with a nearby crowbar. One hand held the torch to the side of the bucket, while the other stirred. "Once this is done, I'm putting it in there. We'll light it, and it'll produce huge clouds of smoke." He stirred the browning caramel-like substance and immediately turned off the flame. He poured in a healthy dose of baking soda and siphoned it into the brown cylinder. He placed a string into the sticky substance and brought the torch up. "Light me."

She twisted the cylinder and the flame sprung anew, lighting the fuse.

He tossed the makeshift bomb about fifteen feet away from Irving and huge rolling clouds of smoke emanated from it.

"Now we can go." Garret turned off the flames and followed Kate over. He got to his knees and pressed down on the river of blood escaping his chest. "No, don't you do this to me."

"His pulse is fading." Kate removed her fingers from his neck.

"Help me get him inside. Keep your hands here." He dragged her hands over and pressed them down. "I'll drag him inside, just keep up and keep the pressure on."

"Got it." She got down on all fours and kept her hands on his chest as they moved forward.

Garret kicked the door once he'd bumped into it and dragged him inside. "Lucien, get your ass over here."

"Jesus Christ." He kneeled. "He needs blood badly."

"Hey open your eyes." Garret slapped Irving's face. "No sleeping on the job."

Irving's glazed eyes opened and fell on Kate in front of him. "I knew angels were real," he gurgled out. "I see one now." He reached a hand out to Kate."

She clasped his hand. "Just be quiet and stay awake."

"You listen to her." Lucien's hands flew across the wounds. "All I can do is close these. He needs a surgeon. Those bullets need to come out."

"The ambulance is on its way." Richard folded up his phone. "How can I help?"

"I'll go open the gate then." Garret stood up. "The smoke's still up. I'll be fine. I'll wave them right in as soon as they get here."

"Stay behind the gate until they arrive."

"I know." Garret exited the room and dashed to the gate. He undid the lock and used his shoulder to push the massive sliding gate open. A new siren intermingled with the police's. A white vehicle with red stripes pulled up on the street. He cupped his hands around his mouth. "Over here. Someone's shot. Hurry up!"

A team of three men jumped out of the back and wheeled a gurney over.

"Follow me." Garret showed them inside.

"This is bad," one said, squatting down. "Get him on the stretcher, and let's get him out of here. Get a bag of O-negative ready," the leader said. "Now, everyone stand back." The remaining two moved Irving's unmoving body onto the gurney and wheeled him back to the ambulance. It peeled out almost immediately with its sirens blaring all the while.

"We're not going to get any sleep tonight," Richard broke the silence. "Get ready for tons of questions once that sicario gets sick of the limelight across the street."

"He'll probably kill himself, if he hasn't already," Lucien said. "Assassins rarely give in peacefully."

"As long as he dies, I'm happy," Garret snarled.

"I hear that." Richard sat down on a nearby seat and hung his head. "Tomorrow is going to be something."

"They'll be watching us like hawks," Lucien said.

"They who?" Garret asked.

"The cops, the cartel - hell pretty much everyone now."

"Then it's a good thing that we won't be anywhere near

it," Richard said. "I'll call and see where we're at tomorrow. I need some rest before the inevitable interrogation."

"I'm going to find Ann." Kate trudged away toward the hallway leading to the back.

"Poor thing." Lucien shook his head. "She doesn't deserve this."

"Neither did Irv." Garret watched her disappear through the door heading toward the alley. "Yet here we are."

21

The gang watched the caravan of police cruisers pull out onto the road. Richard stepped forward. "I thought they were never going to leave." He brought his wrist up and checked his watch. "We still have two hours before your friend shows up at his new job."

"You're still sending him in?" Lucien asked. "You don't seriously think they're going to show up?"

"Why wouldn't they?" Richard asked. "When I call to confirm the meet, I'll tell them we know it was a local psychopath who had his sights set on us for a deal gone wrong. They'll come and make a show of a peace truce. Then they'll get a nice ride to jail."

"It's the best shot we've got." Garret flicked the end of the cigarette in his hands. "We can't take them head on anymore. It brings down too much heat."

"Which is precisely why I'm confirming now." He brought the phone to his ear. "Good morning."

"Is it?" the voice asked. "I heard you boys had a rough night."

"You heard about that? Yeah. We had a crazy customer try and get even with us last night, but we took care of it."

"You're sure on your intel?"

"We got our information from a reliable source. Are we still on for today?"

"We're on alright. I'll text you the location. Can't wait to see you." The line went dead with a click.

"That was short." He hung up and held the phone out. "We're on." His phone lit up with a chirp. "Text this to Frank. Make sure he's not late." He handed his phone to Garret. "Are there any volunteers on observers?"

"I'll see how everything goes down." Garret raised his hand. He held up the binoculars hung around his neck. "I'll go bird watching near the meet. Just let me go look up the most populous birds in case anybody actually asks."

"That's why I pay for internet in this place, for instances like this." Richard gave a mirthful chuckle. "We'll be nearby a few miles away in case anything happens."

"Sounds good." Garret took a seat in the corner of the room and turned on the computer.

A door slammed from down the hall. Ann took one look at the group and then toward Garret in the corner. She came up behind him and placed her hands on his shoulders, leaning forward. "Birds? What the hell?"

"It's my cover." One hand held up the binoculars.

"At least you get points for thinking ahead a little. It's amazing what you plan ahead for. But then you forget the actually important stuff."

"You mean like my life outside the club? I've always been that way. You give me a job, and I'll stay up all night prepping. My personal life, however, is a different story."

"We'll have to fix that." She lowered her cheek next to

his and looked at the screen. "That's my favorite one. The gila woodpecker is adorable."

"Interesting take. I prefer the great blue heron."

"What is it with men and their obsession with size?"

"I just like being able to tell what something is at a glance. What were you imagining? If anyone asks, I'm trying to trail the elusive hybrid hummingbird." He exited the browser and got out of the chair. "Let me guess what you're here for."

"I'm trying to find Kate."

"Oh, the last we saw her she said she was heading out for a little while. It was right after last night's events. We gave her the keys for the training bike. She should be back any time now."

"She couldn't have gotten out from the front."

"That's a good point." Garret made for the door. "Let's see where she went then." The pair exited the clubhouse and found that the bike normally in the corner of the lot was indeed missing. "If she didn't go out the front," he looked behind the building, "she must have rolled it under here." He got to a knee and looked through the large hole. "She could have maybe fit it through here."

"Check it out. Here's a note." She pulled a note taped to the nearby wall.

"I went to check on Irving at the hospital. I won't be coming back. Thank you for everything. I'll post mark some cash for the bike once I get a job. Take care of Ann. I cannot be a part of this anymore. Best regards, Kate."

"Is she the joking type?"

"Not really. She's serious." She crumpled up the piece of paper and spiked it into the ground. "Why wouldn't she tell me before she took off?"

"I can't presume to tell you her reasons, but she must

have had good ones. I'll stop by the hospital after this and see if I can catch her."

"Can you drop me off on the way?"

"It's on the opposite side of town. You can ride along, but I don't have any more bikes to lend. You can ask one of the other guys to loan you one, but I doubt they'll oblige."

"She'd better be there."

"I'm more worried about Irv," Garret said. "He's sitting in a bed somewhere with no protection other than rent-a-cops."

"The sooner we get going, the sooner we can go check. Right?" She clenched onto his arm and dragged him back out front. "Let's stop wasting time."

"Easy." Garret disentangled himself and brushed off his sleeves. "We'll make sure Frank doesn't get himself into too much shit, and then do the same for Irving and Kate. Deal?"

"I'm holding you to that."

A mile away from the meeting spot...

"You're in place?" Garret asked into the phone.

"We're three minutes away, hiding in plain sight. Let us know if you need us," Richard's voice said.

"I'll send a text if anything goes down. Once we do, we should all head over to the hospital and visit Irv."

"That's a great idea." Richard's voice became muffled. "How do you all feel about visiting old Irv after this?" A raucous round of affirmatives flooded his ear. "We're in."

"Can't wait. I'll text you when to call in the cavalry. Later." He hung up and looked over at Ann. "What's up?"

"I see someone." She stuck close to the nearby tree. "Looks like they're pulling off the main road."

Garret came over and held out his hand. "Let me see."

She handed him the binoculars.

"Yeah, that's his car alright." He followed the road to the abandoned clearing nearby. "He's right on time." He lowered the binoculars and typed on his phone. "They should be here in a few minutes, so it's time to call in backup."

"This is definitely one of the more ambitious plans I've ever seen implemented. I'll be impressed if this works," Ann said at his side.

"There's no reason it shouldn't. They'll show up to rob us and find a nice surprise."

"That's the best case. I don't see that happening. I imagine they'll show up and immediately turn poor Frank inside out when they find out he's not Richard."

"That is a possibility."

"What are you going to do if he does get in trouble?"

"What can I do?" Garret asked. "Go charging over there and take on trucks full of pissed off gangbangers? I don't think so. I'll have to sit and watch."

"There's nothing worse than that."

"You're telling me." Garret scanned the roads. He reached over and nudged her shoulder. "Check it out." He pointed toward the road and handed her the binoculars. "I think they're here."

She saw three vans pull off the road and approach Frank's position. "They're here alright. You'd best get to praying, because I don't see the boys in blue anywhere. I sincerely hope he's good at talking his way out of things."

"He's an actor and a smooth talker. If anyone can, it's him."

The caravan came to a stop across the clearing. A group of visibly armed men filed out.

"Oh shit," Ann muttered under her breath. "You'd better hope they get here inside of a minute."

Garret snatched the tool and looked through. "Don't get out of the car, Frank."

Frank exited the car and stood with the door between him and the new guests. Garret could see his mouth moving. "You moron, let them speak first. You don't even know who they are."

"I told you to stay in the car and stay quiet. Stop improvising. This isn't some local play."

One of the armed men made his way across the divide and came face to face with Frank.

"This isn't right." Garret continued staring through the binoculars.

The man's hand shot forward toward Frank who stumbled back. Garret saw an object gleaming in the afternoon sun. "Son of a bitch." The rest of the group dashed over and formed a circle around the now hunched over Frank leaning against his car. Their arms pivoted back and forth. "They're turning him into a shiv cushion."

The distant sound of sirens met their ears.

"Of course you fucking come now."

The men opened Frank's trunk, took the large cardboard box inside, and loaded it into their front van before filing in and trying to pull out, only to be blocked by a blockade of police cruisers.

"I'd say that plan worked about halfway," Ann said. "Maybe they can save him if they get an ambulance here fast enough."

"Not with that many stabbings. He'll be lucky if he's still

breathing." Garret lowered his hands and turned away. "It's my fault this happened."

"Yeah. What do you want me to say? You knew this was a possibility. Take responsibility."

"I know. All that matters is the good of the club. It still doesn't mean I have to like it." He dragged his feet all the way back to his ride. He put on his helmet, sat on the seat, and pulled out his phone. "I've got good news and bad news."

"Good news first."

"The plan worked. I'm watching them get down on the ground right now."

"The bad news?" Richard asked.

"Right after they arrived, they filled Frank with their favorite knives."

"God damn," Richard said.

"Yeah."

"We'll figure it out tonight. For now, get over to the hospital. We need to let Irv know what's happened."

"I'm not sure he'll be thrilled, but yeah. You got it." He hung up.

"We're heading over to the hospital now, right?" Ann asked. "There's not much left to do here."

"Sure." He tossed her the helmet.

"Take it as a lesson." She hopped onto the back of the bike and wrapped her arms around his waist. "As sergeant, you're going to be making life and death decisions every day. Never underestimate your opponent, and shit like this won't happen."

"I'll take it under advisement." He started the engine and pulled out onto the dirt path leading back to town. They passed a familiar white van that pulled out behind them.

Half an hour later...

The group marched up the stairs. "At least one good thing happened today." Richard led them through the door at the top. "There he is." He pointed ahead through a glass door. They could see Irving splayed out on a hospital bed connected to all manner of electronics. "They really did a number on him." Richard stood in front of the glass. "Hey, what's that?" He pointed inside the room toward a lone note sitting on the table beside the bed. A lipstick smeared kiss could be seen on the outside.

"That's Kate's alright," Ann said. "She must be long gone. She must have come here earlier and left already."

"If it's any consolation, it was probably in the wee hours of the morning while we were being interrogated," Garret said.

"He's still breathing though." Skuz placed a palm on the glass when his phone vibrated in his pocket. "Seriously?"

"What is it now?" Garret peered over his shoulder. "You're kidding."

"What?"

"Tell me she's joking," Garret said. "She wouldn't actually snitch on her brother, right?"

Richard ripped the phone from Skuz's grasp and glared at the screen. "You'd better go straighten this out right now." He gripped Skuz's collar. "I don't normally tell people what to do in their personal life, but it's now officially affecting the club. Get some distance between her and us."

"I'm on top of it." Skuz pulled away from Richard. "I'll make sure nothing's connecting us."

"You'd better," Richard said. "We can't afford to give the cops any more ammunition for their investigation. If they connect Jerry to us, we're finished. We'll have homeland security up our ass for years, if we don't end up in irons first."

"This is why you don't stick your dick in crazy." Lucien shoved Skuz toward the exit. "You should have listened to me."

"I'll go with him and make sure it gets done." Garret backed away from the window. "Let Irv know I send my best."

"Guess I'll stick around too, since you're my ride." Ann said. "You don't mind do you, Lucien?"

"I'll drop you off tonight, sure."

Garret and Skuz left the group and disappeared into the stairwell.

Lucien stopped a nearby nurse. "Excuse me, dear. Is that young man allowed visitation?"

"Only family." She shifted the linens in her arms.

"He doesn't have family." Lucien looked down. "I'm the closest thing he has."

The nurse looked back at the nursing station then back at Lucien. "I shouldn't, but go ahead. Don't tell anyone I let you."

"I can keep a secret. Thank you, sweetie." He slid the door open and went to the foot of the bed. He took the chart and brought it close to his eyes. His face contorted into a grimace. He slid it back into place and headed back outside. "It doesn't look good. I'll tell you what, I'll stay here with the kid."

"Good call," Richard said. "Tony, I guess that means we're holding down the clubhouse until everyone gets back."

Tony took one last longing stare at the beeping form of Irving. "Yeah, I guess so."

Lucien headed back inside. The numerous machines littering his bedside beeped. He squeezed past them and sat in the lone seat. He grabbed the letter on the nearby stand and opened it. "Kid, your girlfriend left you a letter. I don't know if you can hear me, but in case something happens, you deserve to know what she wrote. Sorry about opening this without your permission." He ripped open the letter and cleared his throat.

"You probably won't be in shape to read this for a while. I need to tell you a few things. First, do not attempt to contact me or find me. This incident is just the last of many. I pray with all my heart you will recover and be made whole once again. I just can't stand to stay in this chaos. I've had my fill. I'll take your secrets to my grave, so rest easy. If we had met in a different life, things would have been different. Maybe we'd have dated, married, had grandchildren and grown old together. I just don't see that being a likely option in the lifestyle you've chosen. If you patch out, look me up - but not before. I wish you the best of luck in your future, Kate."

"There's a kiss mark here in lipstick too." Lucien held the card above Irving's face. "I guess you'll see it later. You need your rest." He placed the letter on the nearby table, grabbed the remote, and turned on the television.

22

"You think you can handle the little woman?" Garret asked. "We wouldn't want a repeat of last time."

"Like your love life holds a candle to mine."

"At least mine doesn't need a scented one to be in the same room with."

"Be quiet," Skuz said. "I've got this." He reached up and pressed the doorbell. He leaned back and looked down the street. "They're always here."

The door unlocked with a quiet click. "Come in," Jerry's voice said.

Skuz pulled open the door and the pair walked in. "Just here to see Mitzi."

"Don't let me keep you. She's been going nuts wanting to see you lately. It's a good thing you're here."

"Has she now?" Garret asked. He started walking down the nearby hallway of the single floor home. "That doesn't sound good."

"Just stay out here. I don't want you to scare her." Skuz threw open the door and saw Mitzi standing in the middle of her cluttered room with her back facing him. "I got the

285

impression you wanted to talk earlier, so here I am." Skuz walked in and plopped down on the bed. "What was the hurry?"

"I'm tired of this." Her voice was sullen. Her arms fell to her sides, red dripping down from her fingertips. She turned to face him and revealed bloodstained arms across both wrists.

"Whoa." Skuz stood up on the bed and backed into the wall. "We need to call somebody. That looks kind of bad."

"This is only skin deep. This is nothing." She took a wobbling step toward him and crawled onto the bed. She clawed a blood soaked path up his clothes until she pinned him against the wall and stood nose to nose.

Garret banged on the wall. "Bro, we have to get out of here. I think we were followed." He busted the door open with his shoulder. "Oh fuck. What did you do?"

"I didn't do anything."

"Exactly," Mitzi said. "You never did anything or followed through with anything." She brought her head to his shoulder."

The front door slammed open. Frantic commands began. "Get down. Get on the ground now."

Garret got onto his knees. "Best do as he says."

"I would if I could."

Mitzi banged her head into the wall. "Why?"

The leading officer yanked Garret's arms behind him and cuffed him. "Stay there."

The second older officer turned the corner into the room. "Great spitting yaks! What in the world? Get away from her, slime ball."

"Officer, please," Mitzi's shaky voice called out. A thump was heard. "He slammed my head into the wall."

"Here we go." Garret rolled his eyes.

"Get an ambulance now," the first officer called out. He pulled Garret up. "Now let's all take a trip down to the precinct and figure out what's happened, huh?"

"Am I under arrest, officer?"

"You care to explain this?" He nodded toward the room.

"I would like to confer with my attorney."

"We can make that happen." He yanked Garret up by his arms. "You and your buddy are going to have a little time out." He pushed Garret toward the front door and guided him into the back of the already open police car. "Scoot over."

Skuz got pushed in beside him and they slammed the door shut. "This is bad."

"You were saying something about my love life being terrible?"

"I don't want to hear it."

"Which is what got us into this mess, as I remember it. What was it the old man said?"

"That doesn't help us right now." Skuz kicked the seat in front. "I didn't even touch her. The bitch slit her wrists. We'll be out inside of a week."

"If common sense prevails, which in the US courts it rarely does in my experience."

Garret watched a van parked on the other side of the street. "Wait a second. Who are they?"

"Who?" Skuz leaned forward and tried to peer past Garret's honey blonde hair. "I can't see."

"Oh my God." Garret looked away from the window and dove into the floor space. "Get down," he shouted.

A hail of bullets and a deafening chorus assaulted all the senses along with shattered glass raining down. Indistinguishable voices could be heard but not made out.

Screeching tires and car alarms were all that was left in the aftermath.

Garret craned his neck up. "Are you dead?"

"Not yet," Skuz said. "He did wing me though."

"What?" Garret sat up. He leaned back and kicked the door. "Get in here."

"He only got me in the shoulder before I was all the way down. I'm not bleeding that bad," Skuz said. "They're probably still shitting their pants outside. We'll be lucky if they check on us before more cops show up."

"Not if I can help it." Garret continued stomping on the door. "Hey, come on. We need medical attention in here. This is a human rights violation. We are in your custody, and this is your responsibility in here."

The door flung open and the first officer's angry voice came. "What is -" he paused. "Oh shit. I'll call in another ambulance." He closed the door and pulled out his radio directly outside the window.

"Maybe next time you'll listen, and we won't have to go through this shit."

"Okay, so I might have been wrong about a few things."

"You don't say."

Meanwhile at the Clubhouse...

Tony pushed the gate open, and Richard pulled inside. Tony drove his bike in and parked bedside him. They shut off their engines and got off. "It's been a hell of a day."

"You said it, and it doesn't look like it's over yet." He pointed ahead toward the open road. A police car pulled into the lot.

"Let's go see what this is about then." The duo approached the car when the front door opened and an officer stepped out. "Afternoon, officer. How can we help you this fine day?"

"I'm here to ask a few questions, given recent events around here."

"I'm not too good with trivia, you see," Richard said. "Maybe Tony here can help you out. He knows every musical since the nineteen-sixties."

"Cut out the shit," the officer said. "Why were my officers shot at during a simple arrest?"

"It's an occupational hazard I guess." Tony shrugged. "It really seems like that should have been a given."

"They specifically went after two of your men, almost like they weren't coming after us. I believe you know them as Garret and Skuz? You know who their attackers are I'm betting. I'm here to find out who."

"I'd love to help you, but my lawyer always said not to talk to strangers with badges. You understand."

"How about you?" The officer looked at Tony. "Are you willing to answer anything?"

"We've said all we're going to say," Richard said. "Now let me ask you something. Are they okay?"

"The stupid haired one caught one in the shoulder, but he'll be fine. You're not going to talk further?"

"We can talk about the weather if you like. I heard it's going to rain later. I hope you brought your umbrella."

"This is useless. Have fun in the pig pen with your new pals." He flopped into the driver's seat and rolled down the window. "You'd better hope no innocents get in the middle of your little beef."

"We would never." Richard took a half step back and

raised a hand to his chest. "I'm offended you'd even suggest such a thing."

"Sure. Try the pearl clutching act with someone else. I'm not buying it."

"I'm hurt." Richard burst into laughter. "Have a nice day now, officer. Be careful out there."

The officer glared at the pair before backing up and leaving the lot.

"Let me figure out what the fuck happened over there. Hopefully they have a bail. We can't afford to lose those two right now," he whipped out his phone, "especially not if they're sending more men after us. Close the shop and the gates. We don't need any more surprises while we're putting out these fires."

"Got it." Tony ran over to the outside of the gate, flipped the sign, and closed it from the inside.

Richard's phone rang as Tony was ready to begin dialing. "That was fast." He answered, "Yes?"

"So this wasn't our fault," Garret said. "I think they might have caught a glance of me leaving the meet this morning and followed us here."

"What the hell would that have accomplished?"

"Events happened here that made it look worse than it really is. The girl slit her wrists and rubbed herself all over Skuz."

"Did the magistrate give you bail?"

"We both got bail. I got twenty-five hundred. Skuz got twenty-five thousand. They're claiming sexual battery, which is bullshit. Forensics will prove it."

"God damn! You two sit tight. We'll get you out."

"The guard says that's all my time anyway. I'll see you later." The line went dead.

"Bad news?" Tony asked.

Richard reached into his vest's pockets and unfolded a pair of sunglasses. "Just the crazy woman living up to her name. She framed Skuz, and Garret got caught in the whirlwind. She slit her wrists."

Tony whistled. "What about bail?"

"Twenty-seven thousand, five hundred combined. Twenty-five of which is for Skuz alone."

"I take it we're going out and collecting for it?"

"Get the van's keys and get changed. I'll grab us a cooler and get the van ready."

"At least they'll be back soon." Tony walked toward the garage.

"Assuming we get that money." Richard went inside the clubhouse and filled the cooler under the bar with ice from the nearby freezer. He stuffed a dozen bottles of water into the freezing receptacle and hefted it up on top of the bar. "I haven't went collecting in a while. I hope I've still got it." He lifted the box off the counter and kicked the door open, bumping it closed behind him. He hauled it to the back of the open van and dumped it. "There."

"We ready?" Tony poked his head out the driver's window.

"Just one last thing." Richard took off his kutte and ran inside the garage. He draped it over the office chair and hurried back outside. "Now we're ready." He shut the back doors and climbed into the front passenger's seat. "Now, who owes us?"

23

"Don't make me ask again." Tony delivered a punch to the man's stomach. "Where's our money?"

"None of us want this." Richard paced back and forth staring out the front door of the store. He opened the door and flipped the sign to closed and closed the blinds. He walked behind the counter and removed the tape from the surveillance apparatus. He walked in front of the pair and waved the vhs in front of the man. "This would be a lot easier if you just paid your debts."

"I need that money for my daughters -" He was interrupted by another haymaker from Tony. He lost his balance and drooped against the wall.

"We're not asking for a story. We're asking for the cash you owe us. Don't forget who fronted you the money to buy this lovely store front. Just give us the three thousand you owe, and we'll keep making sure nothing happens here."

His head hung down. "Check the safe in the back. It's in the wall. The combo is nine, fourteen, five, and seven. Start going to the right first."

"Was that so hard?" Richard walked forward and gave a

light tap to the man's cheek. "We all could have been spared this ugliness if you'd just said so in the first place. He circled around the glass counter and entered the back room. He saw the black safe in the wall and set to work spinning the dial. A click indicated he'd entered the combination correctly. He twisted the handle and pulled to see a small pile of wrapped cash. "There we go." He snatched the green bills and stuffed them in his pockets. He closed the safe and came back into the front room. "We're done here. I even left the remainder. What a nice guy I am."

"You did?"

"Of course we did." Tony pulled him up and got him to his feet. "We're not animals. We're businessmen. We'd appreciate being treated like one. Just don't forget to pay, and we don't have a problem."

"He's right." Richard sauntered past Tony toward the door. "Let's take our leave so our friend can continue his workday in peace." He opened the blinds and gripped the handle of the door. "Just remember we value our privacy, and don't go getting talkative or we'll have to pay another visit."

"I got it." The man rubbed his stomach.

"I bet you do." Richard pushed the door open and flipped the outside sign back to open. "That's it. We're finally done." Richard yawned. "We got the full twenty-eight thousand."

"I thought it was twenty-seven and a half," Tony said.

"He only had stacks of a thousand. I couldn't bear to undo his craftsmanship. It was a thing of beauty."

"It'd have been a real shame. We're going to the bail office next, right?" He climbed into the driver's side door.

"That's the plan." Richard pulled himself into the

remaining front seat. He reached forward and twisted on the radio.

"Police report that they have finally apprehended two suspects in a local drive by chase. The alleged event took place earlier today in our very own town. Suspects then tried to evade police but ultimately failed."

"Sounds like Garret and Skuz's friends are finished. I wonder how many more goons they sent up north. Their ranks have got to be depleted by now, wouldn't you think?"

"Depends how many they sent up. I doubt they sent up an army for only Enrique's crew."

"That's what I'm saying. Still, we shouldn't get complacent." Richard's head rolled to the right and his eyes focused on the mirror.

"They should get the message already," Tony said, stepping on the brakes. "Stay down south and things are a lot simpler. They own the law down there, so I don't even know why they bother coming up here."

"Bigger market share. Mexico is a developed nation and all, but they don't have near the buying power the good old US does. It's always about the money."

"I guess you're right. It just seems like more of a hassle than it's worth."

"That's for them to decide." Richard's brows furrowed. "I think we're being followed."

"What makes you say that?"

"Call it a hunch. It doesn't look like many people though. I only see one truck following us about three cars back. I only see two inside, but they're tailing us alright. Take us somewhere isolated, and when we get there stay behind cover in case this goes to shit. We can't afford them following us to the station and taking out all four of us in one fell swoop. We'll nip this in the bud right now."

"I guess we can take a little detour out into the country. I love a good walk." Tony turned the wheel and pulled off onto the exit.

"They're following. Let's see how far they're willing to chase." Richard slid down in his seat, his eyes glued to the mirror to his right. "Why aren't there more of them?"

"Maybe it's all they have left after today."

"Until they send more grunts up north."

"I have a feeling their little war is going to be keeping them busy after this news hits Mexico City. They just got busted and had a loss of manpower. Why wouldn't their competition take advantage?"

"You're quite the optimist," Richard said. He reached into his jacket and readied his 9mm. He pulled down the hammer and rested the weapon in his lap. "I guess we should pull over and see what they want then. As soon as we pull to a stop, get out and get to cover."

"They could be friendly." He turned onto a dirt path that twisted around some trees and led to a meadow. "Just throwing that out there."

"We'll find out." Richard threw open the door and bolted toward the nearby tree line.

Tony went across the way and took cover behind a fallen trunk.

The truck came into view and stopped once they were halfway down the path. Three men filed out and took cover behind the pickup. "It all ends today." Enrique's baritone voice echoed in the meadow.

"You under some pressure from your jefe?" Richard asked. "Let me guess. He said if you massacre us you're cool?"

"This isn't business anymore."

"Personal huh?" Richard knocked his head back against

the bark. "You always were too serious for your own good." He flinched when he heard a shot fire behind him.

"There is one good thing about having a rich benefactor. Here, check it out."

Richard peaked around the ficus tree and saw Enrique at the corner of the vehicle fiddling with something in his hands. "They didn't give him..." He reared his hands up and Richard caught a glint of green. "They did." He took off in a dead sprint and ended up behind a huge tree a dozen yards away from a monstrous explosion. Dirt, leaves, wood, and even a few body parts from the local wild life fell around him. "Jesus Christ in heaven."

"Don't tell me you're dead already? Hey, we might at least not have to do anything with the body. The animals will eat the remains." A snarky laugh rang out.

"Yeah," Richard muttered. "Keep laughing, jackass."

"Go see if he's dead, and be careful. He might have one more with him, so keep your head on a swivel. It's our asses if not."

Richard leaned against the tree and raised his arm out, taking aim toward the recent blast zone.

Another gunshot ended in a scream. "That wasn't me."

"Then get your head down," Enrique said. "No doubt he has backup. You, come with me. We're checking this side.

Richard lowered himself and braced his aim. "Guess I've got the lone man." He lined up his shot. Once the man stopped and scanned the nearby area, he squeezed the trigger. His legs crumpled under him, and he fell straight down. Bits of skull fell beside his feet along with brain matter. The remainder of the back of his head banged against the earth.

"Your boy's dead," Richard said. "Your turn's next."

"Don't get cocky just because you nailed one guy." Another shot cracked off in the wooded area. "You, take the one over there. I've got the old man." Richard saw Enrique duck behind a tree on his side of the clearing.

"You want a one-on-one?" Richard asked. "I always was the better shot."

"Age beats aim in a duel, Grandpa. You can't hit someone as fast as me." He dashed from tree to tree with Richard firing and missing.

"All it takes is one. You're playing a dangerous game."

"I think it's exciting." Enrique poked his weapon's muzzle around the tree and squeezed a round off in Richard's direction. "Who's going to find their target first? Will my man kill yours first and flank you, or vice versa? Doesn't it just get your blood pumping?"

A shot rang out in the distance. "I think your man's dead." Richard ejected the magazine and injected a new one. He pulled the hammer down.

"I sincerely doubt that. That wasn't just any rank-and-file grunt I brought along with me. It was the cartel's greatest hit man. He never misses."

"Well, ain't that grand?" Richard hissed. He took off in a dead heat toward where he last saw Tony, ducking into cover at every opportunity. He waited until the shots ended before taking off toward the next one.

"Where you going, old man?" Enrique's voice haunted him from behind between every volley of lead. "You worried your man's not up to the task suddenly? You should worry about yourself more." He trailed behind Richard, staying behind cover every time Richard took some himself. "You're not going to be able to outrun me. I've already gained. Keep it up and exhaust yourself. It'd just make my job easier."

"Be smart about this." Richard shook his head. "He's younger than you, more fit, and cocky. I have to use that," he whispered.

"What are you muttering to yourself about? I can hear you over there," Enrique grunted, and a click met Richard's ear.

Without bothering to look at his adversary, Richard bolted toward a nearby huge boulder and dove behind it.

The tree he was behind exploded, resulting in a shower of lumber.

"How many did those lunatics equip you with?"

"More than enough to take care of you. I'm just getting started. You'd best keep moving if you don't want to find out."

"I can't do this all day." Richard was breathing hard as he got to his feet behind the giant rock.

"But I can. If you can't move, I've got just the thing for you. Here, catch."

Richard popped up from behind his cover, already taking aim toward Enrique's exposed body out of cover. He shot without pause.

Enrique pulled the pin in his hands. His legs fell out from under him. His arm whirled to the side, tossing the explosive as far away as he could.

Another earth rumbling explosion and another shower of debris littered the once pristine wilderness.

Richard ducked behind his cover. "The first tip in a duel is not to telegraph your moves, you fucking moron. You're lucky that grenade didn't catch you in it."

More gunshots echoed in the distance.

"This doesn't matter."

"I disagree entirely. Once you can't move, you're easy pickings out here."

"Then do it, old man. I dare you."

"With you doing nothing but aiming at my cover? You must think I'm as stupid as you are."

"Then I guess you must be fine with your man going alone against the terror of the south," Enrique said. "He must be a real sharpshooter for you to have that much faith in him."

"You piece of shit." Richard got to a knee and picked up a large twig. He poked it out of cover to his right only for the tip to get shot off and fly out of his hand.

"Why not try that again? I'm just warming up. If you'd shot me in the arms this wouldn't be a problem, but you chose my mobility instead."

"You can't aim in two places at once." He picked up the remaining stick and repeated the action, but as soon as the sound met his ears he took off low to the ground out the other side of his cover. He heard multiple gunshots behind him and managed to crash into another tree to take as cover.

"Nice moves, but you're running out of tricks here. How long can you keep this up?"

"More than your bleeding carcass can. You'll bleed out before long."

"We'll see about that," Enrique roared and stumbled to his feet. He leaned against the nearby trunk. "This much is nothing."

"Keep bluffing. You're just causing more damage the harder you act."

"Shut up!" Splinters shot out beside Richard's head as he flinched away instinctively.

"I'm tired of this." He ejected his magazine and peered into the bottom. "Two left," he said under his breath. "I wasn't expecting a war out here. This has to end now." He banged on the lumber. "Enough play time. Let's end this once and for all."

"I couldn't agree more." More shots whizzed by Richard's ear with a whistle.

Richard pressed his belly against the soil beneath, extended both of his arms in front of him, and called out. "One last volley and let's finish this. I'm getting too old for this shit."

"Sure, whatever you say," Enrique said with a dark laugh.

"It's now or never. I can't stay here all day," he whispered to himself. He rolled out of cover and kept rolling as more shots narrowly missed his lowered profile. He eventually heard a click and stopped on his stomach. He leveled his muzzle at Enrique's center mass and squeezed off a lone round.

Enrique fell onto his back and let loose a loud groan. "Nice try."

Richard got to his feet and zig zagged toward Enrique's downed form. He ducked behind trees as he got closer until he came within striking distance. He delivered a football kick to his right hand and knocked the pistol away. He looked down at Enrique and nudged his chest. "Bulletproof vest huh? I should have figured." He raised his sights to his forehead. "Let's see how it works now."

"Wait a minute, man."

He squeezed the trigger, and Enrique went quiet. His head slumped back against the earth and went still.

Richard got to one knee, his face red with exertion. "Let me take that off your hands." He grabbed the weapon and frisked his belt line. "Hello there. What have we here?" He found two more grenades waiting to be used. "This will be useful. There's no extra ammo though. He must have been running low too. I'll have to make sure these count."

More gunfire broke his concentration. "No time for dawdling." He jogged off in the direction of the noise. He heard Tony's voice off in the distance ahead of him.

"I hope you know how to camp pendejo because we're going to be out here all night."

Richard didn't hear any reply. He simply continued bobbing and weaving between cover toward the direction where he'd heard his voice.

He leaned out of cover and saw a man holding a large rifle in his hands marching through the environment. "That's him. We damn sure don't have that kind of firepower on us."

This time a hail of bullets broke the silence instead of a single shot. The man took off into a sprint sideways as he ejected the magazine and inserted a new one.

"That's some firepower there. Is that all just for me? You must not believe in your aiming."

"Keep talking, we'll see what happens."

When the assassin peeked around the corner, Richard took the opportunity to inch ever closer while staying behind the natural foliage. Once within a stone's throw he hunkered down in some nearby bushes. "As good a place as any." He took out one of the grenades he'd looted from Enrique. He poked his head up to confirm his target's location, pulled the pin, and chucked it in his direction without any verbal call out.

"Motherfucker!" his voice rang out. He moved but he was only a few yards away when it went off. His body went flying and crashed against a nearby tree.

"Jesus," Tony said. "You have a misfire over there or something?"

"Or something," Richard said loud enough for Tony to hear. "Hold your fire and stay there for now."

"Got it."

Richard approached the tree from behind, stalking as he went. He pressed his ear to the tree and listened. He backed away from the tree and readied Enrique's loaded weapon. He circled around the tree and stepped on the rifle, sliding it behind him.

Hateful eyes glared daggers up at him. Gurgling breaths escaped his lips. "This ain't over. More will come up here eventually. You know that."

"We'll burn that bridge when we come to it." His eyes trailed down the man's body to his missing leg. "Is that bone?" Richard's foot kicked the exposed wound. "That's nasty. That's why you don't play around with explosives. Didn't your mother teach you anything? Anything could happen." He jammed the pistol into the numerous fragment wounds peppering his entire body.

"Just finish me already. I'm tired of this shit."

"Hey Tony, you can come over here already."

Tony appeared from behind a large tree some distance away and jogged over. "Holy hell. Is that his leg over there? What happened over here? I heard an explosion."

"You can thank Enrique for that." Richard removed the gun and stood up. He brought a hand up to his ear. "He nearly deafened me with his little toys earlier. Since he was coming after you, I figured you should get the honor."

"With pleasure." Tony raised his weapon and fired, ending the assassin's life.

"It looks like we've got a lot to clean up today before we head home." Richard walked away from the body, back to their van. "We can use the cooler as a digging implement."

"Graves with a cooler and it's lid? Seriously?"

"Don't bitch. We're lucky to be alive."

"That's true. I call the lid."

"Any reason?"

"It's lighter than using the rest as a digging implement."

"I knew we should have brought the shovels today."

Richard pulled open the large double doors at the back of the van and climbed inside. He dragged the cooler over and ripped it open. He tossed a bottle of water over to Tony and took one himself. They both opened theirs and took a big swig. "Enjoy it, cause those were the last." He knocked the container to its side and ripped the lid off its hinges. He tossed the now disconnected lid over to Tony. "Here you go. I'll make due with this. We'll just dig one grave. There's no time for two since we must dispose of their truck as well. We'll just burn that for good measure afterward."

"We don't have anything to burn it with though."

"It has gas and our van has matches. I'm sure I can figure something out."

"We should gather them first and then start digging. I'll start while you go gather Enrique's remains."

"Sounds like a plan." Richard hopped out of the van and made his way back to Enrique's body. "What a pain in the ass you are, even in death." He grabbed him by his shoes and dragged him while looking over his shoulder. "You're heavier than you look." He heard the shuffling of earth behind him. "How's it going so far?"

"I think I'd rather have literally any other tool for digging."

"We make due with what we have." Richard dropped Enrique's limp leg over top of the other bodies leg. "Let me go get mine and I'll join you." He hurried back, grabbed the main body of the cooler, and ran back. "My back's not looking forward to this."

Later that night...

"I'll be glad to never see another cooler lid for the rest of my life." Tony tossed the white implement to the side and wiped his forehead.

Richard dumped the last load of dirt onto the grave and discarded it. "Now for the easy part, taking care of the truck."

"We can't burn it here, we'll have to move it."

"Why?"

"Because, Pres, I don't know if you noticed, but we're surrounded by foliage. We'd be lucky if we didn't start a brush fire. That'd attract the authorities really quick."

"Good point. What do you propose?"

"Take it to the usual spot."

"I'll drive the van, and you take the truck. I'll follow you. We'll torch it and then finally be done with the night."

"It's not that far away, so yeah that would work. Let's get this done with already." He led the way to the vehicles. He climbed into the van's driver's seat, hovered his foot over the brake, and twisted the key already in the ignition. He looked up and saw Tony doing the same across the meadow. He leaned to his left out the window and gave a thumbs up after switching his lights on.

Tony turned around and led the two out onto the road. Richard kept his eyes on the road ahead but retrieved his phone with his other hand. He diverted his attention just long enough to dial. "Are you back in the club yet?"

"We just made it back," Lucien's gruff voice answered. "Where in the world are you?"

"We ran into some problems with Enrique earlier, but we took care of it. We're cleaning it up right now and will be heading back soon. How's Irv and Skuz doing? Did they move him to the same place?"

"Of course they did. They weren't going to take him all

the way to Phoenix. He didn't get it nearly as bad as Irving did. It grazed his shoulder. He'll be fine inside of a week, then they'll send him back behind bars."

"We got the money for bail anyway, so he won't have to put up with it for long. We'll get Garret out tomorrow since it's too late today."

"He'll survive one night in lockup. He's used to much longer periods," Lucien said. "I won't ask what trouble that punk gave you on a phone, but I'll ask when you get back. I'm interested now."

"Anything to keep me from sleeping," Richard laughed. "Fine, you got it. Alright, I've got to go. We're almost at the place."

"Be thorough and don't forget anything. Remember what I taught you."

"I don't want to be in Garret's shoes right now. Trust me, we're on top of it."

"Good. Talk to you soon," Lucien said before hanging up.

Richard watched the truck turn right, following the sign to the nearby quarry. He turned the wheel and followed closely behind. They passed through an old decrepit chain link fence that had numerous signs plastered to deter people from entering. The truck stopped in front of the giant gulch, and Tony hopped out.

Richard opened the door and stepped out. "Now for the fun part."

"How do you prefer?"

Richard walked up to the back of the van and opened the doors. He reached inside the back so far his belly ended up on the cabin. He pulled out a long discarded cloth. "First we set the fuse, make sure it's not in park, light it, and then push it in. Easy enough."

Tony accepted the cloth. "I'll take care of the gas tank, and it's not in park so pushing will be a breeze."

"Good. Just make sure you get it deep enough in there that it's in the gas. If not, it'll take a while longer for the evidence to go up in smoke."

Tony shoved the cloth down into the gas tank. "It's in there as far as I can get it." He stepped to the side. "You're free to check my work if you please."

"It looks fine." Richard gave it a cursory glance. "Now as soon as I light this, we're on a timer."

"I figured as much."

Richard extracted the box of matches from his pocket and struck one against the back of the box. A small flicker of flame engulfed the tiny red end of the stick. "Ready?"

"Ready for this to be over."

"You and me both." Richard ignited the cloth and ran back to Tony. The pair pressed their shoulders against the back of the truck. They dug their heels into the gravel and grunted as the truck inched forward.

"Watch out." Richard said as the truck neared the edge. "Back up a step. It's going on its own."

The truck toppled over the edge and went vertical. Crashing glass and metal filled the air as it tumbled down to the already crowded quarry below. The pair looked over the edge and saw the fire disappear into the gas tank. A fireball expanded around the truck and died out in a moment in a blaze. They covered their eyes and backed off a step until the glow died down a moment later. The boom below was replaced with a constant sizzling.

"There," Richard said. "It's burning good and steady now. We're done here." He turned away. "What do you make of today?"

"You mean with Enrique and that assassin guy?" Tony took the lead as they headed back to the van.

"Was there any other life and death struggle I don't know about?"

"It shows how weak we made him look," Tony said. "He didn't have much choice and came at us with everything he had. They probably threatened his family, if I had to guess. Which is why he never even attempted to get away once he lost his first man."

"That makes sense. The assassin would know he'd be dead if he came back empty handed. It's almost like they were a suicide squad."

"When you're desperate, you'll do anything when you're told to."

"It also would explain why they loaded them up with so much fire power for little old us. It's not everyday you come across fragmentation grenades." Richard removed the cylinder from his pocket, tossed it up, and caught it.

"I wonder where they got it." Tony opened the driver's side and climbed in.

"Probably from a corrupt Mexican infantryman, if I had to guess. They must cost a pretty peso down there. If not for the money, then to keep his family safe. Rumor has it the government down there is run by cartels." He shoved the explosive back into his jacket pocket.

"Hell," the engine roared to life, "it could have been an order if that's the case."

"However they got it, it just shows we need to step our game up before they can recover. We need to find a heavier weapon supplier who's willing to sell."

"Allies might not be such a bad thing as well." The van lurched forward and shook over the gravel road. "We've made a blood enemy with this. We need a deterrent, and there's little better than allies. God knows they have enough enemies who would be willing to sell to their enemy."

"I have a few groups in mind. The enemy of my enemy is my friend as they say. We might have to open up our meth market to gain access, but I have a feeling they'll join us."

"Money really is the greatest motivator known to mankind."

"I'll deal with that tomorrow after I've had a full night's rest."

"You've gotten used to sleeping on the floor on a sleeping bag?" Tony asked.

"Hell no. We're going back to our homes tonight. We can't stay there forever and ES-15 is crippled in the states now thanks to us. We're not cowering in our fortress any longer than we need to."

"Thank Christ." Tony turned into the nearby exit. "All we need is for Irv to get better and we'll be whole again."

"It still would be prudent to recruit more. You have any favorite hang arounds?"

"I know a few who would kill for a chance to prospect. You want me to give them a call tonight?"

"Sure. Wake them up. We'll see how dedicated they really are."

"I'll ring three and tell them to haul their ass over and put them to work."

Richard reached down between the seats and reclined his seat back. "Sounds like a plan."

24

"What took you so long?" Richard asked with arms wide open.

Garret stepped into the hug and returned it before taking a step back. "You know how slow guards are on release day." He looked at the rest of the group. "How did everything go yesterday?"

The group headed inside the clubhouse and sat around a nearby table.

Garret noticed Ann standing off in the corner. "I'll be right back."

"Don't take too long now," Richard said.

"No promises." Garret approached her. "It's been a while since I've seen that beautiful face."

"Not really."

"Oh yeah. You know how it is. Jail always makes time seem slower. Still, I am serious when I say it's good to see you again." He reached forward and engulfed her right hand in both of his. "Don't say you didn't miss me."

"Don't put words in my mouth now." Ann gave a small smile. "I was just thinking about the future."

"Come to any conclusions?" Garret asked, pulling out a seat for Ann before sitting down himself beside her.

"That's the infuriating thing. No."

"Now you know why I love planning for jobs. It's easy, concrete, to come up with a plan of attack. Your actual life always throws wrenches into the plans, so I just stopped trying. It usually ends up more fun in my experience."

"Yeah, I bet last night really exemplified that train of thought."

"Okay, to be fair, that wasn't my fault, and you know it. That was Skuz's crazy bitch."

"Fine. Come with me then." She grabbed his hand and dragged him back into the bedroom amidst a chorus of wolf whistles.

"She missed you last night it looks like," Richard called out with a laugh.

He closed the door behind him and turned back. Ann's face was inches away with her palms on either side of his head on the door.

"What about me?"

"Excuse me?"

"Are you planning on including me in your life? Or did you not think that through either?"

"I guess this was coming eventually. He reached up and grabbed her right hand. He held it in his hand as he spoke. "That depends on you. You know you'll never be a member here, correct?"

"Obviously."

"Then are you fine being my old lady?"

"I..." she looked away, "maybe."

"Then yes. If you're willing, I'd be happy if you were to stay."

"Just know if you ever did cheat on me, she wouldn't stay alive very long."

"That went dark. You're the jealous type eh? I'll remember that." Garret took the initiative and picked her up. He walked forward as she squealed in his arms. He dumped her on her back onto the bed. "Let's just see where this goes then, shall we?"

"What the hell? Why not?"

"That's the spirit." He lowered his head and captured her lips. He inserted his tongue inside, licking the top of her mouth. His hand danced up her side and flicked her ear lobe causing her to mumble into his mouth. He rose up. "Now, where was I? Oh right. I think the boys wanted me for something."

"They'll fucking wait." She reached up behind his head and pulled him back. "Don't even think of leaving me here wanting."

"A gentleman would never." He snaked one hand around her core and pulled her body closer. "Now just relax. I'll take care of you real good today."

A knock interrupted them along with Lucien's voice. "Don't get too comfortable in there. We still have business."

"So do we," Ann said. "Go away."

"Alright, damn." Footsteps faded away. "They're getting it on. We'll just have to wait."

"Have I ever mentioned how much I hate him sometimes?" She climbed off him. "Go ahead, but don't be too long. The last thing I want is them talking in there."

"I'll hurry it along." Garret exited the door and came back to the table in the main room. "What was so important that couldn't wait?"

"It's time to pick up the pieces. Your little bonding exercise in there can wait," Richard said. "Going forward, we're stepping up our recruiting. You know what that means."

"I do need another prospect to fetch me things," Garret said. "Now that Irv's patched in, I have to go pick up my own orders."

"Your lazy ass needs to do it yourself. Back in my day-"

"You had to go to the dealers house uphill both ways in the snow?" Tony asked with a smile. "I think I've heard this one before."

"I'm thinking we prospect three at a time given the situation." Richard looked around at the men sitting around the table. "Let's not mince words. We need bodies if ES-15 is sending more north of the border eventually. If nothing else, they can watch the clubhouse while we take care of business."

"Even if we get three more, we still need allies. We can't hope to take on a well-organized cartel on our own," Tony said. "You said you had ideas on who that might be before?"

"That's right. I know we generally operate alone, and that's the way we like it. I'm not suggesting a joint venture with another charter, more of a mutual defense pact."

"Meaning they wouldn't be able to fuck up our business?" Lucien asked. "There's a reason we never aligned with the morons around here."

"They're not afraid to pick up a gun. That's all that matters here, let's be real."

"At least you're right about that." Lucien wiped his nose. "Just make sure we don't give up too much."

"Negotiating is my specialty," Richard said. "I was thinking of the Outback Boys."

"Those crazy foreigners?" Garret asked. "You're sure they can be trusted?"

"They're honorable in their dealings." Lucien's nails dug

into the wood of the table. "A little crazy, but they're always up for a fight. They're wild though. We'd have to keep them at arm's length."

"Which is precisely the goal. We give them what they want, our drugs, in exchange for some protection."

"We might even get some of that famous weed they're always bragging about, enriching our own business at the same time," Garret said. "I'm all for it."

"That makes two. How about you two?" Richard asked Tony and Lucien.

"It makes sense to me," Tony said.

"We'll hold the vote off until we have enough members present, but in the meantime, let's set it all up. I'll go get their lead office's number. Moving on," he slammed his fist down on the table, "what's the ETA on Irving getting out?"

"That shot nearly hit his heart." Lucien's face contorted. "He'll be lucky to be up and moving inside of two months. It's not pretty. In maybe a month he'll be able to come back here, but he won't be in shape to do much of anything."

"That's fine. He'll be able to boss the new prospects around and have them wait on him hand and foot," Tony said.

"Agreed," Richard said. "Then the only other thing on the docket is Skuz. As soon as he's able, we'll bail him out too. We should also get him a nice lawyer for that stupid case of his."

"It should be a slam dunk," Garret said. "I saw the cut marks myself. No semi-intelligent jury will ever convict him for this one."

"That's worrying," Lucien said. "Most juries are cherry picked by the lawyers to keep the dumbest, most impressionable ones."

"Which is precisely why we're calling in our best

attorney for this one. We don't cheap out on legal funds. It's one of the rules we were founded on, as you were so fond of reminding me when I was younger." Richard looked at Lucien. "Never leave a man behind on the battlefield, or one behind bars, if at all possible."

"At least you were listening."

A buzzing sound interrupted the group. "That's me." Richard pulled out his phone. "Yes?"

"You've been causing us no end of trouble," an older Hispanic voice said. "That stops now."

"Who is this?" Richard asked. "How did you get this number?"

"You know who I am. As far as your number, we have our ways."

"You probably just got it from Enrique, right? The mysterious bit's not playing."

"That's not what you should be focusing on right now. The boss said we'd be paying you a visit soon enough. We owe you from before, and we always pay back our debts." The line went dead.

"Who was that?" Garret asked.

"Take a guess."

"They're already calling? What'd they say?"

"He said they'd be paying us a visit soon. We need to get busy if we're going to be ready. I'll contact the Outback Boys. Garret, go look for a new apartment nearby or something. Everyone else, focus on recruitment. I'll handle it if the bondsman calls here."

Garret ran back toward the bedroom in the back and opened the door. He pulled her off the bed and wrapped his arms around her tall form. He leaned forward and they touched foreheads. "We're going house hunting, honey."

"Together?"

"I am. I'd appreciate a little help if you'd be so kind, my old lady."

"What would you do without me?" She stood up and captured his lips. "Lead the way."

The end

THANKS FOR READING!

The adventures of the club continues in Vengeance Above All coming out next month. If you'd like to support this work, please feel free to leave an honest review on Amazon. Have a great day!

ALSO BY ALEX J FISCHER